MW01419876

Stephen Ford, retired from a career in information technology, is now an author, with *No Free Speech for Hate* being his fourth published novel.

The son of a geologist, he had a varied and nomadic childhood in Africa and the Middle East. Since childhood, Stephen has been inspired by wild places, mountains, rivers and forests—places where nature reigns, not people.

Now inspired to write, Stephen explores these themes: What forces shape human society? What is the future of humanity? Is human development driven by reason and logic, or are reason and logic mere tools used to justify people's choices?

Stephen Ford

No Free Speech for Hate

Austin Macauley Publishers®
London * Cambridge * New York * Sharjah

A CIP catalogue record for this title is available from the British Library.

ISBN 9781035877645 (Paperback)
ISBN 9781035877652 (ePub e-book)

www.austinmacauley.com

First Published 2024
Austin Macauley Publishers Ltd®
1 Canada Square
Canary Wharf
London
E14 5AA

Table of Contents

Chapter 1
Safe Learning Environment

The notice declared the campus to be a motor-free zone, so my Autocab dropped me off outside.

"*Committed to Safe Learning*" stated another sign beneath the name identifying the Willow Brook entrance of Slough University.

A menacing-looking group of men with shaven heads and lightning flash tattoos surrounded me as I stepped out of the vehicle. A leaflet, thrust into my hand, emblazoned with "*Forward England*" demanded "*Vehicle Rights for All*", the right for every member of English society to own a vehicle and drive it themselves.

I edged my way through the shouting mob of "Forward England" supporters to reach the metal turntable security gates. A sign warned: '*Zero tolerance for promotion of hate. Any person expressing hate or bringing hateful material on campus will be ejected and banned from the premises. No exceptions.*'

Having let myself in with my pass, I squelched a few yards through the sodden, spongy accumulation of fallen leaves to where a lightweight wheelchair-accessible tram was just coming into one of the ten stops on the circular route around the campus.

I needed to be at the clinic in Dunwick Park General Hospital later on. But for being summoned to an irritating administrative meeting, I would have gone straight there.

Alighting at the Oppressed Peoples Memorial Complex, a covered walkway saved me from the damp autumnal drizzle to reach a centuries-old arch surrounded by a Tudor gatehouse embellished with diamond shapes formed into the brickwork. Glass-fronted modernist blocks rose up from behind a medieval and Tudor frontage to a confusing labyrinth of interconnected old and new buildings. The gateway that would have once led into an open-air courtyard now covered over to form an atrium in the style of a modern shopping mall. Newly built entrances formed into gothic arches were interspersed between ancient stone and brickwork from previous centuries. Sloping floors laid in concrete, patterned to resemble flagstones allowed for wheelchairs to negotiate the changes in levels. I zigzagged my way through the maze of access ways to reach the old entrance into the university library and crossed the historic room forming the reception area through into the modern library facilities.

I found my way downstairs to Seminar Room B4 in the basement where two women, or rather persons, who, from their appearance, were biologically female, were already present.

'Sorry, I'm not late, am I?' I enquired.

'No, Professor Hubbings; bang on time,' said an immaculately presented biological female in her thirties, sleekly clad in a sober, perfectly tailored business outfit. 'Shall we make a start?'

'Yes, that's fine.'

'First things first, introductions and pronouns. I'm Cheryl Biggetty, Academic Accuracy Officer, pronouns she/her.'

'Shamina Chakrabarti, Learning Safety Officer, pronouns ze/zir,' announced the other person. I reflected that despite her declaration of preferred non-binary identity, she would always look female to me, and a rather attractive if intimidating one, too. In zir late twenties, ze was dressed in faded tightly fitted jeans that showed off zir feminine-looking curves and a close-fitting T-shirt emblazoned across zir prominent breasts with the logo for leading "Diversity, Equity and Inclusion" champion Rockface and the slogan "Proud to be Inclusive".

'Jim Hubbings, Professor of Pharmacology,' I announced.

'Professor Hubbings, please, your pronouns,' chided Ms Biggetty.

'Sorry. He/him.'

'So, to the business in hand,' said Ms Biggetty. 'As you know, our Safe Learning Environment policy requires us to protect our students from hateful material, to which end, as directed by the university Senate, in reviewing the contents of the university library and teaching curriculum, we have identified some questionable material within your remit, Professor.'

I looked at her questioningly. I had always felt reassured that a science subject like pharmacology, unlike the arts and social sciences, would be unaffected by such contentious issues.

'What material do you have in mind?'

'A number of publications within the undergraduate study material feature the work of Herbert Pethering.'

I was aghast. 'Well, of course, they do. Professor Pethering was one of the leading pioneers of the whole field of modern pharmacology. You couldn't possibly understand the subject without studying his work.'

'The Pethering family had shares in slave-owning plantations in Jamaica and Barbados,' explained Mz Chakrabarti.

'But Herbert Pethering devoted his entire life to the discovery of life-saving pharmaceuticals, saving millions of lives.'

'His work is tainted, financed by slavery,' insisted Mz Chakrabarti.

'Professor Pethering's work took place in the late nineteenth century, long after slavery had been abolished within the British empire.'

'It doesn't alter the fact that he could not have done what he did without his family wealth, wealth obtained by exploitation and slavery.'

'But he wasn't responsible for creating that wealth. It would have been his ancestors, grandparents and great-grandparents who did that.'

'The fact remains that the wealth derived from slavery.'

I frowned, grappling for a solution. 'Could we not just put in an explanatory introduction explaining Professor Pethering's family background and the source of his wealth?'

Ms Biggetty shook her head. 'The mention of a hateful matter such as slavery could trigger trauma in some of our students. We have a duty of care to protect their mental health.'

Lost for words, I looked in turn at the implacable expressions on each of my protagonists.

'I'm flummoxed,' I confessed eventually. 'I really can't imagine how we could put a course together that doesn't feature Herbert Pethering. His work is fundamental to the whole pharmacology field.'

'We have a suggestion,' said Mz Chakrabarti.

'Oh, what's that?'

'There was a Miss Enid Clompton who worked with Pethering.'

'Well, yes. She was his secretarial assistant,' I observed. 'Kept records for him, took dictation and looked after the filing.'

'It was her who wrote out all his papers,' said Mz Chakrabarti, 'but due to the sexism prevailing at the time, she was never given any of the credit for it.'

'But she was writing down his ideas rather than her own.'

'How do you know that?' retorted Mz Chakrabarti. 'She worked with Pethering for twenty years. She would have come to know the field intimately and contributed greatly to his work.'

'Yes, she probably did,' I acknowledged.

'So, we suggest you adjust the teaching material to remove the slavery-tainted Pethering and instead give Enid Clompton the credit she was denied due to the blatant sexism prevalent at the time.'

'There are difficulties with this suggestion,' I argued.

'What sort of difficulties?' enquired Ms Biggetty testily.

'For one thing, Miss Clompton wasn't around during at least the first decade of Pethering's career. She would have still been a child when he first started his work.'

'I'm sure you'll be able to think of something,' said Ms Biggetty.

'Such as?'

'He must have had one or more other collaborators in the early years. You could bring them in.'

'I don't like it,' I protested. 'It feels like rewriting history to suit modern tastes.'

'So, you think your personal feelings should stand in the way of our duty to provide a safe learning environment for our students,' said Mz Chakrabarti sharply.

'Supposing I don't feel I can do this?'

'You would have to consider your position,' said Ms Biggetty. 'I can't imagine, however well respected you are in your field, the university could allow you to stand in the way of ensuring a safe learning environment.'

I gritted my teeth. I clearly couldn't win in this situation, and I was mindful of my family commitments. 'Very well. I'll make the necessary adjustments to the teaching material. Only one thing: what do we do about the reference books describing Pethering's achievements?'

'You'll have to talk to the publishers about getting new editions published with Pethering removed from the text.'

'What if the publishers don't agree?'

'They will. It isn't only us here in Slough who require this change. Other institutions both here in the UK and elsewhere require it.'

'All right. I'll get on to it,' I accepted.

'There is one other thing,' said Mz Chakrabarti. 'I understand that there is a statue, a bust of Herbert Pethering on a pedestal in the entrance foyer of the pharmacology faculty.'

'Yes, there is.'

'It'll have to go.'

'What should we put in its place?'

'I think that Enid Clompton should be commemorated, don't you?'

'I suppose so,' I acknowledged. 'But we don't have a statue of her, do we?'

'I have already looked into that,' said Ms Biggetty. 'The technology faculty have assured me that their artificial intelligence engine can produce a spatial reconstruction of her based on some contemporary photos and feed this to a 3D printer to produce a synthetic stone-effect bust.'

Just in time to meet my Liz, I reflected as I emerged from the meeting for a quick bite of lunch before my visit to the clinic, only to notice a message from my daughter Amelia's school, requesting I call back urgently.

'Professor Hubbings, thanks for calling back. I'm Celia Englebury, School Safety Officer.'

'Has something happened to Amelia?'

'Well, in a sense, yes.'

'What exactly?'

'It is a safety issue.'

'She's alright, isn't she?'

'Physically, she is alright, but we have some other concerns.'

'What other concerns?'

'It's a delicate matter, not something I can go over on the phone.'

'When, then?'

'Today, if you can spare the time.'

'At the school?'

'No, I'd like to see you at your home, if that's alright.'

'I'm quite busy. Could you possibly pop over to the university?'

'No, I'm sorry, but this is an urgent matter requiring a home visit.'

'This evening then, when Amelia gets back home.'

'No, best do it without Amelia.'

'I see. When do you want to come round?'

'Could you be home in an hour or so?'

'Yes, of course.'

Damn, I'd have to call off my lunch date with Liz Entworthy, a history lecturer and my romantic partner. We had been close for a year or so, but we were still at the dating stage, not yet attached on any permanent basis.

'Liz, look, I'm sorry but I have to duck out from our lunch date,' I explained over the phone.

'That's a shame. What's up?'

'The school called me. Something to do with Amelia.'

'Is she alright?'

'I think so, but they need me to go over to deal with something or other.'

'Couldn't it wait until after lunch?'

'Afraid not.'

'When are we going to see each other, then?'

'Same time tomorrow. Does that suit?'

'Yes, alright.'

A notice in the library reception area announced non-competitive football due to take place later in the afternoon on the university Outdoor Health playing field, suitable for anyone, no experience necessary, spectators welcome.

I turned to see my friend Harvey Bentling, the university's history professor, striding in hurriedly through the entrance. Preoccupied, he didn't notice me, so I called out a greeting.

'Harvey, fancy seeing you here.'

'Oh, Jim,' he reached out to shake my hand, 'this isn't your usual haunt.'

'I've been over here for a meeting.'

'Likewise. Something to do with safe learning environments, or some such.'

Harvey, an energetic man in his forties, semi-formally dressed in a non-matching jacket and trousers with an open-necked check shirt, his glasses giving him a studious look, didn't look as if he was looking forward to this particular meeting.

'I've just been to one of those.'

'Oh, you too! What happened?'

'I'm having to purge one of pharmacology's leading figures from the curriculum due to his connections with slavery.'

Harvey narrowed his eyes and gritted his teeth. 'What'll that do to your study programme?'

‘We are still going to cover the technical aspects of his work, but we’ll be giving someone else the credit for his discoveries…and we’re taking away his statue.’

Harvey shook his head. ‘God only knows what they are going to do to the history syllabus.’

‘Well, good luck.’

‘I’ll need it, Jim. Anyway, best be getting on.’

As the Autocab pulled up outside our home in a nice suburban neighbourhood in Datchet, my heart sank as I noticed some fresh graffiti along our garden fence: a lightning flash and “*FORWARD ENGLAND*” spray-painted in bright dayglo orange.

It wasn’t the first time it had been defaced. I had dealt with it by painting the whole fence in a dull military-style green, making it easy to paint out fresh scrawling, but with Ms Englebury due to descend upon me imminently, I would have no time for that now.

Sure enough, on my computer screen, I saw the image from the security CCTV of her arrival, scowling her disapproval as she observed the symbol and slogan.

‘Professor Hubbings?’ she enquired as I opened the door.

She was, subject to the formalities about pronouns, a woman, aged around forty, with short, dark, unstyled hair, a plain, round, unadorned face with thick, dark-framed glasses, short and stout in stature, dressed in a baggy polo-necked sweater and loose trousers.

‘Yes. Ms Englebury, I presume.’

She looked at me with irritation. ‘Yes, Professor, my pronouns are she/her, but I would prefer you didn’t make assumptions. And your pronouns are?’

‘He/him.’

‘Is that something that reflects the views of this household?’ she enquired, looking over with distaste at the writing scrawled on the fence.

‘No, local vandals. Found it like that when I arrived. Must have been done earlier this morning.’

‘May I come in?’

‘Sure,’ I said, standing aside. ‘May I offer you a cup of tea or anything?’

‘No, thanks.’

‘Would you like to come through?’ I said, indicating the way into the lounge as we stood in the hallway.

‘Not just yet, thank you. I am here to conduct an inspection of these premises.’

‘What do you mean, inspection? What are you looking for?’

‘A document by a Toxic Influence has been found on Amelia’s tablet computer.’

‘What sort of a Toxic Influence?’

‘A piece written by Kate Stillworthy classified as Category-A Toxic Influence.’

‘Oh, I see. But it’s her own personal computer, not the school’s. How come you’re looking at her personal property?’

Ms Englebury sighed heavily. ‘We have to safeguard the school from Toxic Influences. Surely, you understand that.’

‘But you can’t look at each pupil’s personal devices, surely. What prompted you to pick out Amelia’s to look at?’

‘We didn’t pick out Amelia specifically. All devices are checked automatically as soon as they connect to the school’s Wi-Fi system.’

‘You mean, if I happened to come to the school as a visitor and my mobile phone connected to the school Wi-Fi, my phone would be checked, too?’

‘Yes, all devices. The school needs to be safeguarded.’

‘As a matter of interest, do you ever find anything on the devices of visiting parents, for example?’

‘Yes. Last year, there were two child pornography prosecutions. One wasn’t even a parent. He was doing repairs to the guttering.’

Much to my embarrassment, I blushed red, which did not escape Ms Englebury’s attention. It wasn’t as if I even had anything to hide or be ashamed of, just the thought the school could see everything about me metaphorically stripping me naked.

‘Well, you found the piece written by Kate Stillworthy. Can’t we just leave it at that?’

‘No, we can’t. Kate Stillworthy is a Category-A Toxic Influence. This is a very serious matter.’

‘What makes her Category-A?’

‘She has been one of the most notorious terfs, a trans-exclusionary radical feminist. Her material could cause severe mental anguish to any trans pupil in the school, scarring their young lives, possibly even ending their lives, should the trauma drive someone to suicide. We must safeguard our pupils from this filth.'

'So, what do you want to do?'

'I need to carry out a home inspection to ensure that Amelia's domestic situation is free of any other hateful material.'

'What if I don't agree to your inspection?'

'Why, do you have something to hide?'

'No, but I certainly don't feel comfortable about this intrusion.'

'When you enrolled Amelia in the school, you signed up to the school safeguarding policy, authorising us to carry out such an inspection whenever we have reasonable cause to do so.'

'Supposing I were to refuse?'

'I could come back within a few minutes with a child protection warrant. If you were to obstruct me in the execution of the warrant, I could have you arrested.'

I knew she was right. 'Very well, what do you need to do?'

'I need to carry out a scan of all electronic equipment on the premises and also to search for any objectionable printed material.'

'Go on, then. Do what you have to do.'

Damn, I thought, *I'll be late for the clinic now*. 'How long will it take?'

'Shouldn't take more than an hour or so.'

If I got straight into an Autocab when she was done, I would only be about half an hour late. That should be alright. Leaving her to set up her equipment, I went through into the lounge and used my smartphone to book my Autocab.

My heart was pounding from the accumulated stress. I reached into my pocket for my packet of Complianx, contemplating the packaging. It would provide relief, that was true, but I'd have brain fog for the rest of the day. Better not. I needed to keep my wits about me in the current situation.

Having poured myself a stiff gin and tonic, I caught up with the television news, according to which, there had been serious disturbances in West London as supporters of the far-right group Forward England set upon student activists.

Eventually, Ms Englebury came into the room.

'I have finished my inspection, Professor Hubbings.'

'Did you find anything?'

'Just one area of concern.'

'Oh, what's that?'

'There was a Hills and Doon romance novel in Amelia's room.'

'Is that a problem?'

'Yes. This material has an age limit of 18. It is unsuitable for minors due to the sexist and heteronormative stereotypes it depicts.'

'So, where do we go from here?'

'For the time being, Amelia's social media access has been suspended in accordance with our "No Free Speech for Hate" policy, to safeguard other pupils from any hate that Amelia may have picked up from exposure to Category-A material. I am sure that you understand why we have to do this.'

'When will her access be restored?'

'She will have to go through some anti-hate training. After that, if she keeps out of trouble for three months, it should be restored.'

'I see. Will that wipe the slate clean?'

'Not exactly. This incident will be on her record. Further occurrences would put her "Ethics and Society qualification" at risk. Without that, she could be classified as Educationally Unsuitable and ineligible for a place in university.'

Ms Englebury's gaze caught a framed photo I had on the mantlepiece.

'Who is in that over there, in the photo?'

'Why do you ask?'

'To me, the person in the photo has a remarkable likeness to Kate Stillworthy.'

'I suppose there is a resemblance, yes.'

'Who is she, may I ask?'

'It is Amelia's mother.'

'Our records have you down as a single parent, Professor.'

'Amelia's mother isn't with us anymore, so now, she only has me.'

'Sorry for your loss, Professor.'

Chapter 2
Order Outside the Law

"No Free Speech for Hate" declared the large advertising poster in giant bold letters across a picture depicting four people, cowering as if terrified, a black man in chains, a white woman with short, cropped hair and an angry-looking well-scrubbed face, a hunched Asian woman in a wheelchair and a tall chunkily built square-jawed figure in a dress.

The poster, in common with the wall of the Dunwick Park General Hospital building behind, had been defaced with a spray-painted, bright orange lightning flash symbol and the words "God Save the King".

Scattered on the ground were some soggy, mud-stained leaflets from Forward England, also adorned with a lightning flash symbol and the grinning face of Gordon Garage wearing a cloth cap and a velvet-collared jacket that might have belonged to a prosperous bookmaker. The headline message was "*Protect Women's Spaces*" above a picture, overlaid with a traffic prohibited symbol, depicting a tall, chunkily built square-jawed figure in a dress, heavily made up with lipstick and mascara and an obvious five o'clock shadow.

I was walking away from the hospital and heading into a rough area of Dunwick, stepping carefully to avoid squirting muddy water from rocking loose paving slabs. Looming behind the older terraced buildings along the street were an austere pair of concrete residential tower blocks. The shops in the street—an Asian food store, a pawn shop, an emporium for mobile phones and cheap watches—were fronted with barred windows and rolldown steel shutters.

I felt under my jacket for the envelope in my inside pocket, glancing under my collar to verify it was safe and secure.

At the end of the street, another poster proclaimed "*Stop Sexual Exploitation*" over an image of a semi-clad woman in fishnet stockings being lecherously groped by a furtive-looking man.

The lower part of the poster was adorned with sticky labels with phone numbers offering such services as massages for generous gentlemen and riding lessons from a frisky filly.

A woman sidled up beside me and tugged my elbow.

'You looking for a bit of fun?' she enquired.

She was heavily made up, dressed in a tight-fitting short skirt, high-heeled boots, a sparkly top that barely covered her protruding goose-pimpled breasts, still young, probably around thirty but looking haggard and care-worn beyond her age.

'No, thanks all the same,' I replied.

'You sure? I'm Fenn. I'd see you right. I'm good, you know.'

'No, really. Not today.'

'If you don't have cash, I can do crypto.'

I reached into my pocket and pulled out my phone. The Crypto Cash app was among the icons on the display.

I looked back at the poster. Under the rain-soaked sticky labels, it said, '*Minimum sentence for sexual harassment: 2 years*.' One might have thought that it would have been this persistent woman risking her freedom, but I knew very well, the political climate being what it was, if the law became involved, it would have been me serving prison time.

'No, I won't, thanks.'

'Well, please yourself.'

A bunch of jeering youths approached us. In the Dunwick neighbourhood, youths often jeered, so I had thought nothing of it.

'That's her, the slag,' shouted out one of the boys.

'Hello, darling,' called out another, 'up for a bit with us, are you?'

The woman looked back, wide-eyed and fearful. She made no response, walking away quickly.

'What's the matter? Aren't we good enough for you, you old slapper?' shouted one of the youths, a lad of about twenty with a shaved head, wearing scruffy jeans and heavy working boots, though I supposed that the only work likely to be done with those boots was probably kicking people. There was something familiar about him, but I couldn't quite place where I might have seen him before.

The woman said nothing but continued walking as hurriedly as her tight skirt would allow. I was concerned for her safety.

'You'll drop your knickers for anybody else soon enough if they're paying,' said the youth. 'But not for us. "Educationally Unsuitable", according to those stuck-up gits at the university. No money, so no one wants us.'

'Leave me alone,' said the woman.

The youths caught up with the woman, crowding around.

'Come on,' said another of the youths. 'You can do it for us.'

The youths jostled her along in the direction of some waste ground.

I was nervous, fearful of what might happen to me if I got involved, but if I did nothing, it would weigh on my conscience. There was going to be a gangrape if I didn't do something about it. Swallowing hard, I stepped out towards the group.

'Look, you heard her,' I said, trying to sound authoritative, but failing. 'She said to leave her alone.'

The leading youth turned towards me with a sneering look of contempt on his face.

'Fuck off, you fucking ponce,' he snarled.

The other youths turned to face me, too, a look of total aggression on each of their faces, like a pack of hungry wolves. The woman tried to take advantage of the temporary distraction to escape, but two of the youths grabbed hold of her.

It was clear that had I persisted, I could not have saved her. At the very least, I would have been beaten to a pulp and quite possibly worse.

'Alright,' I said, backing away. 'None of my business.'

Some of the youths made to follow me, but as I slunk away meekly, they returned their attention to the woman.

As soon as I could, I ducked away around a corner so as to be out of sight. I pulled out my phone and began to dial 999. I felt the presence of someone behind me. It was one of those huge men who act as doormen on clubs situated in rough neighbourhoods.

The man reached across, taking hold of my phone with an enormous hairy hand that wouldn't have looked out of place on a gorilla. For a moment, I tried to hold tight onto my phone, but it quickly became clear that I was not going to win a tug-of-war with this individual.

'No need for that,' said the man in a deep, gruff voice. 'We'll take care of this ourselves.'

He still had hold of my phone. I looked at it expectantly. He ignored me.

'Is it okay if I have my phone back?' I asked.

'Not right now. You can have it back later.'

I hesitated. It was an intimidating situation, but it would have been very inconvenient for me to lose my phone.

'When do you imagine giving it back to me?' I asked.

'Not just yet. We've got some business to deal with first. Wait here. Best if you don't look. You know what I'm saying?'

I was confused, but it seemed best to agree. I nodded. 'Well, okay, but if you've got my phone, who are you?'

'I'm Nelson. I'm one of Mr Sharmoni's minders.'

'But why is Mr Sharmoni involved?'

'Mr Sharmoni likes things kept orderly on his manor.'

'Oh, I see.'

'You really don't want to see what's happening,' Nelson reiterated. 'It could be dangerous for you if you did. Do you get me?'

He looked at me expectantly for an answer.

'Yes. I get you,' I agreed eventually.

'Stay here. Out of sight. Don't move. I'll be back with your phone later on. Understand?'

I nodded. Nelson moved on around the corner in the direction of the errant youths.

I held back out of sight. I was looking out at the damp, mouldy blank wall at the end of a terrace of small shops upon which a large hoarding promised in large text, '*A Community Safe from Hate.*' Smaller text elaborated on the Liberal Socialist Party's promise of a harmonious society with universal free education, social care, equality and respect for all.

On the opposite side of the road, I could hear the raised voices of tiny children from a kindergarten nursery and primary school. The introduction of compulsory free nursery education by the Liberal Socialist government had been a boon, enabling parents to pursue their careers, as well as ensuring young kids were instilled with correct thinking from a young age.

I could hear the youths still jeering and chanting. The woman they had been harassing screamed. I probably should have done as I was told, but curiosity got the better of me. I stuck my head around the corner to take a look.

By now, the youths had hauled the woman out onto the waste ground and had her sprawled out on the floor. Intent on what they were doing, they did not notice the group of four huge men closing in on them until they were literally right on top of them, picking up their scrawny frames by the scruff of their necks.

One of the large men helped the woman onto her feet.

'You shouldn't have been out on your own,' I heard him say to her. 'It's not safe.'

Nelson spoke to the hooligan that they had just hauled up from sexually assaulting the woman. He was being held by two of the other men, while the fourth tended to the woman.

'You have been a naughty boy,' said Nelson. He looked around at the other youths. 'The rest of you, fuck off out of here and don't do anything like this again.'

The remaining youths didn't have to be told twice. They rapidly scattered away.

'I'll take you home and get you looked after,' said the bulky man who had been attending to the woman. He must have been around six feet four in height, with a neck that went straight down from his craggy jaw mounted on shoulders wide enough to block a doorway. Nobody was likely to risk giving the woman any more trouble on her way home. He held her by the arm and guided her away.

'Mr Sharmoni expects women to be treated with respect,' said Nelson to the young thug now in the clutches of the other two equally large minders.

I could see that the young man was the one who had been leading the group of youths. He definitely looked familiar, but for the moment, I couldn't quite figure out where I might have previously encountered him. In his current predicament, he looked pathetic, weak and terrified, his earlier arrogance and bravado now all gone.

'Leave it out. I didn't mean anything, just a bit of fun, that's all,' the youth pleaded plaintively.

'Nah,' said the man. 'That was bang out of order, what you did. Diabolical. Mr Sharmoni won't stand for that sort of thing.'

With the assaulted woman now out of sight, Nelson swung a heavy punch into the youth's guts. The other two men let go of the youth's arms and joined in the beating, systematically swinging powerful punches into his face and body. I heard crunching noises consistent with ribs being splintered and the cracking of his jaw. The youth's knees crumpled, but the men wouldn't let him down just yet, taking it in turns to drag him upright while the other two swung into him with their enormous fists.

Eventually, they let his now unconscious body slump down, completing the beating with their heavy boots as he lay on the wet ground.

It was then that Nelson glanced across, noticing me looking on open-mouthed. He strode over towards me purposefully. After having observed what they had done, my heart pounded in fright, wondering what they might have in store for me.

'I told you to keep out of sight and not to look, didn't I?' he said with menace in his voice.

'Sorry, I heard noises,' I said. 'I didn't know what they were.'

'You just had to look, to stick your nose in where it's not wanted.'

'Did you really have to do that?' I asked.

'There was a gangrape going on. We couldn't allow that to happen, could we? Mr Sharmoni won't tolerate that sort of thing.'

'But you didn't have to do what you did. Two wrongs don't make a right.'

'We have to make an example, to make sure others know they can't do things like that.'

'But we have the law for these situations, don't we?' I insisted.

'Don't make me laugh. The law went out the window when the Liberal Socialists defunded the police.'

I didn't know what to say. It was clear that what Mr Sharmoni said was now what passed for the law, at least within the confines of the Dunwick manor.

'Could I have my phone back, do you think?' I asked.

'Before that, we need to sort a few things out, Professor Hubbings.'

I was taken aback by him using my name and title. He must have checked me out after getting hold of my phone.

'Oh, what sort of things?'

'Getting the law involved would not be a good idea.'

'How so?'

'It's a funny thing, but people who might have given evidence against Mr Sharmoni never seem to be there when the cases get to court. They get very accident-prone for some reason.'

Nelson looked at me intently, legs apart and shoulders back, to emphasise his bulky frame, conveying his threatening message more clearly than any words could have done.

'I see,' I acknowledged.

'Sometimes, their loved ones are accident-prone, too. Wouldn't like anything to happen to Amelia, would we?'

I blanched in shock. It was one thing to be concerned about my own safety, but the threat to Amelia, my daughter, came like a heavy fist in the guts.

'Please, leave her out of it,' I pleaded.

'Keep your mouth shut, and nothing will happen. Here's your phone.'

I stood stunned for a few minutes. The bulky men went on their way, presumably on other enforcement duties on Mr Sharmoni's behalf.

The men had gone, but I hadn't seen what had happened to the youth that they had been beating up. I wandered over towards the waste ground where the events had taken place. The youth's battered body lay still in the churned-up mud. I wondered whether he might still be alive, but seeing him inert, it was near-certain that life was extinct. Now lacking his earlier front of cockiness, I suddenly realised where I had seen him before. It had been at the clinic. Name of Johnie Dorritt, as I recalled.

Nearby lay a crumpled and torn pair of women's knickers, the dampness on the gusset suggesting that it had only recently been left on the scene.

I felt conflicted, knowing that the moral thing as a citizen would have been for me to summon assistance, yet the need to protect my own and especially Amelia's welfare was of paramount importance. Besides, nothing could have helped poor Johnie now.

I felt an urgency to distance myself from the scene. Forcing my shaky legs into action, I walked away. It was only the forward motion of my legs preventing the weight of my body from pulling me forward face down onto the pavement, my feet thumping into the ground as I went. I felt lightheaded, and the street scene spun around my head as if I was on a fairground ride.

I had not gone more than fifty yards before I had to throw up onto the grass verge, my puke spilling out over discarded drinks cans, needles and a used condom.

I needed something to alleviate the shock from the violence I had witnessed. I felt in my pocket for the Complianx tablets I had from the clinic. It would calm me down, that much was true, but did I really want to be little more than a zombie for the next 24 hours? That wouldn't do. I had things to attend to. I pushed the packet back into my pocket.

I took some deep breaths, and my head felt clearer. I resumed walking, not fast, but more steadily than before.

Feeling shaky, I considered calling up an Autocab, but I rejected the idea. It could look bad for me and be hard to explain, were such a trip to be on record.

A large, forlorn and defaced building announced itself Dunwick Sports Complex. With sweeping extravagant forms, it must have been designed by some prestigious architect with no expense spared, but now it was dirty, scrawled with graffiti, windows broken, dark and without any sign of life. A faded poster offered non-competitive basketball, yoga and five-a-side football. A sticker on the bottom of the poster offered *Real Sport, Cage Fight* and a number.

I emerged from the Dunwick residential area, along the side of a main road, passing by some derelict land. A piece of plywood tied onto the surrounding fence said *Cage Fight Here Tonight*, scrawled on in white with a paintbrush.

In front of me, the road passed alongside a high fence topped with razor wire, marking the perimeter of what now had the appearance of a military camp, but I recalled had once been the site of Aspen Grove Studios, where many great and not so great movies had been produced.

As I reached the fence, my phone bleeped. I checked the message. It informed me that I was approaching a Toxic Influence Containment Area and, in accordance with the government's "No Free Speech for Hate" policy, Internet access was now restricted to only authorised channels.

A notice in front of the high fence reiterated the message, stipulating that unauthorised persons were prohibited from entry to the Toxic Influence Containment Area, or TICA, for their own protection.

I skirted around the perimeter of the TICA. On the other side of the road, a sign marked the entrance to Lakeside Caravan Park. I avoided the surveillance from CCTV cameras covering the driveway by taking an adjacent footpath leading across a neighbouring field towards a woodland park, from where I could duck back onto the driveway through a gap in the hedge.

Perhaps I was being a bit paranoid, I reflected. The cameras would have been there to record the fly-tippers who commonly dumped debris from building work and old household appliances onto the land. Law-abiding citizens going for a stroll in the countryside would not have attracted anybody's attention. Nevertheless, those cameras made me uneasy.

The lake referred to in the caravan park's promotional material was an old gravel pit, now full of water. There were rentable plots available for people to bring along their own caravans, tents or camper vans as well as semi-permanently installed caravans enjoying the benefits of installed electricity and piped water.

I knocked on the flimsy door of the rickety reception hut. A tired-looking man of about sixty let me in.

'Hello, Sid,' I said. I pulled out the envelope from my inside pocket. 'Do you mind if I leave this with you to give to Kate?'

'No problem. I'll see that she gets it.'

Chapter 3
In the Lab

"*Jezza is right*" said the placard held by one of the shaven-headed men braving the drizzly rain around Slough University's Willow Brook entrance.

Right about what? I wondered as I stepped out of my Autocab. One of the men shoved a leaflet into my hand. Beneath the Forward England lightning flash logo, the headline said, "*British empire done good*". The text below claimed that Britain held India together and abolished the slave trade, quoting Jeremy Fitzregal, described as a leading academic from Slough University. *Mr Fitzregal won't be lasting much longer in the university*, I reflected.

A group of four of the university security team emerged to confront the group of men.

'Move along, please,' said the leading security guard, a stolid, rotund man of around fifty years of age.

'This is a peaceful protest,' objected one of the demonstrators.

'It stopped being peaceful when you handed out hateful material,' retorted the security guard.

'We have the right to free speech.'

'You know perfectly well, there is "No Free Speech for Hate".'

'Hate? I don't know what you're talking about!'

The security guard waved a copy of the leaflet at the bullet-headed man. 'This.'

'What's hateful about that?'

'It is triggering for people of colour.'

'How come?'

'It is a reminder for them of how their parents and grandparents were oppressed by British imperialism.'

'What are you going to do about it?' jeered another of the demonstrators.

‘Look, I don’t want to get the police involved,’ said the long-suffering security guard. ‘Just move along, and we won’t have any trouble.’

‘Could I come through, please?’ I intervened.

‘No unauthorised personnel allowed on university premises,’ said the guard, blocking my way.

‘I am authorised. I’m Professor Hubbings. Here is my pass.’

He checked my pass. ‘Alright, Professor, come on through.’ I squeezed through towards the security barrier.

‘No, not you,’ said the security guard as one of the protesters tried to follow along behind me.

‘Special delivery,’ said the man, who was carrying a large cardboard box.

The guard looked over towards his colleague, who nodded.

‘Alright, put it down there, behind the counter,’ said the guard, looking around furtively.

There was no need for me to catch the campus tram on this occasion because the Asima Shankar Laboratory Complex was situated nearby, a conglomeration of modernist buildings built over what had once been playing fields for sports such as cricket and rugby.

Today, on the one remaining playing field, there was a motley collection of people of all shapes, sizes and genders, including one individual in a motorised wheelchair, assembled for a game of non-competitive football. A butch-looking person of feminine appearance was randomly selecting them into two teams. Nobody seemed too concerned as to which team they were assigned; not that it would matter much because the teams would be re-selected at half time, and every time somebody scored, they were obliged to change places with the opposing team’s goalkeeper.

Having reached my office, a message marked urgent pushed itself to the top of my agenda. The teaching laboratory would not be available today for student practical work because it hadn’t been cleaned. I called the facilities manager.

‘Kyle, what is happening about the laboratory cleaning?’ I enquired.

‘Sorry, but we simply don’t have the staff at the moment.’

‘Surely there is something we can do to get the lab open.’

‘I’m sorry, but that won’t be possible.’

‘Look, we’ve got to do something.’

‘Nothing we can do, sorry.’

I am talking to a brick wall, I reflected.

'Kyle, I understand getting these things organised can be tough. How about we have a chat about it over a coffee?'

'I'm a bit rushed at the moment.'

'Look, we both need a break. Let's meet in the cafeteria. I'll buy you a cake.'

'Alright then, see you there in a few minutes.'

'Hello, Kyle,' I greeted as he arrived. His unisex overalls and close-cropped hair did not disguise his obviously female figure. *I'll have to be careful with my pronouns*, I reflected. I paid for our fairtrade cappuccinos and vegan banana cake slices at the checkout.

'Thanks for the coffee and cake,' Kyle acknowledged.

Not being mealtime, the cafeteria was nearly empty. 'Shall we go over there?' I suggested, nodding towards an alcove away from the main thoroughfare.

A portly security guard, one of those who had been holding the fort earlier at the Willow Brook entrance, was hovering nearby, holding a cardboard box looking remarkably like the one I had seen being delivered as I came in.

'Special delivery for you,' he said to Kyle.

Kyle looked around nervously. 'Okay, thanks; just drop it down there, please.'

'So, you're struggling for staff at the moment?' I observed once we had settled ourselves down.

'Not half.'

'Why has it suddenly become a problem today?'

'I've had a problem with Lisa, my senior laboratory cleaner. For safety reasons, we need at least two people on each job, and I've only got one other suitably qualified person.'

'What was Lisa's problem?'

'There was an allegation of fat-shaming.'

'I see.'

'It was all I could do to stop her from being sacked. She got a final warning.'

'So, she is still with you? Why is it a problem?'

'This whole week she is on a "Diversity, Equity and Inclusion" refresher course.'

'Couldn't the course be rescheduled?'

'No, she isn't allowed back to work until she successfully passes the course.'

'But there is always the chance that someone has to take time off. Don't you have any cover?'

'I'd love to, but we haven't been able to recruit.'

'So, what's making it difficult?'

'We advertise for people, but we are just not getting enough suitable applicants.'

'There must be people out there who could do the work. I've seen them myself.'

'Well, I haven't been able to find any. Where have you seen them?'

'Just wandering about the place, I suppose. Unemployed, in places like Dunwick.'

Kyle frowned and looked uneasy. 'Don't get me wrong. I'm not assuming anything, but we can't employ them if they are Unsuitables.'

It was my turn to feel uneasy, but to hell with it; sometimes, assumptions had to be challenged. 'Cleaning isn't rocket science, is it? I mean, Unsuitables could do the work, couldn't they? If they are properly supervised, of course.'

'Oh no, cleaning in a laboratory is skilled work. Professional work. The staff need to know about health and safety, dealing with chemical spills, first aid, that sort of thing. That's why we insist upon a degree in hygiene and cleanliness and a postgraduate diploma in hazardous substance disposal.'

'That must narrow the field a bit.'

'It does. We're just not training enough people in this specialism.'

'What about non-graduates, if they were supervised by a qualified person? That would be alright, wouldn't it?'

'Oh no, it would put people at risk. Anyway, it wouldn't help very much because, even if we were to employ non-graduates, that would leave us only with students, and they could only work part-time.'

'Why would it only be students?'

'Think about it. Before they come to university, they are too young, then when they leave, they are graduates.'

'What about those who don't go to university?'

'Well, obviously that would be because they are Educationally Unsuitable.'

'But we wouldn't be educating them, just employing them as cleaners.'

'It is strict university policy. No Unsuitables to be permitted on site in any capacity, no exceptions.'

'Couldn't an exception be made? It isn't right for us to be closing the laboratories that the students need for their studies.'

'Even if we did, the administration couldn't handle it.'

'Why not?'

'Unsuitables, being Ethically Unapproved Persons, are not able to have bank accounts. They would need a bank account for the university payroll system to pay them.'

'Suppose I could get the chemistry students to do their own cleaning to help us out.'

Kyle nearly fell off his chair in horror. 'Out of the question. Employing unqualified scab labour. Don't even think about it.'

No sooner had I broken the news that a video and theoretical demonstration of the equipment would be substituting for the day's practical work, having already missed my discussion with Eddie Donagal, one of my PhD students, than I was informed of the arrival of Robin Smith, my mysterious visitor from the Health Security Agency, at the main Willow Brook entrance.

I met Mr Smith in the Asima Shankar Laboratory Complex reception area. We exchanged pleasantries as I saw to the issuing of his visitor's pass. He was a short, smooth-looking, well-spoken individual of South-Asian extraction. I very much doubted that Robin Smith was his real name.

'Come far today?' I enquired conversationally as we walked up towards my office.

'About average.'

'From the Salisbury direction, I suppose,' I ventured, having surmised that he was probably from the government establishment at Porton Down.

A momentary grimace of annoyance flickered on Mr Smith's otherwise inscrutable face before he changed the subject. 'There were some demonstrators outside the university entrance when I arrived.'

'Yes, they were around when I came in earlier.'

'Does this happen often?'

'Yes, from time to time.'

'Do they ever manage to get in here, into the laboratories?'

'No, that's never happened. The campus security team do a good job at keeping them outside.'

'Could they get in as staff or contractors?'

'Shouldn't think so. Most of them will be Unsuitables, which means they aren't allowed access.'

'How firmly is that policy applied?'

'I can personally vouch that the policy is applied rigorously,' I said with feeling.

We passed by the coffee machine to pick up some refreshments. Two of the PhD students were close by, chatting about their work. I looked around, thinking I might see Eddie Donagal to apologise for having missed him earlier, but I didn't see him.

'Do the staff often talk about their work like that?' enquired Mr Smith.

'Yes, it often helps to bounce ideas around with colleagues.'

'Aren't there confidentiality concerns?'

'I hadn't really thought about it. I shouldn't think so.'

We walked on through with our coffees, and I put out a half-consumed packet of chocolate digestive biscuits on my desk. Mr Smith gazed out of the window from my upper-floor office.

'Good view, isn't it?' I observed.

'Yes, stunning.'

'In the middle there, that's the old historic chapel within our Oppressed Peoples Memorial Complex, now swamped a bit by some of the new administrative buildings.'

'An interesting blend of old and new.'

'Interesting is one way of describing it. Rising up behind it in the distance on the other side of the river, that's Windsor Castle.'

'A lot of history out there.'

'Yes, but some of it is history we can't talk about.'

Mr Smith looked at me with a wry smile. 'Good that you appreciate the need for discretion.'

'Well, what can I do for you, Mr Smith?'

'How feasible would it be to genetically engineer somebody's body to produce a drug?'

'Quite feasible, actually. We are already doing work which demonstrates this concept.'

'So I've heard. Which is why I'm here. Can you give me an idea of what it would involve?'

'You know about mRNA vaccines, I assume.'

'Yes, of course.'

'The injected RNA inserts itself into muscle cells, which produce a protein to stimulate the immune system. Well, it could equally well stimulate the cells to produce a drug.'

'Is it really that simple?'

'Well, no, first the mRNA vaccines are only a one-off. They only work as long as the RNA is there and then stop. For a vaccine, that's fine, because you only need to stimulate the immune system, and then the job is done. For a drug, you probably want the effect to be sustained over a longer period.'

'Sustained for life, perhaps?'

'Yes, that would be good. One injection for a permanent effect. For that, you need the code for the drug production to be incorporated into the body's DNA.'

'How would that be done?'

'With a vector, such as a retrovirus.'

'So, it's simple, then. Inject someone with the appropriate retrovirus, and their body will make the drug indefinitely.'

'Not quite that simple. You need to have a process for controlling the drug dosage.'

'How would that work?'

'The body would need to produce something that inhibits further drug production when the dosage reaches the desired level.'

'What would that involve?'

'You need to introduce the DNA for both the drug and inhibitor production at the same time and in the correct proportions. It's quite tricky to set up.'

'And you have been working on this, Professor?'

'Yes, absolutely. I like to think we are someway ahead of the field in this area.'

'That's why we're talking.'

'The field has fantastic promise. Insulin for those with Type-1 diabetes, blood pressure control, statins to name a few.'

'This is something we would like to do ourselves in the Health Security Agency.'

'What particular drug did you have in mind?'

'That's classified.'

'Why does the Health Security Agency need to get involved? We could do the work here if you like.'

'It is a matter of national security. We'd like your help.'

'Why should we help? What's in it for us?'

'It is in the national interest.'

'So, you want us to help without even knowing what it is about.'

'This programme is on a strictly need-to-know basis.'

'To be honest, I would rather not get involved if I don't know what it is for.'

'It isn't about what you would rather do. National security comes first.'

'Supposing I don't cooperate?'

'It really would be better if you did cooperate. If you don't, your entire work in this area could be declared an official secret. The Health Security Agency has the statutory powers to seize all your material on national security grounds. Were you to divulge anything about it, including our conversation today, you could be prosecuted under the Official Secrets Act.'

I looked into Mr Smith's eyes. He was implacable. I had heard of this happening in the past. Eminent scientists were being silenced and marginalised because some aspect of their work was to be incorporated into a secret weapon system.

'Alright, what do you want from us?'

'You are to provide us with the framework for the drug/inhibitor mechanism. We'll take it from there.'

'I would need to bring in Eddie Donagal, one of my PhD students, to assist in this. He has done some key work in this area.'

'That won't be possible.'

'Why not?'

'He doesn't have security clearance.'

'But I don't, either.'

'You do, actually.'

'How is that?'

'We have checked you out, Professor.'

'When did that happen?'

'We were discreet. You wouldn't have been aware of it.'

'Well, I'm damned.'

'You like walking in the countryside, Professor, don't you?'

'Yes, as a matter of fact, I do.'

'Some concerns were raised about you sometimes getting close to the Toxic Influence Containment Area on the former site of Aspen Grove Studios.

However, you were on foot and took the footpath opposite, so we assumed that you just enjoy walking in the woods. That is right, isn't it?'

I was shocked. Big Brother was watching me at all times, it seemed. Did he know anything about the killing of Johnie Dorritt? Mr Smith looked at me expectantly.

'Yes, that's right,' I concurred after a pause.

'Please keep our conversation today confidential.'

'Well, okay.'

'It's not to be mentioned to anyone. Not your boss, not Liz Entworthy.'

'What has Liz got to do with it?'

'She is your romantic partner, isn't she?'

'Well, yes.'

'And especially do not discuss this with Eddie Donagal.'

'Very well.'

'By the way, Eddie isn't in today, so we wouldn't have been able to see him.'

'Where is he?'

'He is attending a "Diversity, Equity and Inclusion" refresher course this week.'

I was shocked. For one thing, Mr Smith was scarily well-informed. Also, these courses were for those who had transgressed in some way. What could Eddie have done? He was outspoken, that's true. Probably spoke out of turn.

'Has that got anything to do with his lack of security clearance?' I enquired.

'I can't comment on that.'

Having seen Robin Smith off the premises, I noticed the time. Damn, I was already late for my lunch date with Liz Entworthy. She would be waiting for me. Then I saw that Professor William Englebirt, head of the Life Sciences Faculty, wanted to see me when it was convenient. With all that was going on, I would have to skip lunch.

'Sorry, Liz, you must have been wondering where I was,' I said over the phone.

'Yes, actually I was.'

'Some things have cropped up.'

'When are you going to be here?'

'I'm afraid I won't be able to make it.'

'What, again?'

'Look, I'm terribly sorry.'

‘So you should be.’

‘I am, honestly.’

‘Twice in a row, Jim. It’s getting to be beyond a joke.’

‘Can we fix another time?’

‘No, you call on a day you can actually be there.’

‘Okay. I’ll call as soon as I can.’

‘Jim, you had better not stand me up again. Understand?’

Suitably chastened, I wandered over the enclosed bridge to Professor Englebirt’s office in the neighbouring building.

‘You wanted to see me, Bill?’

Professor Englebirt was aged around seventy, spectacled with a permanently cheerful grin, balding on top with his remaining grey hair in two tousled mounds of fuzz on the sides of his head, a throwback to a bygone age and dressed formally in a crumpled jacket and shirt adorned with a bowtie.

‘Yes, Jim. It’s about the coming Rockface audit. We need to get our ducks in a row.’

‘Yes, of course.’

‘They’ll be checking our diversity. I’ve been looking at the numbers for ethnic minorities, gender balance, LGBTQ plus and challenged people. I think we may have a few problems.’

‘Right. What are the concerns?’

‘We have a real issue on the challenged people’s side.’

‘How is that? We have wheelchair access everywhere, provision for guide dogs and all signs are in braille. We have installed all the facilities that have been requested. The upgrade programme for the whole Asima Shankar Laboratory Complex cost us £4 million.’

‘That’s no good if we don’t actually have anyone who is in an actual wheelchair or blind.’

‘I see your point.’

‘It won’t look good for us.’

I pondered for a moment. ‘As I understand it, you don’t have to be completely blind to be registered visually challenged.’

‘No, just a degree of visual impairment qualifies as visually challenged.’

‘I was thinking, Ruth in the records office has those very thick glasses. Is she on the list as visually challenged?’

Bill scanned through his papers. ‘No, she isn’t on the list as such.’

'Suppose we enquire whether we could get her registered as visually challenged. I don't suppose she would object because, at the very least, it would qualify her for a mobility allowance.'

'Great, Jim. Could you look into it? It still won't look good, though, unless we can get at least one wheelchair around the place.'

'Jackie twisted her ankle playing football, and it's been giving her a bit of trouble. Suppose she were to need a wheelchair to get around, just on a temporary basis.'

'Could she be persuaded to do that?'

'I'll ask. She'll want a favour, I should think.'

'I'm sure you'll think of something. LGBTQ+ is a problem. We've got nobody at all whose gender isn't as recorded at birth. That's going to look really bad. Is there anyone we can persuade to go non-binary? Doesn't have to be for long. Just until the audit is completed.'

'You're suggesting I have that conversation with someone?'

'Well, yes, if you can think of someone. It could save us from an "unsatisfactory" rating.'

'It's not exactly a conversation I relish having. It could be misconstrued as sexual harassment or some such.'

'It's what they pay us for, unfortunately.'

'I could have a word with one of my PhD students, Eddie Donagal. We are quite close, and I don't think he would take offence if it was me who suggested it.'

Bill winced. 'I've just had a report about him. He's been a naughty boy and been sent on a "Diversity, Equity and Inclusion" refresher course.'

'Yes, I heard that. Didn't hear what he did, though, that was so bad.'

'Hateful material found on his mobile phone is what it said.'

'I see. Didn't say what the hateful material was, I suppose.'

'No. Could have been almost anything, there is much these days that is classified as hateful. I can't keep up.'

'Well, it does mean he'll probably be amenable. He needs to keep in our favour, given his situation. I'll raise it with him.'

'Would you? That would be great. Overall, we're alright on the ethnic and gender balance split, except in the leadership category.'

'How come?'

'Well, look at us two. Both of us, white, male and straight.'

'You're not suggesting we resign, are you?'

'No, we'll just have to take the hit on that one. We won't be getting an "outstanding" rating, that's for sure, but we might just scrape in as "good". How soon could you get those things moving?'

'It won't be for a couple of days. As you know, tomorrow, I'm at the WRLP party conference.'

'Oh, the Workers Revolutionary Liberation lot, or whatever it is they call themselves.'

'Yes, that's right.'

'I don't know what you see in them.'

'They're not the Liberal Socialist Party, that's one thing in their favour.'

'But they're even more fanatical, aren't they? As far they are concerned, aren't the LSP proto fascists?'

'To tell the truth, I joined them when I was a student, and I've really just stayed along for the ride.'

'I keep out of politics myself,' Bill confessed. 'Far too dangerous these days.'

'I'm kind of stuck with them, to tell the truth.'

'How's that?'

'If I were to leave the WRLP, it would be noticed, which, in my situation, I can't afford.'

'Why not?'

'It's Amelia. She depends upon me. I couldn't bear the thought of her being taken away.'

'Why might that happen?'

'It was only really my credentials as an active WRLP member that saved me from the suspicion of being in league with Amelia's mother when she had her bit of difficulty. Amelia effectively lost her mother at that point. She really needs me now.'

'Your Liz isn't involved with the WRLP, is she?'

'She is like you; she keeps herself out of politics.'

'Wise lady. How are things between you and Liz?'

'A bit dicey, to tell the truth. I've stood her up for lunch twice running.'

'Pity. Hope you can smooth things over. Amelia could do with a mother figure.'

I grimaced. 'Not sure we're quite ready for that.'

'This thing with the WRLP, you're not stuck with them, are you?'

'Where else could I go? I could switch to the LSP, but they're the government. I'd quickly get sucked into implementing their policies, which I would rather not do.'

'So, you don't like their policies?'

'Of course, I love them. How could I say otherwise?'

'So, why wouldn't you want to implement them?'

'I have to say I love them; doesn't mean I like them, though.'

'I get it. You dare not be opposed, yet you would rather they weren't as they are.'

'You know how it is. There are things we just cannot say.'

'But aren't the WRLP policies even more radical than the LSP's?'

'Yes, they are, but in the WRLP, we can talk about things and be as radical as we like with no danger of our policies actually being implemented.'

'Indulging in idealistic fantasies by the sound of it.'

'Yes, I guess that is about what it is.'

'Isn't all that talking just a waste of time then?'

'No more so than, say, going to a Star Wars convention dressed up as Darth Vader, which lots of people do.'

'Isn't that for people who have nothing else in their lives? You're running a department working on the cutting edge of science. I'm struggling to see the point.'

'In my case, it is risk management. As a WRLP member, nobody doubts my progressive credentials.'

'Why don't you do what I've done, keep out of politics completely?'

'I would immediately be suspected of having conservative sympathies. Once you have been in politics, nobody believes you're neutral.'

'There are several other left-wing factions. There seem to be more splinter groups every day.'

'They would forgive moving to the LSP because many do that, and they would see it as a desire to actually get things done, which you can't in a minor party. But if I were to move over to a different faction on the left, I would automatically be seen as a traitor by the WRLP and with suspicion in my new party until I demonstrate myself as worthy by some act of fanaticism.'

'I can't see you wanting to do anything fanatical.'

'Exactly.'

'No possibility of joining anything relatively moderate, I suppose.'

‘You’re not serious, are you? You know perfectly well that were I to show any support for any party to the right of the LSP, I’d be condemned as a Toxic Influence and thrown into outer darkness so fast my feet wouldn’t touch the ground, especially with the lingering suspicion from things in the past.’

‘Yes, I see that,’ Bill mused. ‘Probably explains why these days, nothing at all really exists between the LSP and Forward England on the political spectrum.’

Chapter 4
Political Conference

The usual crowd of rough-looking, shaven-headed men jostled around the university's Willow Brook entrance.

I squeezed my way through the throng only to find the entrance turnstile dented and scratched with its metalwork bent out of shape, unresponsive to my pass. A handwritten notice was propped up out of reach on the campus side of the barrier.

'*Due to vandalism, this entrance is out of use. For admittance, please show your passes to the security staff at the public entrance.*'

With the crowd of men in front of me, that was going to be easier said than done.

'We have invitations to the conference, so what's the problem?' asked one of the men.

'You aren't on our list of conference attendees,' said the leading member of the security staff, a solidly built middle-aged man. 'You need to have been registered in advance.'

'We did register. Look, it says so here.'

'If you were, the WRLP would have put you on the list.'

'Look, we're members of the Workers Revolutionary Liberation Party. Here are our membership cards.'

I had a look at the man doing the talking. I could have sworn that I had seen him before, thrusting a Forward England leaflet into my hand. *Quite a leap from supporting Forward England to being a member of the WRLP*, I reflected.

'I can't help that,' said the security guard. 'It doesn't mean you're registered for the conference.'

'The conference is open to all WRLP members.'

'But you need to be registered. We can't just let anybody in.'

‘We did register. It says so here. Look at the invitation.’

The security guard looked at the paperwork. ‘Alright. Wait here a moment and let me check.’ He disappeared into the security kiosk by the entrance.

‘I’ve checked. I’m afraid your registration was disallowed by the university,’ he explained when he emerged.

‘Why’s that?’

‘You are recorded on the system as Educationally Unsuitable, which means that you are not permitted on university premises.’

‘So, that makes me a non-person, does it? As far as the university and the WRLP are concerned, we don’t matter and have no rights; is that it?’

‘No good having a go at me. I don’t make the rules.’

‘Do you mind if I come through?’ I intervened, holding up my pass.

‘Let the gentleman through, please,’ said the obliging security guard.

‘You let posh gits in then, do you?’ shouted one of the men.

‘Think you’re better than us, do you?’ shouted another.

The Workers Revolutionary Liberation Party conference was taking place in the Diverse Community Conference Hall, the largest and most imposing of the old buildings within the Oppressed Peoples Memorial Complex.

Coming in through the modern atrium, WRLP members checked in at a reception desk near the building entrance before congregating in an open area where coffee and other beverages such as herbal tea were being served.

Shamina Chakrabarti, the Learning Safety Officer with the curious non-binary pronouns was there. I caught zir eye, nodded and smiled slightly. Ze looked back at me with an unsmiling air of suspicion. In the absence of anyone else, I knew it seemed polite to greet zir.

‘Hello,’ I said.

Ze looked at me for a few seconds, grilling me with zir eyes. ‘Hello,’ ze acknowledged eventually.

‘I saw you on the programme, proposing a resolution against fascism,’ I said.

‘Yes, that’s right.’

‘I’ll be interested.’

Zir eyes nailed me again. ‘I hope I can count on your support.’

‘Don’t know. I’ll have to hear the discussion.’

Zir lip curled in annoyance. I was relieved to spot someone else I knew: George Dennigg.

‘George, how are you?’ I said. He was with his partner, who I also recognised. ‘And Imogen, good to see you again.’

George, a short, chirpy man in his fifties, with sparse, shoulder-length greying hair tied back into a ponytail, was one of those acquaintances whom I only ever saw once a year at WRLP conferences, yet we felt like old friends. I only really knew Imogen because she was his partner. I would have said wife, but these days, you could never really know what people’s pronouns were going to be, and besides, I didn’t even know for sure if they were married.

Imogen was a slimly built woman in her fifties, standing tall and straight, not quite my height but tall enough to look down on George.

George reached forward and clasped my hand firmly in his. ‘Jim, glad to see you.’

‘How are things with you up in Aintree?’ I enquired.

‘Same as always,’ George replied. ‘I’m out in the fresh air a lot these days, tending our vegetables, which is nice.’

‘Vegetables! Tell me more.’

‘It’s part of our Food Miles Initiative with the Horticultural Studies programme. Improving people’s lives with wholesome locally grown organic produce, that’s the idea.’

‘How’s it going?’

‘Problem is, most of the produce gets pinched.’

‘That’s a shame.’

‘It’s those Unsuitables,’ Imogen intervened. ‘They’ve got no respect.’

‘They don’t have much,’ I observed. ‘The nice fresh veg must be a temptation for them.’

‘You don’t imagine they eat it themselves, do you?’ said Imogen.

‘Why not? I expect it’s jolly good.’

‘All their sort eat is chips and burgers,’ Imogen scoffed. ‘They’ll be selling it at the farmers’ market.’

‘I imagine the students learn something from growing it,’ I suggested, ‘even if it does end up getting stolen.’

‘Hopefully so,’ said George.

‘I see you have your own Unsuitables problem here, too,’ said Imogen.

‘You mean the protesters at the front gate?’ I said.

‘Yes, that disgusting bunch of fascists,’ said Imogen.

‘They are claiming to be WRLP members,’ I said.

‘What a cheek!’ Imogen exclaimed.

‘Actually, we felt quite at home,’ said George. ‘We’ve got our own mob of protesters back at Aintree.’

‘What are they protesting about?’

‘They are demanding the restoration of traditional sports.’

‘What, bringing back horseracing?’

‘Yes, exactly. Pointless, though. Apart from being an infringement of animal rights, Aintree University has built all over the old racecourse.’

‘Imogen, your Women’s Studies Faculty is where the parade ring was, isn’t it?’

‘Yes, I believe so,’ said Imogen, ‘although I never saw it before the building went up.’

‘I expect you’re too busy running the faculty to get involved in George’s vegetable planting.’

‘Vegetables aren’t really my thing.’

‘I guess you’re going to be busy, being in the conference chair.’

‘Yes, we’ve got a lot of important business to cover this year,’ said Imogen, her posh accent giving her an air of dominance and certainty.

‘Yes, of course, very important issues,’ I acknowledged.

‘Any issue in particular that you find important?’

‘The debate on zero tolerance for microaggressions should be interesting.’

‘In what way, interesting?’

‘The legal definition of a microaggression could be tricky.’

‘How would it be tricky?’

‘How do you formulate what might reasonably be construed as aggressive?’

‘If someone hearing something said and observing some behaviour feels it as being aggressive, then it is aggressive.’

‘But it might not have been intended that way.’

‘What was intended is not the point. If someone is hurt by it, it is wrong.’

‘Won’t that make it difficult to have any kind of interaction between people?’

‘Why?’

‘People will be scared of saying or doing anything, in case it might cause offence.’

‘People need to be educated better about unconscious bias.’

‘I’m struggling to see how it would work, to be honest.’

‘That’s because it wouldn’t apply to you.’

'How do you mean?'

'You are never going to be a victim of microaggression.'

'Why not?'

'You have white privilege, male privilege, ableist privilege. What microaggressions could you be subjected to?'

'People could still be aggressive towards me, couldn't they?'

'Not unless you are a member of a disadvantaged group.'

'So, I could be held accountable for committing a microaggression against someone in a disadvantaged group, but they can say what they like to me?'

'I am worried about you. You really need to learn more about your privilege.'

'I might want to say something about this in the debate.'

'You need to be qualified to participate.'

'I'm a member; doesn't that qualify me?'

'You need to have the lived experience, which you couldn't have unless you were in a disadvantaged group. Are you in a disadvantaged category?'

'Well, I suppose, not really.'

'In that case, as chair, I would have to rule your participation as being out of order.'

'So, I'm not allowed to take part; is that it?'

'Excuse me,' said Imogen, 'things to do.'

'Not sure why I'm here, really, if I am not allowed to say anything,' I complained to George after Imogen had departed.

'Same as me, probably; here to do Imogen's bidding.'

'She may be the conference chair, but that doesn't make her a dictator.'

'That's what you think.'

Imogen's voice came over the intercom. 'Comrades, please take your seats in the auditorium.'

The comrades wandered through the space that had been the extravagantly vast fifteenth-century chapel. Soaring pillars framed expanses of leaded stained-glass windows beneath a gothic-style, fan-vaulted ceiling. Above the stone entrance arch loomed gigantic banks of cylindrically arranged organ pipes reaching up almost to the roof.

The conference attendees took their places, occupying fewer than half of the stackable chairs laid out in rows spread out over less than half of what had originally been the nave in front of a podium where the altar had once been. George and I found a spot together about halfway back on one side.

'Comrades, as we all seem to be here, perhaps we could make a start,' said Imogen into her microphone from her central position on the platform. 'I am your chair for the conference, Imogen Chumley. As for my background, I am a professor of women's studies at Aintree University, and my pronouns are she/her.'

'Our first item on the agenda is the following resolution: *Conference calls for effective action to suppress fascist influence in all its forms.*'

I stood up, signalling with an outstretched arm. 'Point of order, comrade chair.'

'What is it?' demanded Imogen icily.

'It would appear that some of our members have been denied the chance to attend the conference today.'

'Who might those be?'

'I observed people with conference invitations being denied entry to the university campus.'

'Were you able to find out why?'

'The security staff said that they were recorded as Educationally Unsuitable and were not permitted on university premises.'

'University admissions policy is outside of our control.'

'That may be,' I persisted, 'but it was the WRLP that decided to hold the conference on these premises.'

'We are at liberty to hold the conference wherever we like.'

'WRLP rules clearly state that conferences must be open for all members to attend. By holding our conference here, are we not in breach of this rule?'

There were murmurs of discontent from around the hall and a distinct air of hostility to my intervention. 'We don't want Unsuitables,' somebody called out. 'Fascists, the lot of them.'

'What evidence do we have that these people attempting to gain entry were genuine members?' asked Imogen.

'They claimed to have both membership cards and conference invitations,' I replied.

'How do we know that they were genuine?'

'I saw these people, too,' said Shamina Chakrabarti, who was also already on the platform. 'I recognised at least one of them as someone from Forward England.'

'That may be,' I admitted. 'But people are allowed to change their allegiance. They may have had a change of heart and are supporting us now.'

Derisive laughter and jeering echoed around the room.

'I find that hard to believe,' said Imogen testily. Several people cheered.

'I am overruling this objection. The people you referred to are clearly not genuine WRLP supporters, and their intention would have been to disrupt our proceedings.' Many people clapped.

'So, without more ado,' Imogen pronounced, glaring in my direction, 'I would like to invite our comrade, Shamina Chakrabarti, to propose the resolution. Mz Chakrabarti is the Learning Safety Officer here at Slough University and the head of the "Diversity, Equity and Inclusion" policy for Rockface.'

'Thank you, Chair,' acknowledged Mz Chakrabarti. 'My pronouns are ze/zir. Comrades, the most important word in this resolution is *effective*. For many years now, we have skirted around this issue, deploring, condemning and discouraging fascism, but we can see all around us that this has been ineffective. We need to do more than just talk about this issue. We need to take effective action to stamp out fascism once and for all.'

Cheering, clapping and stamping of feet supported Mz Chakrabarti's words.

'The other important point in this resolution is the suppression of *fascist influence in all its forms*. We have seen that fascism often does not call itself by its true name; rather, it insinuates itself often masquerading itself in liberal clothing. We have already heard that today just now when our comrade reported the attempted infiltration of our conference today by Forward England fascists.'

There was clapping and shouts of "Fascist scum".

'It seems that these would-be disrupters of our proceedings succeeded in fooling at least one of our comrades…' giggles and snorts of derision could be heard '…though thankfully, most of us could see through their vile plot.' More clapping ensued.

'Every day in the streets, we see the image of Gordon Garage on leaflets such as these.' Mz Chakrabarti waved one of the Forward England leaflets I had seen myself. 'Leaflets being distributed by the very same fascists who attempted to wheedle their way into our conference today.'

Low, concerned groans emanated from the seated conferencegoers.

'Garage and his supporters are out there, blatantly calling for the restoration of the monarchy, a feudal tyranny we had to fight so hard to overturn, whipping up nostalgic emotions with jingoistic displays celebrating imperialistic wars.'

'Most shocking of all, this particular leaflet features one of our own from this university.'

'Who?' someone shouted.

'A PhD student by the name of Jeremy Fitzregal, using his influential position to publish revisionist views about British imperialism, which are then put to use by Forward England.'

'Cancel him!' shouted someone from the floor.

'More insidious, we saw the works of trans-exclusionist Kate Stillworthy attempting to seduce us by dressing up her hateful aims in feminist attire.'

Boos and jeers echoed up into the vast space above our heads.

'Both Garage and Stillworthy are classified as Toxic Influences, yet Garage continues to get his vile message out, and hate-filled documents from Stillworthy continue to circulate. It is clear that our existing anti-fascist measures are inadequate and ineffective.'

Voices of agreement called out from among the audience.

'So, what we need now is an effective and decisive solution. We need to take the likes of Garage and Stillworthy out of circulation permanently.'

Harrumphs of agreement could be heard.

'There can be no free speech for hate. It has got to be stopped, for good. We have tried Toxic Influence Containment Areas, but that clearly hasn't worked. We have tried re-education, but compulsory course attendance fails to reach hardened fascists. We need to try something else, something more permanent.'

'Shoot the bastards!' shouted someone from within the hall.

'We have rejected the death penalty,' Imogen intervened from the chair.

'I accept what you say, Chair,' Mz Chakrabarti concurred. 'Although it is a question, we might want to revisit in an emergency situation such as we see today. No, my suggestion would be a more humane method using a modern pharmaceutical.'

I stood up. 'May I enquire what pharmaceutical you had in mind?'

'I have been advised that Complianx would be suitable.'

'There are serious ethical concerns with this proposal,' I pointed out.

'What ethical concerns?' enquired Imogen.

'Administration of a pharmaceutical without the informed consent of the patient.'

'They aren't patients,' spat back Mz Chakrabarti. 'They are fascists.'

There was more clapping and cheering from the audience.

'At this point,' said Imogen, 'I would like to put the resolution to the floor. All those in favour raise your hand.'

A mass of hands went up.

'Any against, please raise your hand.'

I looked around to see if anyone else would raise their hand. Nobody did. I decided perhaps it was best not to raise mine.

'Passed unanimously,' Imogen announced.

Mz Chakrabarti took a seat on the platform.

'We now move on to the next resolution,' Imogen continued. '*Conference calls for the total suppression of all aspects toxic masculinity*, to be proposed by our comrade Harriet Henpuddle, the convenor for the Lewisham Socialist Women's Collective and Refuge.'

A corpulent woman in her late forties stood up from her chair and approached the rostrum. She was clad in baggy trousers and a working man's style loud check shirt. Her large mass of unruly wavy hair flopped about her head as if it had a life of its own.

'Thank you, Chair. My pronouns are she/her. Comrades, we have tolerated the patriarchy for far too long. It is time for us to stamp it out once and for all. Containment, admonishment, and calling it out simply isn't enough. It needs to be eradicated, root and branch. Anything less than the *total suppression* called for in this resolution is not enough.'

A handful of radical-looking women from around the room clapped, and a couple stood up. George and I, in common with the other men in the room, remained squirming in our seats, staring nervously at the floor.

'As the resolution states, the measures against patriarchy must cover *all aspects* of this oppression. Clearly, we must stamp out violence against women including sexual violence, but that isn't enough. Toxic masculinity is responsible for so much that is wrong with our society. Inequality, violence, war and environmental catastrophe all stem from the dominance and greed inherent in patriarchy.'

The coterie of radical feminists around the room again clapped and cheered.

‘A primary source of these aggressive tendencies is violent pornography, the type that depicts and normalises sexual violence. We need to purge this unacceptable material from the Internet. This needs to be classified as hateful material.’

A small number of people clapped, but most sat, still looking embarrassed.

‘Furthermore, we need to close any loopholes, in particular, letting disgusting images of sexual violence go on display by masquerading as artworks. Did you know that *The Rape of the Sabine Women* by Rubens is on display at the National Gallery? Did you know that Picasso’s work includes depictions of bestialism and rape?’

There was an intake of breath from around the room.

‘We must stamp out women being pestered for sex. To that end, an approach of a sexual nature may only be initiated by a woman.’

I stood up. ‘Chair, if I may.’

‘Yes, what is it?’ Imogen enquired.

‘Would it be permissible for a woman who was recorded as male at birth to make an approach of a sexual nature towards another woman?’

Imogen turned to Ms Henpuddle. ‘Transwomen are women, are they not?’

Ms Henpuddle looked uncomfortable and then combative. ‘Any sexual approach to a woman that makes her feel threatened must be disallowed, regardless of the gender of the person making the approach.’

‘Would the person, such as another woman formerly recorded male at birth, know that they would be threatening?’ I enquired.

‘We believe women,’ declared Ms Henpuddle. ‘If she feels threatened, we believe her, and whoever caused that must be breaking the law.’

‘In the interests of equality,’ I persisted, ‘shouldn’t men and non-binary people be afforded the same protection?’

‘Toxic masculinity applies only to men,’ replied Ms Henpuddle.

‘Could not a man be subjected to toxic masculinity from another man?’ I enquired.

There were groans from around the room.

‘I am ruling this out of order,’ said Imogen, followed by cheers. ‘The scope of this resolution is toxic masculinity, not gay rights.’

I started to formulate a retort. ‘Sit down, please,’ said Imogen firmly. I waved my hand in defeat and sat back down.

‘We also need to firm up on consent,’ continued Ms Henpuddle. ‘*No means No* is not sufficient. We need it to be *Yes means Yes*. Silence does not constitute consent.’

The feminist activists around the room clapped enthusiastically.

‘Misogyny of all kinds must be stamped out. In particular, incels must be denied any kind of a platform and purged from social media.’

There was a stamping of feet and shouts of ‘Yes.’

‘Women must feel safe from toxic masculinity. To that end, single unaccompanied men should be denied entry to designated women’s safe spaces such as public parks.’

I stood up again. ‘Chair, can I just clarify?’

‘Yes, very well.’ said Imogen testily.

‘Did I just hear that men are to be denied access to public parks?’

‘No, not at all,’ said Ms Henpuddle. ‘Provided they are accompanied by a supervising woman, men will be free to enter.’

‘Equality is a key tenet of the WRLP constitution,’ I pointed out. ‘This proposal is clearly in breach.’

‘It is also in the WRLP constitution that we make appropriate provision for underprivileged groups,’ said Imogen.

‘Can I just clarify?’ I continued. ‘I take it, women recorded as male at birth will be allowed into women’s safe spaces.’

‘Of course, transwomen are women,’ said Imogen.

‘And anybody may identify as the gender of their choice and enjoy the full rights accorded to that gender?’

‘Yes, of course. Trans rights are human rights.’

‘I suggest that this could sometimes result in women feeling unsafe.’

One of the feminists in the audience stood up. ‘Point of order. This man has no right to participate in this discussion.’

‘Excuse me, why not?’ I retorted.

‘As a man, he does not have the lived experience of being a woman.’

‘What does it matter whether I have the lived experience, so long as what I say makes sense?’

‘Patriarchy culturally marginalises the feminine lived experience.’

‘I can still apply logic and reason to this discussion, can’t I?’

‘You are applying the tyranny of logic,’ the woman asserted.

‘What is wrong with logic? It’s how we arrive at the truth.’

‘There is more to truth than logic.’

‘How do you mean?’

‘Truth is lived experience, arrived at with empathy and feeling; logic is hard and cold, denying those essentials.’

‘Nevertheless, if it is objectively true, it is still true, isn’t it?’

‘It is weak objectivity.’

‘How is it weak?’

‘Strong objectivity requires you to have had lived experience to support what you are saying, which as a man you don’t have.’

‘Point upheld,’ ruled Imogen. ‘Comrade Hubbings, you are excluded from the discussion of this resolution.’

I sat down. George nudged and whispered in my ear. ‘The bar is open, I think. Fancy a drink?’

‘Not half. May as well, because they won’t let me talk.’

‘Best you do not go just yet,’ said George, ‘because it’ll look defiant. I’ll slip out and you join me in a couple of minutes.’

I nodded and George quietly eased himself away.

The woman who had shut me down intervened again. ‘Chair, I have a query. We have had laws against sexual violence for many years, yet men still commit these acts. I suggest the law on its own is insufficient.’

‘I suppose so,’ Ms Henpuddle acknowledged. ‘What did you have in mind to supplement the law?’

‘Men could be treated using medical science. A drug such as Complianx could be used to curb their toxic masculinity.’

My cheeks puffed with indignation, but, being now barred from further participation, I had to swallow the objections poised on my lips about medical ethics.

As I slipped out to join George, Ms Henpuddle was replying enthusiastically that this was an interesting and useful idea.

There was a message from Liz on my phone. ‘Have you changed the world yet?’

‘No, apparently I don’t have the lived experience, so I’m not allowed to change the world,’ I replied.

George already had two foaming pints of Meadow Dew ale waiting for us at the bar.

‘Thanks. Don’t know about you,’ I said, ‘but after that I need a drink.’

'You had a rough time,' George acknowledged.

'I've found that I always do when I try to apply reason and logic. I should have learned by now.'

'What delights are we missing?'

'There's a resolution calling out microaggressions and another one condemning Zionism.'

'There always is,' George observed. 'We never seem to bother about Rohingyas or Uighurs and other such suffering folk, just Zionists for some reason.'

I looked around the room, the same one where we had earlier gathered for coffee, herbal tea or whatever. A few other folks, all men, had had the same idea as us and were sipping pints of ale.

'I sometimes wonder why I bother to participate anymore,' I mused philosophically.

'It doesn't make any difference, anyway,' George observed. 'No resolution that gets passed here is going to be put into effect.'

'Sometimes, it does. I've known the Liberal Socialists adopt some of our ideas.'

'They'd have done those things, anyway.'

'Possibly. Anyway, I don't like to see things go unchallenged.'

'I've learned that it's best to keep quiet, or else just agree.'

'I can't do that.'

'You should know by now what happens when you take part.'

'What?'

'They gang up and humiliate you.'

'That's true.'

'Yet you keep coming back for more.'

'I suppose I do.'

'Go on, admit it, you must like it.'

'How do you mean, like it?'

'Being humiliated by the women; it turns you on, doesn't it?'

'Not really.'

'Come off it.'

'Alright, what makes you keep coming here for this annual ritual?'

'Same as you.'

'But you don't participate, so nothing happens to you.'

'Don't you believe it? She deals with me afterwards, when we're alone.'

'Who?'

'Imogen.'

'Right. Is that why you married her?'

'No, we're not married. She considers marriage to be patriarchal oppression.'

'So, she deals with you, as you say?'

'Yes, she certainly does.'

'She makes a thorough job of it, I suppose.'

'Oh yes,' said George with feeling. 'She calls it suppressing my toxic masculinity.'

'More than just verbal suppression, I'm guessing.'

'Yes.'

'Look, sorry, I've been prying. None of my business.'

'Don't worry about it. No offence taken. I don't mind confiding with like-minded people.'

'What makes you think I'm like-minded?'

'Well, you came here to be humiliated, didn't you? Come on, don't deny it.'

Chapter 5
The Clinic

There may have been some truth in George Dennigg's suggestion that I was a glutton for punishment. Having established myself as a professor in pharmacology, there wasn't any need for me to maintain a part-time practice in my first medical specialisation as a psychiatrist, yet I persisted in holding my weekly clinic at Dunwick Park General Hospital.

I told myself I did it to give something back to the community, but perhaps, George was onto something, and I got some kind of sado-masochistic kick out of wallowing in the misery of others.

In its favour, keeping my clinic going maintained me with a foothold in the medical profession and drew me out of the rarified isolation of research science by keeping me in contact with ordinary people.

My consulting room was small, plain and antiseptic, with two standard-issue hospital chairs upholstered in wipe-down bright blue vinyl and a height-adjustable hospital bed mounted on large wheels serving as a consulting couch. There was a cupboard containing various items such as dressings, disposable gloves and syringes. When I say my consulting room, it didn't really belong to me, being mine only for the duration of my weekly clinic. It wasn't any particular consulting room, being whichever of the multiple almost identical consulting rooms was allocated by the hospital administration for that particular day.

First on my list was a new patient with anxiety, depression and suicidal thoughts, twenty years old, but as usual, of unspecified gender.

As the patient came in, I was nearly certain I recognised them. They looked like one of the group of youths I had seen participating in the gangrape of the prostitute the last time I had been in Dunwick. He, sorry, they at this point, looked at me quizzically, as if wondering if we had met before.

The patient was of medium height with a slim superficially male-looking figure, short, cropped hair and signs of stubble on their jaw, but in our modern world, it was never safe to make assumptions. They had a lightning flash tattooed on the back of their hand.

'Hello, I'm Jim Hubbings, one of the doctors, pronouns he/him. Do come in and take a seat. Can I just check on your details, name and date of birth?'

'Carl Gellsten.'

I checked their date of birth. 'And, if you don't mind my asking, your preferred pronouns?'

Carl looked uncertain. 'Well, I want to be she, really.'

'Of course, do I take it you have been he up to now, but would like to change?'

'Yes. I don't like being a man anymore.'

'You've been feeling anxious recently, I understand?'

'Yes.'

'Is there anything in particular that makes you anxious?'

'Everything, really.'

'But some things more than others, I suppose.'

Carl looked nervously from side to side. 'Not really.'

'You can speak freely. Everything you say is confidential. Just between us.'

Carl's lips curled as if he didn't believe me. 'I don't care, anyway.'

'There must have been something that made you feel like this.'

Carl screwed up her face, looked at me and then looked away. 'One of my mates got killed.'

'Oh, I'm sorry. How did it happen?'

'Got beaten up. Really thumped him, broke his ribs and that. So bad he died.'

'You saw it happen?'

'Nah. I'd run away, with the others. Happened after we'd gone.'

'Same could have happened to you if you hadn't run; is that it?'

'Nah. Don't think so. They told us to scarper before they topped Johnie.'

'Who was it that topped Johnie?'

'Mr Sharmoni's geezers.'

'What made them do that to Johnie?'

'He was fucking that woman, wasn't he?'

'Which woman?'

'Some tart, name of Fenn.' She looked at me through narrowed eyes. 'We saw her with a bloke.' She looked embarrassed, looked away, then at me again, questioningly.

'With someone who looked a bit like me.'

'Yes, that's right. Looked like you.'

'How come Johnie was…er…having sex with her?'

'Fenn was happy to let posh blokes shag her if they paid, but blokes like us, Unsuitables, didn't have a chance.'

'So, what happened?'

Carl made a face. 'What are you asking for? You already know, don'tcha?'

'You thought you'd have sex with her whether she wanted to or not.'

'Well, the others, perhaps; not me.'

'Why not you?'

'I haven't got a proper cock, have I? Doesn't really do it for me, does it?'

'Oh, I see. When you say, not a proper cock?'

'Well, mine doesn't go up on its own. I've got this pump thing. And even when I do get it up, I don't come or anything. Not like ordinary blokes.'

I quickly typed on the computer screen to bring up Carl's medical history. Damn, I should have done it before. She was recorded as female at birth but had undergone a transformation to male at the age of ten.

'You had an operation when you were ten, to make you into a boy, is that right?'

'I was already a boy.'

'But you had girl's, you know, sexual parts?'

'Still got them, tucked away underneath.'

'So, how is it you were a boy?'

'When I was young, I played with boy's things, so my mum took me to this clinic place. They said I was a boy.'

'How old were you?'

'Dunno. I don't really remember. Must have been about four, I suppose. It was before I went to school.'

'And what then?'

'Well, I was a boy. That's it. I was always a boy. At school and with my mates, I was a boy.'

'And then when you were ten?'

'They gave me pills. Said it would block puberty and make sure I would be a real boy. Then I had this operation. They took some flesh from my arm and made a cock out of it.' Carl rolled up her sleeve to reveal a scar on her forearm that had been partially disguised with skin grafts. 'It looks alright. I can pee out of it and everything, and I've got this pump thing that makes it go up and down.'

'And you've always been a boy, or man, since?'

'Oh yes, nobody knows that I'm different.'

'But, when it comes to sex, it would be a bit different, wouldn't it?'

'Huh! What sex? Nobody wants to have sex with Unsuitables like us, do they?'

'You haven't had any sex, then?'

'I did once. Wanted to know what it would be like. Went alright. Did the business. She never knew I was any different. Didn't really do anything for me, though. I don't even fancy girls that much, truth be said.'

'If Mr Sharmoni's men hadn't been there, were you all going to have sex with her?'

'Yes, Johnie first, then the rest of us.'

'And you would have done, too?'

'Would have had to, wouldn't I? Wouldn't have looked right with me mates, if I hadn't.'

'But it must have upset you, with what happened?'

Carl stared at the floor with a look of despair on her face. 'Yes. After what happened to Johnie and what we did to Fenn, I don't want to be like that anymore. I want to be a girl.'

'Would you like me to refer you for gender affirmation as female?'

'What do you mean, gender affirmation?'

'Transitioning to female.'

'What would that involve?'

'In broad terms, taking hormones and some surgery, to reconstruct your breasts, vagina and so on, and removal of your male genitals, penis and so on.'

'Male genitals, ha! They're fake, anyway, in my case.'

'Is this something you would want to explore?'

'Not sure I care. I don't think it would be any better, really.'

'It might make you feel better.'

'Nah. What have I got? I'm an Unsuitable. I'll never be anything.'

'How was it that they said you were Unsuitable?'

‘I got onto this website for blokes who can’t get a girlfriend.’

‘What was the problem with the website?’

‘They said some nasty things about girls on it. Then the school saw my search history. The School Safety Officer said I was an incel.’

‘You couldn’t persuade them that you were just curious?’

‘No. I liked some of the posts on there. The Safety Officer said I must have agreed with them. Women wouldn’t be safe with me around, is what they said.’

Anger was building up inside me, but I knew I must suppress any urge to comment. ‘It needn’t be so bad as an Unsuitable,’ I lied, not very convincingly.

‘I’m never even going to have proper sex.’ Carl paused and stared at the floor. ‘Best if I just end it, really.’

‘Ending it would be a permanent solution for a temporary problem. We can make you feel better, trust me.’

‘Can’t see it myself.’

‘Look, I’ll put in a referral to the Tavidown Clinic for possible gender affirmation as female, and we’ll see what they can do. In the meantime, I’ll make out a prescription for Complianx. That’ll help you through how you’re feeling right now.’

‘Don’t let him in here,’ said the next patient as they came in.

‘Who mustn’t we let in?’ I enquired.

‘He’s obsessed with me, keeps following me.’

‘How long has he been doing this?’

‘Don’t know, some weeks now.’

I went over to the door and looked out along the corridor.

‘Nobody there now,’ I assured them.

‘I called Mr Sharmoni. He’ll get him sorted out.’

‘Please take a seat. You’re safe now.’

The patient sat down. I already knew her. She was the prostitute I had seen being raped a couple of days earlier after approaching me in the street. She was in her usual brashly sexual working attire. I wondered whether I might be wise to get in a chaperone, a nurse or a trainee perhaps. I gave her smile, ambiguous but which could have been taken as recognition.

‘I’m Jim Hubbings, one of the doctors, pronouns he/him. If I could just check on your details, name and date of birth.’

‘Fenn Holby, and my date of birth is none of your business.’

‘Sorry, but I do need your date of birth for identification purposes.’

She twisted her face but gave it to me.

‘And your preferred pronouns?’

‘Ain’t it bloody obvious. Out there on the street, you blokes recognise that I’ve got a fanny right enough. You don’t need to ask out there. Why all this toffee-nosed crap in ’ere?’

‘These days, we have to ask because people don’t always identify the way they appear to others.’

‘What is all this “identify” bollocks? If you’ve got tits and a fanny, you’re a woman. If you’ve got a cock you’re not.’

‘So, I take it that you prefer she/her as your pronouns.’

‘What do you think?’

‘It isn’t what I think, it’s what you prefer.’

‘Yes, of course, I prefer she/her.’

‘So, this person, you said him, so a man I guess, has been following you.’

‘Yes, it was him who caused the bother, why I’m here now.’

‘How did he do that?’

‘Well, you must have seen what happened, you were there.’

I blanched. I feigned ignorance. ‘Where was that?’

‘You know, just outside here, you was looking for some company, and we was talking about it.’

‘Actually I wasn’t looking for company, as you put it.’

‘They all say that.’

‘Really, I wasn’t. But yes, I did see those youths giving you some trouble.’

Fenn’s bravado evaporated and tears welled up in her eyes. ‘It was more than trouble. They fucking raped me, that’s what they did.’

‘I’m so sorry. It must have been horrible.’

‘You probably think that because I fuck for a living, it doesn’t hurt, but it bloody well does.’

‘I know it must do.’

‘Thing is, it isn’t the being fucked that was so bad. It was what they did to Johnie, the one was doing it. I can’t get it out of my head.’

I decided not to let on that I knew what happened to Johnie. ‘What did they do to Johnie?’

‘They topped him, didn’t they?’

‘Who did that?’

'Mr Sharmoni's boys. They look after me, see, protect me. I don't blame them. Only doing their job.'

'You said you can't get it out of your head.'

'No, I just think of him being killed, and it was all because of me. I hate myself. It would be better if I wasn't here no more. Then nobody else would have to be killed like that.'

'It wasn't anything you did.'

'But it happened because of me. If I wasn't here, Johnie would still be alive.'

'Johnie raped you. He died because of what he did. You had no part in it. You don't owe him anything.'

'It was because of what I do, though. If I weren't such a slag, he wouldn't have done it.'

'You have to make a living somehow.'

'That's not what they say. They say that being on the game is not allowed.'

'It isn't you that is doing anything illegal. It's being a client that is illegal.'

'Yeah, but it's the same thing. Being illegal for the punters means I can't be upfront about it. It has to be in the street, all surreptitious. If it weren't for Mr Sharmoni's boys minding us, we couldn't do it at all.'

'It's very understandable for you to be upset by this. How much is it affecting you?'

'I can't sleep. I get nightmares, imagining Johnie raping me and then getting killed. I can't get it out of my mind.'

'Yes, that is to be expected. Post-traumatic stress. We can work on that.'

'Then, I'm frightened to go out to work. I get the shakes. Punters make me nervous.'

'We can give you something to make you calmer. Tell me about this man who is stalking you.'

'He's the one who caused all this. He's been following me, trying to get me to go with him. Then, when I wouldn't, he got his mates together, and then, you know, they did what they did.'

'So, this man arranged the whole thing?'

'Yes, he did.'

'I'd like to put you on a course of Complianx, just until things settle down for you. Then, if you come back in a week or so, we can talk some more about this man who follows you and see whether we can do something about him.'

I made out the prescription and prepared to end the consultation.

‘Would you come out with me?’ asked Fenn. ‘Just in case he’s still there.’

‘Yes, of course,’ I replied, humouring what I took to be her delusion.

As we approached the reception area, we heard a commotion. Two huge men were grappling with a young man who I recognised as being one of the noisier of the youths who had mobbed and attacked Fenn. One of the large men was Nelson, the leader of those who had earlier intervened on Fenn’s behalf.

‘Keep out of this, Professor Hubbings,’ said Nelson. ‘We’ll just get rid of this scrote, and it’ll all be quiet again. Alright?’

I nodded and backed off with Fenn a little bit down the corridor.

‘That was him,’ said Fenn. ‘The one been following me. Don’t worry, Mr Sharmoni’s boys will deal with him.’

There had I been, wondering about what anti-psychosis medication to prescribe for Fenn’s delusions about a stalker, and he had been real all the time! But the downside was, Mr Sharmoni’s boys being as they were, Fenn could soon have culpability for another death weighing her down.

We allowed a couple of minutes for Nelson and his rough-looking colleague to hustle the hapless youth away before seeing Fenn out of the building.

These days, the precautions against the rising violence in the neighbourhood made the reception area less than welcoming, with security barriers separating the publicly accessible reception area from the rest of the hospital and nursing and reception staff sitting behind security screens. Along the corridors, beside every desk, and in each consulting room were panic buttons. Every nook and cranny of the hospital was monitored by CCTV. The only reassurance was a framed Rockface certificate rating the hospital as “good” from a “Diversity, Equity and Inclusion” perspective.

I ambled over to see Benny, the psychiatric department charge nurse, a smart, man in his mid-thirties with neatly trimmed hair, his thick-framed glasses giving him a serious look.

‘That was a bit of a commotion,’ I remarked.

‘Certainly was,’ Benny agreed. ‘Should we do something, do you think?’

‘That young lad who they dragged off, he wasn’t a patient, was he?’

‘No, an intruder. He followed in behind that last patient, Ms Holby. She was frightened of him. I stopped him coming in, while she was in with you.’

‘Well done. It could have got ugly.’

‘So, what should we do?’

‘I think nothing. It would be different if any of the staff or patients had been involved, but it was only an intruder.’

‘He could be in danger, that lad.’

‘I don’t think we can do anything about that.’

‘We could call the police, I suppose,’ Benny suggested.

‘Ha! What would they do?’

‘From past experience, nothing. Last time we called the police, they didn’t come in until the next day and then wasted an hour of our time filling in pointless forms about the racial classification, sexual orientation and preferred gender of everyone involved.’

‘I remember. I had made a complaint, but that only meant I had to spend a further two hours while more forms were completed.’

‘Since they were defunded, they’ve been useless,’ observed Benny. ‘They don’t arrest anybody, just do pointless paperwork. The only ones who are any use are Mr Sharmoni’s boys.’

‘They’re sometimes not very nice, Mr Sharmoni’s lot. People get hurt, or worse.’

‘They’re effective, though. Ms Holby made a call while she was waiting to see you, and Mr Sharmoni’s boys were here within five minutes.’

‘So, who else have I got to see today?’

‘There were a couple more, but they scarpered when Mr Sharmoni’s boys arrived.’

‘Okay, not so good then. Frightening away the patients.’

Being done for the day in good time, I messaged Liz to confirm our lunch appointment, which was just as well having stood her up twice running. I walked out past the kiosk housing the hospital security guards and out onto the streets.

As I waited on the corner for my Autocab, another vehicle pulled up next to me, splashing my feet as its tyres rolled into a puddle, a gleaming black prestige limousine that you didn’t often see these days. Mr Sharmoni’s man, Nelson, stepped out from the passenger side and opened the back door.

‘Professor, would you mind stepping into the motor for a moment?’

‘What’s this about?’ I enquired.

‘Just want to have a quick word, that’s all.’

With Nelson standing close, his towering stature blocking out the light, it would not have been wise to argue. I slid into the plush and spacious interior.

Nelson closed the door behind me and resumed his place in the front passenger seat.

'Professor, it would be best to keep today's incident with the intruder between ourselves.'

'Any particular reason?'

'Getting the authorities involved would get us all unnecessarily bogged down with a lot of paperwork, don't you think?'

'What happened to the young lad you took away?'

'What young lad?'

'The one who came into the hospital.'

'If anyone asks, he wasn't there, got it?'

'Alright, but what did actually happen to him?'

'We persuaded him to keep away from Fenn. That's all you need to know.'

'Alright, I won't be saying anything.'

'One other thing. I don't know what Fenn has been telling you.'

'Everything she says is covered by medical confidentiality. It's between her and me and nobody else.'

'That's the ticket. But if she were to have said anything about Mr Sharmoni, we just look out for ordinary people in the neighbourhood, got it? Mr Sharmoni does it out of the goodness of his heart. Wouldn't like anyone to get any ideas about Mr Sharmoni having any business interest in Fenn's work, would we?'

'I won't be saying anything about it.'

'Good, Professor. Glad we got that straight. Please remember, Mr Sharmoni doesn't like people who say unpleasant things about him. It doesn't do to disrespect Mr Sharmoni. Trust me on that.'

Nelson stepped out of the car and politely held the door for me to exit.

Looking out over the limousine as it departed, I saw my friend and colleague Professor Bill Englebirt a little distance away, close to the large hoarding proclaiming, '*Stop Sexual Exploitation*' beneath which stickers offered various intimate services. I was wondering whether to greet him but deciding against it when I noticed him in conversation with my patient, Fenn, her short skirt hitched up suggestively.

Chapter 6
Academic Accuracy

The group of Forward England supporters usually had the area in front of the Willow Brook entrance to themselves, but on this occasion, they had opposition.

"Let Jezza Speak" and "Justice for Jezza" proclaimed placards held by the Forward England supporters, mainly shaven-headed men with beer bellies, separated by a thin line of security guards from an assortment of young people, mainly students from the university, shouting slogans such as "Racists Out!" "Colonialist Scum!" and "No Platform for Imperialists", their placards declaring "No Free Speech for Hate" and "Zero Tolerance for Fascism".

Stepping cautiously against protruding wet, thorny shrubbery to manoeuvre myself around the jostling demonstrators, I made my way onto the campus via the now-repaired turnstile security gate.

Liz was already waiting for me in the Cloister Cafeteria in Seacole Square, an open area once part of a quadrangle within the Oppressed Peoples Memorial Complex.

The wipe-clean tables and brightly coloured dining chairs fashioned out of moulded recycled plastic looked out of place with the medieval brick and stone archways once forming the cloisters. The college cafeteria extended from the original brick building out through the arched openings into the covered atrium, in past times open to the sky. In place of the original lawn, there was a paved area surrounding a central well within which two floors had been built below ground. The atrium roof, winner of a prestigious architectural award, was formed in undulating folds of glass panels supported by a tilted framework of sweeping curved steel girders.

'Hello, stranger,' said Liz. Her sleek blonde hair framed her pretty face, animated by her bright flashing eyes and mouth crinkled into a challenging smile.

'Alright, I'm sorry. I know it must feel like that.'

'You managed to get away from your clinic, then. You often get held up.'

'Only because some heavies came in and cleared the waiting room for me.'

Liz sat up with a start and turned towards me. 'Good God! Couldn't security keep them out?'

'They were Mr Sharmoni's minders. I don't think the security fellows would dare stand in their way.'

'What were they there for?'

'Someone was stalking one of my patients. She put in a call to Mr Sharmoni, and that was the result.'

Liz slumped back down and breathed out with a huff. 'She must have been someone important to get that sort of service.'

I shook my head. 'Not so much important, more that Mr Sharmoni has a business interest in her welfare.'

Liz narrowed her eyes and leaned in towards me. 'What sort of business interest?'

'You really don't want to know.'

Liz's face suggested that actually she did want to know.

'Look, shall we get something to eat?' I suggested by way of deflection.

We selected from the wide choice of vegan and gluten-free culinary options and resumed our places.

'I must say,' Liz remarked. 'I admire your courage. Dunwick scares me to death. I certainly wouldn't go there if I could avoid it.'

'Enough about me. What have you been up to?'

'More changing around of the history syllabus.'

'What now?'

'Certain artists and works are to be erased from the history of art.'

'Who and what?'

'Rubens and Picasso, for example.'

'Why?'

'Use of sexually explicit images.'

'Why is that a problem?'

'According to Professor Bentling, it is a safety concern. It might trigger students who have experienced sexual violence.'

'That's sad. How does Harvey Bentling feel about it?'

'He isn't happy about it all. It was imposed on him by the Safe Learning Environment folk. They aren't his favourite people at the moment.'

'I don't suppose they are.'

'Also, coverage of the Greek and Roman classical period is being cut back to make room for more on African affairs, such as Zimbabwe, Benin and so on.'

'Is there much historical material from Zimbabwe and Benin to actually work on?'

'Not much, a small fraction of what there is on classical Greece and Rome, but that's all right. We just fill in with speculation about what there might have been.'

'I suppose it's going to look better for the coming Rockface audit if the curriculum was more balanced racially and geographically.'

'You may think that,' said Liz with a wry smile, 'but I couldn't possibly comment.'

'I don't think anything,' I said, struggling to keep a deadpan look on my face. Liz giggled.

'I should really be preparing my underprivileged balance statistics tonight,' said Liz. She looked at me askance, brushed her hair off her ear, tilting her body so as to present me with a better view of her breasts as they bulged from under her T-shirt.

As she no doubt intended, I admired her bosom as I chewed on a mouthful of my black lentil, pistachio and shiitake mushroom burger. Looking beyond her more obvious carnal attractions, she had a general beauty about her, a pretty, smiling face and an elegant gracefulness in the way she moved.

'Are those statistics needed urgently?' I asked.

'Not really,' she admitted. 'Good to get them out of the way, though, if there is nothing else I could be doing.'

Her face crinkled into a provocative smile as her eyes caught mine feasting themselves on her well-formed figure, challenging me to pick up on her cue.

'What could you be doing instead?' I asked.

'Oh, I don't know,' she said, pausing for a moment. 'Do you have any ideas?'

We were getting into dangerous territory. While she was giving all the indications of flirting, were I to respond in a suggestive fashion, it could be construed as sexual harassment, a potentially career and reputation-destroying move.

I was saved from having to answer right away by a commotion in the central paved area of the cloisters as three burly-looking men with shaved heads, visible lightning flash tattoos and spare tyres of flesh bulging out over jeans that were too small for their overweight frames rushed in shouting 'Let Jezza Speak!' and 'What about free speech?'

A young woman, probably one of our students, rushed in after them shrieking "No to Hate Speech".

Five or six security guards followed, blocking and scuffling with the troublemakers.

'Horrible having people like that in here,' said Liz. 'They shouldn't be able to get in.'

'Always a way, if you are determined enough.'

'It ruins the learning ambience, having Unsuitables around the place.'

'Maybe the Unsuitables would like to learn, too.'

'I don't think so,' said Liz. 'All they do is make trouble.'

'Being excluded as they are, perhaps there isn't anything else for them apart from making trouble.'

'Making trouble is all they know how to do.'

'We don't teach them to do anything else.'

'Those security people were struggling to control the situation,' Liz observed. 'They could really do with some assistance from the police.'

'Ha,' I observed. 'What police?'

'Okay, I know,' said Liz. 'Institutionally racist. Defunded.'

After some jostling and more shouting, the security guards managed to hustle the demonstrators away from the cafeteria.

'Well, do you have any ideas?' Liz wanted to know after the furore had subsided.

'About what?'

'Do you have any ideas about what I might do instead of doing my stats?'

I looked at her, my eyebrows raised quizzically in an attempt to check her intentions. She looked back expectantly, clearly wanting me to suggest something.

'You have been giving me some ideas but I probably shouldn't say what they are,' I said.

'What sort of ideas?'

'I think that you probably already know.'

She looked at me and wrinkled her face. She leaned in close.

'How would I know?' she cooed softly.

'Liz, love, you know about these things.'

She pulled back in mock outrage.

'You misogynist swine,' she exclaimed. 'How dare you call me love!'

I twisted my face and glanced up at the ceiling.

'Oink,' I replied.

'What do you mean, oink?'

'I'm a swine, aren't I? Oink.'

Her eyes narrowed. She shrugged in acknowledgement that her attempt to wrongfoot me had failed.

'You still haven't told me what those ideas of yours are,' she observed.

'Since I am a swine, my thoughts are likely to be dirty ones.'

'Yes, I imagine that they would be,' she agreed.

I took another bite of my vegan burger and chewed. For some seconds, nothing more was said.

'Well, what are these smutty ideas of yours?' Liz insisted eventually.

'I couldn't possibly say.'

'Why not?'

'Let's say, it might be the sort of thing that could get me into trouble.'

'Give me a clue.'

'Something which requires affirmative consent ongoing throughout,' I said obtusely.

I knew what she had in mind, and she knew that I knew, but she remained determined to manoeuvre me into being the first of us to make an explicit indecent proposal. That was a man's job, after all, to have his toxic masculinity take the blame.

'And what might that something be?' she enquired.

'I'll have to issue a trigger warning first.'

For a few seconds, she didn't say anything, waiting for my next move. 'Go on, then, what are you going to warn me about?' she enquired eventually.

'I might be about to say something of an intimate and sexual nature that some viewers might find uncomfortable.'

'Okay, I've been warned. What is your suggestion?'

'I could distract you from preparing your statistics by kissing your neck and nibbling your ear.'

'Is that all?'

'Well, after I've done that, I could take you away from your statistics completely by putting my arms around you and giving a good snog.'

'That wouldn't distract me for long.'

'Things could go further, but we'd have to have a negotiation about affirmative consent first, according to the university's published guidelines on sexual relations.'

Liz's face was flushed. 'So, my place at six,' she panted.

'I'm sorry, I can't do it tonight. Amelia's expecting me to be home to help her with her project at school.'

Liz puffed in frustration. 'Can't Amelia look after herself for once? She's old enough.'

'I'm sorry. I promised her.'

Liz screwed up her face. 'You are a bastard. You got me all turned on and then you back out. You knew all along that you wouldn't be able to make it.'

'Look, I'm sorry. Let's do it tomorrow evening instead. We can have a cosy meal first, my treat, and then we can take our time and make it really romantic.'

'Not sure that I'm in the mood anymore, after you let me down like that. Again.'

'Come on, get your statistics done this evening and then relax with me tomorrow. You know it makes sense.'

Liz pouted. Still annoyed with me, she said nothing.

'Alright,' I said, 'just let me know what you want to do. I've got to go now. I'm due at one of those adjudication panels.'

'What are they accusing you of?'

'Nothing, I'm on the panel. Someone accused of historical misrepresentation apparently.'

'I've got to dash, too,' said Liz. 'I've got a lecture to give.'

'What on?'

'Role of women in the Renaissance period.'

'Why women in particular?' I enquired provocatively.

'You know perfectly well,' Liz replied testily. 'Gender balance. For every Leonardo da Vinci, Galileo and Christopher Columbus, the course has to provide female counterparts.'

The Platform Safety Adjudication Panel convened in the upper room of Lupton Tower. We avoided the noisy demonstration still underway in Seacole Square by entering via the high-level walkway, a steel and glass tube that bridged across from the main administration block, a brutalist concrete building erected within what had once been the quadrangle.

The panel was chaired by the university's provost and deputy vice chancellor, Dr Jenny Colepepper, a commanding woman in her mid-fifties with lines on her face engraved into a permanently stern expression.

I was one of the two other panel members there, in my capacity as a professor in the pharmacology department, to represent the university's academic staff. The other panel member was Shamina Chakrabarti, representing the student body in her, sorry, zir role as the Learning Safety Officer in the Student Union, a postgraduate student in zir late twenties with dark features and a magnetism that drew in energy remorselessly from anyone or anything that came within zir orbit.

We had been assembled to hear the case against Jeremy Fitzregal, a PhD student, short in stature with a skinny frame, hunched shoulders and a thin bony face that made him look underfed. He was accused of academic misconduct, specifically imperialist denial by suggesting that some good things had arisen from the existence of the British empire.

Presenting the case was Dr Cheryl Biggetty holding the post of Academic Accuracy Officer, a woman in her mid-thirties with an air of unstoppable commitment and sleek professionalism, with straight brown shoulder-length hair tidily combed back and a pretty but ice-cold face that could freeze with a single glance.

According to Dr Biggetty, Mr Fitzregal had published an article where his position in the university was mentioned, having not only failed to obtain academic accuracy approval but had not even sought approval, knowing that such approval was certain to be denied due to the false claims that he was making. In so doing, he had brought the university into disrepute and triggered distress among members of the community.

Mz Chakrabarti nodded vigorously when distress was mentioned, zir eyebrows furrowed with indignation.

'Is this true, Mr Fitzregal?' demanded Dr Colepepper. 'That you published without seeking approval?'

Jeremy Fitzregal opened his mouth to answer, but Tania Tenby, a diffident woman of about twenty-five, the academician's advocate appointed by the Student Union to represent him, gestured to him to leave this to her.

‘I submit that Mr Fitzregal did not publish an article that could reasonably be expected to require formal approval,’ asserted Ms Tenby, her glasses giving her a studious look.

‘The rules are clear,’ replied Dr Biggetty. ‘All publications must be approved for academic accuracy prior to submission.’

‘In the case of the alleged infringement, Mr Fitzregal was responding to an online query on a discussion website,’ stated Ms Tenby. ‘I submit that this does not constitute the publication of an article as intended within the university regulations.’

‘Mr Fitzregal put out his piece on a prominent website that was available for all to read,’ responded Dr Biggetty. ‘I submit that it was clearly publication.’

‘Members of the university staff and students interact on websites every single day,’ insisted Ms Tenby, her voice trembling. She was clearly nervous, overawed by the collection of big egos surrounding her.

Ms Tenby forced herself to continue. ‘It would be unworkable for them to seek and obtain formal approval every time they answered a query from someone. It just doesn’t happen.’

Her voice was getting shrill, prompting me to intervene. ‘Ms Tenby has a point. We must all be infringing the regulation every time we answer something that we get asked online. I know I must be.’

‘Which website was this published on?’ Dr Colepepper enquired.

‘Champions of Saint George,’ said Dr Biggetty.

‘Nothing academic then,’ said Dr Colepepper.

‘Certainly not,’ said Dr Biggetty. ‘It is a forum for English nationalism with a membership tending to promote far-right-wing views.’

‘This is a hate site,’ said Mz Chakrabarti. ‘The Student Union has cancelled it in accordance with our “No Free Speech for Hate” policy.’

‘Professor Hubbings,’ said Dr Colepepper addressing me, ‘there is a difference between simply answering a question in an academic context and making a pronouncement on an overtly political platform, wouldn’t you agree?’

I had to concede the point.

‘Furthermore, Mr Fitzregal’s piece was over 5000 words long and clearly presented in a publication format,’ Dr Biggetty insisted. She called up the piece on the room’s display screen.

‘I think we can agree therefore that this does constitute publication as intended in the university regulations,’ said Dr Colepepper.

Dr Biggetty was uncompromising as she continued, outlining the shameful catalogue of alleged falsehoods in Mr Fitzregal's scurrilous piece with forensic precision. She had a relentless drive that defied interruption and a serious demeanour that deterred anybody else from the slightest jocularity. I could not imagine a light-hearted side to her in any setting, let alone the present circumstances.

Allegedly, Mr Fitzregal had placed the blame for the partition of India on those representing the Indian people, Nehru and Jinnah, failing to reach an agreement rather than with the imperialist British administration where it belonged, a clear case of victim blaming.

Furthermore, Mr Fitzregal had perpetuated the myth that the British had ended the slave trade when in reality, the whole imperial edifice had been built on the triangular trade between Africa, the Americas and Europe.

The railway system built in India was portrayed by Mr Fitzregal as an example of Britain benefiting the empire, while in reality, it had been an example of ruthless exploitation of Indian resources for the benefit of the British imperialist elite.

As Dr Biggetty set out the full extent of Mr Fitzregal's inaccuracies, Mz Chakrabarti could barely contain the swelling intensity of zir indignation.

'This is gaslighting of the oppressed people of the British empire,' ze exclaimed. 'Telling us that the suffering of our forebears was somehow imagined or for our own good.'

'The issue here,' intervened Ms Tenby on Mr Fitzregal's behalf, 'is not whether the members of the panel agree with Mr Fitzregal or find his views to their liking. The point is whether we should support his right to free speech. Debate and discussion are fundamental to education, are they not?'

'Most fundamental of all is the protection of the student body from hate speech,' responded Mz Chakrabarti. 'I have had several students come to me deeply traumatised by what they have read. There wasn't even a trigger warning given about the content. It's unacceptable.'

'Students can't be protected from distasteful matters if those matters are historical facts,' I said.

'If the matters concerned are indeed accepted historical facts,' replied Dr Biggetty, 'then of course, they may be presented, subject, of course, to an appropriate trigger warning. The issue here is that Mr Fitzregal is perpetuating myths, dangerous fringe ideas that can only cause harm.'

‘But who gets to decide on what is the accepted truth?’ I asked. ‘Doesn’t it have to be debated first?’

‘The Academic Accuracy History Sub-committee has reviewed these matters at length and laid down very clear guidelines,’ insisted Dr Biggetty.

‘But you can’t set these things in stone,’ I asserted. ‘There must be a possibility to challenge accepted ideas. Otherwise, we could never move forward in our knowledge.’

Dr Colepepper, fixing me with the penetrative gaze of her piercing blue eyes, gestured to curtail the discussion.

‘The proper channel for such a challenge would have been a submission to the academic accuracy committee, not broadcast irresponsibly on the Internet,’ she pronounced so as to end this thread of discussion, the toughness of her tone echoed by the prominent sinews in her neck and wiry tendons on the back of her hands.

Ms Tenby looked about to argue the point further but decided to withdraw from the field. I felt the same. It was not an issue for which I was prepared to die in a ditch. Seeing that his allies had abandoned him, Jeremy Fitzregal decided to enter the fray on his own behalf.

‘I have done the research,’ he said in a high-pitched whining voice. ‘The accuracy committee is wrong in this regard. I have the documents and figures to prove it.’

Ms Tenby tugged his arm in an attempt to stop his onslaught, but he ignored her.

‘It was African rulers who enriched themselves by sending their own people into slavery,’ he continued. ‘The British traders did not actually enslave anyone, only shipping those who were already enslaved.’

Ms Tenby put her hand to her face. No doubt she had been hoping to minimise the damage to Mr Fitzregal by emphasising his remorse for his mistake and undertaking not to repeat it, but he had just blown that possibility.

Dr Colepepper’s face glowered her disapproval. Her hairstyle, iron grey disguised by a brown tint, cropped off at neck length, forming the shape of a German military helmet, emphasised her authority.

‘That’ll do,’ she said. ‘We have heard enough. The panel will now consider the matter.’

Dr Colepepper, Mz Chakrabarti and I withdrew into the modernist glass bubble of an office that had been built up on the very top of the old brick Lupton's Tower.

Below us in Seacole Square, we could see the still-ongoing demonstration, although the chanting was barely audible through the soundproofed windows.

'Mr Fitzregal evidently has his supporters,' observed Dr Colepepper.

'Fascist scum,' said Mz Chakrabarti.

'They must be Unsuitables, surely,' mused Dr Colepepper.

'I'd have thought so,' I concurred.

'Are they here supporting him spontaneously, or did he put them up it?' mused Dr Colepepper.

'It only goes to show him in his true colours,' said Mz Chakrabarti.

'How did they get in?' pondered Dr Colepepper. 'We're supposed to have security.'

'We need to be tougher on these fascists,' said Mz Chakrabarti. 'And on those who foment fascism. Zero tolerance.'

'We can't allow this demonstration to influence us,' said Dr Colepepper. 'Must do this by the book, based on the facts of the case.'

'I agree,' I confirmed.

'Well, what are your views?' asked Dr Colepepper.

Before I could say anything, an irate Mz Chakrabarti launched into a tirade.

'This is a clear case of historical denialism. Totally unacceptable. None of the students or university community could be safe while Mr Fitzregal remains at large to propagate his venomous and distressing falsehoods. There must be zero tolerance for hate. He must go. We must de-platform him and cancel his presence completely.'

'Professor Hubbings, what do you think?' Dr Colepepper enquired.

'I feel uneasy about suppressing free speech and debate,' I confessed.

'This is outrageous,' Mz Chakrabarti shrieked. 'It's unacceptable for the university academic staff to support hate speech like this. I'll be taking it up with the Student Union.'

'Enough! Professor Hubbings is allowed to speak his mind,' insisted Dr Colepepper. 'Could you enlarge upon that please, Professor?'

'To understand something, you need to look at it from multiple points of view,' I explained. 'It must be possible for someone to challenge the orthodox position.'

‘I suppose that you would defend the holocaust denial as well,’ said Chakrabarti in a sarcastic tone. ‘The Nazis were wonderful, really, just misunderstood.’

‘Well, I wouldn’t encourage that,’ I replied. ‘But I would rather defeat it with reason and evidence than suppress it as if it was heresy.’

‘Alright,’ said Dr Colepepper, the clarity of her thought matching the sharp precise edges of the dark red lipstick applied to her lips. ‘Let’s take a situation closer to home, Professor. Suppose someone were to suggest that vaccines were a plot to implant microchips and made vaccinated people magnetic, would you want to have to waste your time defeating that notion with reason and evidence?’

I mused for a moment.

‘I can see what you are saying,’ I conceded. ‘There are indeed some things that really do not justify a platform.’

‘Not only that,’ said Dr Colepepper, ‘the proper channel for Mr Fitzregal to pursue his ideas was through the academic accuracy committee, not irresponsibly shouting them from the rooftops and rabble-rousing a fascist mob into a frenzy.’

I reflected to myself that there was a snowball’s chance in hell of the academic accuracy committee agreeing to consider a submission from Mr Fitzregal, but I decided against sharing that particular thought.

‘You are right,’ I conceded. ‘Mr Fitzregal should have followed proper protocol.’

We moved on to consider what sanction to apply to Mr Fitzregal. A lenient approach was ruled out on account of his lack of contrition. Mz Chakrabarti demanded that he be permanently de-platformed and cancelled from academic life.

‘That seems draconian, doesn’t it?’ I intervened. ‘Permanent and irrevocable termination of the man’s career for having expressed what would seem to be an honestly held opinion, even if the way that he expressed it was inappropriate.’

Before I had spoken, I knew that my intervention was not going to be well received, but I felt that I could not in good conscience remain silent while this process was developing into a lynching.

‘I represent the student body,’ hissed Mz Chakrabarti, ‘and we will not accept the propagation of fascism and imperialism. We must hold the line. Zero tolerance for hate.’

‘What Mr Fitzregal has done is suggest a more nuanced perception of imperialism,’ I argued. ‘There wasn’t any evidence presented of actual incitement of hatred.’

‘But those people of his shouting outside are hateful,’ asserted Mz Chakrabarti.

‘We can’t allow ourselves to be influenced by them,’ said Dr Colepepper, ‘only the facts and evidence presented in the hearing.’

‘We can’t allow fascists to operate within our midst,’ shrieked Mz Chakrabarti.

‘We don’t have evidence that Mr Fitzregal is a fascist, and even if we did, his political views are not relevant to this case,’ asserted Dr Colepepper. ‘What do you suggest, Professor?’

‘I think that we can agree that Mr Fitzregal cannot be permitted to continue or repeat what he has done,’ I said.

Mz Chakrabarti nodded vigorously and Dr Colepepper indicated her assent.

‘However, I think that it would be unreasonable of us not to allow for Mr Fitzregal to fall back into line and rehabilitate himself,’ I continued.

‘No, absolutely not,’ yelled Mz Chakrabarti. ‘He is toxic. We must root him out.’

‘Let Professor Hubbings speak,’ said Dr Colepepper sharply.

‘I suggest that Mr Fitzregal be suspended,’ I continued, ‘then obliged to attend a historical accuracy education course, on completion of which, he may be re-admitted to his position subject to him formally undertaking to abide by the university regulations.’

Mz Chakrabarti was about to shout out again, but she was silenced by a stern glare from Dr Colepepper.

‘I concur,’ said Dr Colepepper, ‘with one proviso. Mr Fitzregal’s suspension should be for a minimum of six months before he may apply for reinstatement.’

‘That’s reasonable,’ I agreed.

‘Mz Chakrabarti?’ said Dr Colepepper.

‘No, he must go. He must be cancelled,’ screeched Mz Chakrabarti, leaping to zir feet.

Dr Colepepper stood up to face her, asserting her authority not only with her rank and position but also with her athletic figure and posture.

‘Professor Hubbings’s suggestion is carried as a majority position of the panel,’ she stated firmly.

Being impotent to change the decision, Mz Chakrabarti withdrew into a sulk so deep it sucked the very oxygen from the air, like a black hole absorbing all around it, radiating nothing.

As I stepped out of the Lupton Tower, I almost collided with Professor Harvey Bentling, who was coming in.

'Harvey, we're going to have to stop meeting like this,' I said cheerily.

'Oh, hello, Jim,' he responded in a dejected tone. More formally dressed than usual, his face pale and haggard his countenance was as if he was facing an ordeal.

'You look down in the dumps. Anything the matter?'

'As a matter of fact, there is.'

'Oh dear, what is it?'

'Sorry, Jim, I can't discuss it, I'm afraid.'

'Well, tell me another time.'

'There may not be another time.'

He cast his eyes to the ground and walked on past me into the building.

Chapter 7
Dictators and Populists

Upon returning to the lab, I saw a message from Robin Smith of the Health Security Agency. He wanted to talk to me at my earliest convenience.

Damn, I hoped he wasn't going to keep me long, because I wanted to be back at home early for some quality time with Amelia to help her with her school project.

'Thanks for getting back to me, Professor,' said Mr Smith. 'I need to discuss with you the equipment we're going to need for the work we talked about during my visit.'

'I'd be happy to, but you weren't particularly forthcoming about what exactly you were doing.'

'It's classified.'

'Yes, but unless you give me a better idea, it is rather difficult for me to help.'

'It was as I mentioned. We are developing a means of making the human body produce a drug so as to maintain a constant dose of the drug for life.'

'Like insulin, then, for curing Type-1 diabetes.'

'Similar idea, but it's not insulin.'

'The specific drug concerned would have quite a bit of impact on what you'd need.'

'Supposing it was a drug that affected the nervous system.'

'Dopamine to treat Parkinson's, perhaps.'

'I can't tell you the exact drug involved.'

'Alright. I could give you a shopping list of the main equipment you'd probably need and a few hints.'

'That would be perfect. What would be the main items?'

'Off the top of my head, spectrophotometers, electrophoresis and vacuum concentrators for customisation of DNA sequencing.'

'Could you be a little more specific?'

'Sorry, Mr Smith, but right now, I'm rather busy. Leave it with me, and I'll email you in greater detail and jot down some thoughts about the best approach.'

'When would you be able to do that?'

'Hopefully, I could do that by the close of play on Monday.'

As I came out of the Asima Shankar Laboratory Complex, Kyle was standing outside, diminutive and feminine in his overalls, passable for a teenage lad, his eyes flitting furtively from side to side.

'Hello, Kyle,' I said as I passed.

'Oh…' exclaimed Kyle, taken aback. 'Hello, Professor.' He quickly looked in another direction and stepped a few steps away from the door.

A young man, presumably one of the students, slunk up beside him and Kyle slipped over a small packet, which the young man shoved into his pocket.

'So, Amelia, what is this project of yours?' I enquired later, as we settled down at home with some tea and toasted muffins.

'Comparison of the dictators of the 20th century and populists of the 21st century,' replied Amelia, a pretty fourteen-year-old, her unisex school attire of trousers and polo top failing to disguise her developing feminine allure.

'I see, so what do they want you to do?'

'To show how these leaders have used hate to advance their cause.'

'Right, so it is a given then that they did all use hate to advance their cause.'

Amelia looked at me questioningly. 'But they did, didn't they?'

'Well, yes, I think that's right. In most cases, they did. But it irritates me when you get told what the answer is in advance without any opportunity to evaluate it for yourself.'

'They always do that.'

'The next question I would have is, what is a dictator and what is a populist?'

'They told us that, too. A dictator is someone who has seized absolute power and uses it for hateful purposes.'

'That would mean that someone with absolute power who doesn't have a hateful agenda would not be a dictator. Not sure if I buy that one. What did they tell you a populist was?'

'Someone who seeks popularity by promoting and inflaming hateful tendencies within the population.'

‘So, it’s not being popular that makes someone a populist, just someone who exploits popular ideas that happen to be hateful. Alright, what material do you have to work with?’

Amelia pulled out her tablet computer. ‘This is what they gave us.’

‘Didn’t they want you to go and find your own material?’

‘Dad, I couldn’t do that because they took away my access.’

‘You can do searches online, can’t you? Browse the online libraries.’

‘Dad, it won’t let me. Look.’ Amelia attempted to do a search.

‘*Search facility disabled,*’ said the screen.

‘The school did this, did they?’

‘Yes, Ms Englebury told me it was suspended until I had completed out-of-hours anti-hate training.’

They could certainly do this, I reflected. Laws limiting access to harmful content meant that a lot of information was filtered out for everyone, adults included. For children, any child, vast swathes of content were off limits. The powers-that-be had unlimited abilities to restrict access even further for particular individuals considered vulnerable. These days, it was no use trying to use someone else’s computer or phone to bypass the restrictions because the identity of anyone attempting to access to search or social media was verified each time using a biometric such as a fingerprint or iris scan.

‘Has anything more happened since your run-in with Ms Englebury?’ I enquired.

‘Yes. I have to stay on after school for anti-hate training.’

‘How have you found it?’

‘I’m not bothered. It means that I don’t have to do sport.’

‘Not letting you do sport, is that part of the punishment?’

‘Not for me, it’s not. Sport is boring.’

‘Why?’

‘Nothing really happens. You get allocated to teams at random, and then, anytime anybody scores, they swap people over between the teams, so nobody really wins or loses.’

‘That’s the point, isn’t it? There aren’t supposed to be any winners or losers because that might damage people psychologically.’

‘Which just makes it boring. Everyone thinks so.’

‘What do they teach you in your anti-hate training?’

'It's funny because it is supposed to be anti-hate, but they tell you people who are supposed to be terrible like you're supposed to hate them.'

'Ah, but that's because those people are the ones doing the hating, which is why they have to be hated; is that right?'

'Yes, I suppose if those people promote hatred, it serves them right if they get hated themselves.'

'I'm not convinced myself that hating is a good way to combat hatred,' I mused.

'What about when the person you are told is hateful is someone close to you?' said Amelia. 'A friend or someone in your own family.'

'Friends and family members can sometimes do bad things. When they do, they have to take the consequences, just like anyone else.'

'It's not very nice when that happens.'

'No, it's not,' I reflected. 'Anyway, let's have a look at what they gave you to work with.'

I scanned through the material displayed on Amelia's screen. 'I can see, by way of examples, they've given you Hitler, Mussolini, Donald Trump, Boris Johnson and Gordon Garage. But I don't see Stalin, Mao, Putin or Castro.'

'Should I put something in about Stalin or Castro?' Amelia asked.

'No, better not,' I conceded.

'Why not?'

'For one thing, they might want to know how you got to find out about Stalin or Castro. You can't search for anything, remember? So, they would put two and two together and assume it must have come from me.'

'Would that be bad?'

'Could be very bad. At the very least, they could classify me as an unfit parent, perhaps even a Toxic Influence, and with your mother gone already, well, you know what that could mean.'

Amelia looked back at me open-eyed with shock. 'What would happen to me?'

'Don't know, taken into so-called care, I suppose. So, don't do it.'

'Why aren't we allowed to think for ourselves, Dad?'

'We *should* think for ourselves, love, but we need to be careful when and how we do it.'

'But if we think for ourselves, terrible things can happen to us.'

'Yes, very much so. Which is why we need to be very careful.'

‘I hate not being able to think my own thoughts.’

‘Nobody can stop you doing that. They can’t look into your head; at least, they can’t yet. Just be careful what you say to people, and don’t write anything down.’

‘But sometimes, I just want to tell someone what I think.’

‘You can always tell me. What we say here, you and me, remains here between us. I won’t tell, and you mustn’t tell either, okay?’

‘Okay, Dad. But why is it that those in authority are telling us, the ordinary people, what we should do and think?’

‘It is for our own good, I suppose, to stop hateful things happening.’

‘We are supposed to be a democracy, aren’t we?’

‘Yes, that is what is claimed.’

‘In a democracy, aren’t the government supposed to do what the people want, not the people having to do what the government want?’

‘Yes, that’s the idea.’

‘If the people like what Putin, Trump or Gordon Garage say and vote for them, shouldn’t they be elected?’

‘If people like them get elected, they tend to oppress people and start wars.’

‘If that’s what people want and vote for, shouldn’t they be allowed to do that?’

‘The issue here is the tyranny of the majority.’

‘What’s that, Dad?’

‘It is when a majority chooses to oppress minorities within the community and justifies it by saying, “We are the majority, so it’s democratic”.’

‘You mean, like Hitler did to the Jews? It was democratic because the majority of the population didn’t like Jews.’

‘Exactly. In a proper democracy, we have freedom and diversity. Minorities should be able to be themselves without being oppressed by the majority.’

‘So, we avoid that by excluding those we think would oppress minorities.’

‘Yes, I would say, that is the justification.’

‘But when we do that, don’t we make those people themselves an oppressed minority?’

‘You know, I’m proud of you. You are very perceptive.’

‘Thanks, Dad.’

‘So, let’s see what they’re saying about these characters.’ I scrolled down on Amelia’s screen. ‘Hmm. Nazis burning books, artworks condemned for being degenerate, ghettos for Jews, people classified as *Untermensch*. I get that bit, but this statement, *"We have to combat hate so that it won't happen again*", that's a bit of a stretch.'

'But we don't want that happening again, do we, Dad?'

'Well, it would be better if it didn't happen again, but there are things happening now that are remarkably similar.'

'What, is that true?'

'On books, you yourself have only recently got into trouble over what you read. I am having to get textbooks altered. I heard that Rubens and Picasso are being dropped from the art history syllabus because they are sexually explicit. We have confined people to Toxic Influence Containment Areas, and we classify people as Educationally Unsuitable.'

'That's not the same as what Hitler did, is it?'

'Explain to me the difference.'

'I see. Should I point that out in my project work?'

'Good God, no. It would get you into all sorts of trouble, and probably me as well for putting the ideas into your head.'

'What should I do then?'

'Read through what they have given you, stir it around a bit, rewrite it in your own words and hand it in. Don't change or add anything.'

'What would be the point of that?'

'It would demonstrate your understanding and loyalty to the cause.'

'What cause?'

'What they are teaching you.'

'What if I don't agree with it?'

'Not agreeing would get you into deep do-do.'

'What sort of do-do?'

'Failing your Ethics and Society qualification, for a start. Without that, you are deemed Educationally Unsuitable and can't get into university.'

'What would happen to me if that happened?'

A graphic image sprang into my mind of Amelia walking scantily clad through the streets of Dunwick as one of Mr Sharmoni's troupe of prostitutes. I shuddered. 'In my work in the psychiatric clinic in Dunwick, I get to meet some of the Unsuitables. Believe me, it isn't very nice, what happens to them.'

'But I'm not mentally ill. I'd be alright.'

'It might make you mentally ill if you were in the situation they are in.'

'What do I have to do to avoid it?'

'Just tell your teachers what they want to hear. Thinking for yourself will get you into trouble unless you keep quiet about it. Above all, keep on the right side of Ms Englebury.'

'Alright, Dad.'

'What was that Hills and Doon novel about, the one Ms Englebury took exception to?'

Amelia blushed a deep crimson. 'You know about that?'

'Yes, she complained about it to me.'

'Well, you know.'

'Young girl gets swept off her feet by handsome prince sort of thing.'

'It was Georgian times; it was an innocent vicar's daughter in a country parish who meets a dashing aristocratic cavalry officer. She is below his station in life, but he doesn't care because he loves her. Then he has to go away to fight Napoleon at Waterloo.'

'Sounds like a good read. Did you imagine yourself as the vicar's daughter?'

Amelia blushed again. 'Yes. It was very romantic.'

'But I'm not a vicar.'

'You're quite forthright and moral, though. You could be, Dad.'

'Never thought of myself like that. Anyway, you enjoyed the book.'

Amelia squirmed, looking at the floor, her face glowing red hot.

'It's perfectly alright,' I reassured her. 'You're allowed to have those feelings.'

'But Ms Englebury doesn't like it. Says it's heteronormative.'

'She would say that.'

'What is heteronormative? I don't even know what it is.'

'Suggesting that straight men and women getting it together is normal.'

'Isn't it?'

'According to the current ethos, it invalidates other types of relationship, gay relationships, trans, non-binary, all that.'

'Does wanting to have a handsome straight man make me a bad person?'

'No, of course not. But, if you do want that, you will need to keep saying stuff about how good other types of relationships are, otherwise Ms Englebury and others like her will give you a hard time.'

'I see. I just need to say the right things.'

'You've got it. By the way, what do you know about Georgian times?'

‘Not much. All they tell us about it is colonialism and slavery.’

‘Would you like to see what it was really like in those days?’

‘Yes, I’d like that. I can’t really picture it at the moment?’

‘Do you fancy seeing a Georgian-style country house, with what they had in it, clothes they used to wear, that sort of thing?’

‘Yes, that would be great.’

‘There is one we could go and see, tomorrow if you like, run by the National Trust.’

I had to look twice as the Autocab swept into the entrance passing a sign announcing itself as Ashanti Abansoro. As we cruised up the long leaf-strewn driveway, I was reassured to see the large Georgian mansion I recognised from pictures I had seen as being Pevening Place.

A sign near the entrance reiterated: *Welcome to Ashanti Abansoro*. A notice next to the sales kiosk informed us that all profits from ticket sales were to go as reparations for slavery to those whose efforts financed the building of this property, namely the Ashanti people of Ghana in West Africa. A subtext explained that *Abansoro* meant mansion in the local Twi language spoken by the Ashanti people.

As we entered the building, a notice told us that the National Trust was proud to represent the former Pevening Place as the Ashanti Abansoro, celebrating the people whose travails had made it possible.

The first room in our tour had been stripped out of its original aristocratic trappings of paintings, classical busts and Chippendale furniture and replaced with West-African Ashanti artefacts, carved wooden stools curved up at the sides with legs in the form of stylised animal figures, primitive looking statuettes, extravagant headdresses and golden facemasks.

The second room portrayed the lives of African slaves on sugar plantations in the West Indies—black people shackled together as they were transported in ships across the Atlantic, labouring in the fields under the hot sun and the rough wooden shacks in which they lived.

The third room depicted the gruesome cruelty of Sir Archibald Pevening and his sadistic overseers, inflicting vicious whippings and tearing infants away from their mothers to be sold on.

Only in the fourth room were we able to see the genteel conditions enjoyed by the Pevening family from the proceeds of their West-Indian plantations, the ornate furniture, fashionable attire and extravagant balls.

As we emerged from the tour, Amelia looked bored, dejected and, in her youthfulness, out of place amongst the mostly elderly folk on a day out in their retirement.

'Sorry,' I said. 'That wasn't quite what I expected.'

'I suppose it wasn't so romantic as I thought in those days,' Amelia reflected.

'Not quite what you read in Hills and Doon.'

'No, it sounded like all fun and romance in the story.'

'The reality was probably more complicated than what the National Trust is portraying,' I observed. 'I doubt whether Sir Archibald Pevening was quite as bad a monster as they are suggesting.'

'Not nice, what happened to those people on the plantations, though.'

'True. But are we so much better today? When we buy clothing, a T-shirt, say, how often do we stop to think about the conditions some seamstress in Bangladesh was working under when she made it?'

Amelia paused to consider. 'No, I never did. Should we stop buying clothes made in Bangladesh, then?'

'No, because if you did, the seamstress would be put out of work and her conditions would be even worse. She would probably starve.'

Amelia stopped and looked at me. 'So, it's wrong whatever we do. Buy stuff, and we make the workers suffer. Don't buy it, and they suffer even more.'

'Welcome to the real world.'

'I don't like the real world very much.'

Chapter 8
Police Enquiries

As usual, I caught up with the news in the Autocab on my commute to the university.

Following the recent propagation of hateful material, a government consultation was underway on the control of hate criminals. Critics complained of the writings of the trans-exclusionist Kate Stillworthy continuing to spread, most shockingly among impressionable school children, while mobs of far-right thugs blatantly propagated toxic filth from Gordon Garage while both were supposedly confined to a Toxic Influence Containment Area. The government clearly needed to act urgently to impose tougher controls.

In other news, the body of the murdered man in Dunwick who had died after being viciously beaten to death had been identified as twenty-year-old Johnie Dorritt.

I didn't want to hear any more, so I switched it off and made a phone call.

'Hello, Liz, it's Jim. Still on for this evening?'

'Oh, yes, long overdue. You're not going to stand me up again, are you?'

'Oh, no. We're definitely on. Nothing's going to stop me this time.'

'It had better not,' she said emphatically.

'It'll be all the sweeter for having waited.'

'Is that your excuse? You'll have to do better than that.'

'Seriously, I can't wait. You're very special, and I love you.'

'You're not bad yourself when you deign to turn up. Don't be late.'

The usual crowd of Forward England protesters braved the weather outside the Willow Brook entrance, protesting against the disciplining of their favourite academic icon, Jeremy Fitzregal. As I idly ran my eyes over the throng, I was taken aback to see one of my own PhD students, Eddie Donagal, a young man in his mid-twenties with an uncombed curly mop of hair, brandishing a *Justice for Jezza* placard.

'Hello Eddie,' I said, restraining myself from shouting at him angrily.

'Hello, Professor,' he replied, peering at me through his steamed-up glasses.

'I need to talk to you, Eddie. Can you spare a moment?'

'I'm busy right now. May I see you later?'

I clenched my jaw and held back from swearing with difficulty. 'Now would be best,' I said in an assertive tone, 'if you can tear yourself away.'

'What, you mean right now?'

'Yes, right now, please.'

Eddie handed his placard back to one of the other demonstrators.

'Well, what is it about?' he enquired, having extricated himself.

I reined back from cursing that it was bloody obvious what I was concerned about. 'Let's go through onto campus, shall we?' I muttered through gritted teeth.

Eddie shrugged and loped along behind me through the turnstile. Once through, he looked at me quizzically. I nodded my head, indicating for us to walk over towards the nearby Asima Shankar Laboratory Complex.

'You are playing with fire by doing what you just did,' I remarked once we were clear of the entrance area.

'That's my business,' Eddie replied defiantly.

'It's my business, too. You are doing some important work, and I don't want to see it jeopardised.'

'It's diabolical what you did to Jeremy. Someone has to make a stand in his support.'

'What do you mean, what I did to Jeremy?'

'You were on the adjudication panel, weren't you?'

'If it weren't for me, instead of a six-month suspension, Mr Fitzregal would probably have been banned from academia for life and very possibly declared a *Toxic Influence* as well.'

We had reached a rain-soaked bench beside the path looking out over the campus overlooked by Windsor Castle with the Great Park stretched out in the distance. 'Let's take a seat here,' I suggested.

Eddie hesitated for a moment at the prospect of wetting his pants on the damp wood before overcoming his misgivings and gingerly sitting down beside me. 'So, you argued on Jeremy's behalf, you say?' he said sulkily.

'Yes, I did.'

'Sorry, I thought you had gone over with the establishment.'

'No, but to have any influence, you have to operate within the system.'

'Doesn't alter the fact that what you…' Eddie hesitated. '…they, did to Jeremy is an attack on academic freedom.'

'Since when has there been academic freedom?' I scoffed.

'Don't you believe in academic freedom?'

'It doesn't matter what I believe in. It doesn't exist. Certainly not these days.'

'We should still aspire to academic freedom, though, shouldn't we?'

'We can aspire all we like, but that won't magic it into existence.'

'We must do something. Make some sort of a stand.'

'Going about it the way you just have out there won't achieve anything. You just set yourself up to go the same way as Jeremy Fitzregal; perhaps, worse.'

'What, just for expressing what I think?'

'You were standing with Forward England and Gordon Garage. I can barely think of anything more likely to get you cancelled. I only hope that nobody else except me noticed you there.'

'What about freedom of speech?'

'I can't believe that you are so naïve. Don't you realise that "No Free Speech for Hate" is one of the tenets of our times?'

'I'm not hating anyone.'

'That's not the point. Hate is anything that does not comply with the established ethos.'

'Could I really be cancelled for that?'

'Of course, you could. Many have been cancelled for much less.'

Eddie pondered. After a few moments, he turned to me. 'On reflection, thanks for getting me out of there.'

'You're welcome. I'd hate to see your career ruined.'

'It was on the spur of the moment. I saw them protesting about Jeremy, and I felt the same as they did.'

'They're dangerous company. Not people you want to be seen with.'

'I suppose they are.'

'You've already been in some trouble, haven't you? How was that "Diversity, Equity and Inclusion" refresher course they sent you on?'

'I did it last week. Bloody waste of time.'

'I hope you didn't say that to anyone.'

'Why not?'

'To redeem yourself, you need to say how valuable it was and how much you learned.'

'If I don't?'

'You would be treading on thin ice. By the way, if you don't mind my asking, what did you do to get sent on the course in the first place?'

'Banned material on my phone.'

'Anything in particular?'

Eddie looked embarrassed.

'It's alright, not really my business,' I reassured him.

'It was an old war film, *The Dam Busters*. They said it was jingoistic and racist.'

'Oh dear, I seem to recall the dog had an unfortunate name, a word we can't use these days.'

'So, it's not just me. You've seen it, too.'

'Yes, but it was a very long time ago, before such films were banned. How did it come to light? Surely you had it encrypted.'

'Yes, I did, but as I was watching, I was called away. I left my player behind with it still playing, and someone saw it.'

'Oh, dear. You really should have been more careful.'

'It was completely private as far as I was concerned. Didn't think I needed to hide it away.'

'Nothing is private on campus. Once you're here, there is always someone who might take offence.'

'I thought I could trust my colleagues, at least.'

'Obviously, you were overly trusting.'

'I realise that now.'

I stood up. 'Come on,' I said. 'Let's get over to the lab. We need to talk about your project work.'

I didn't get to discuss Eddie's work because I had a visitor waiting for me in reception, a police officer.

'Professor James Hubbings?' enquired the officer, a feminine-looking person with a serious disposition.

'Yes, that's me.'

'I am Detective Sergeant Travers. Pronouns she/her.'

'He/him,' I acknowledged. 'What can I do for you?'

'I need to ask you a few questions,' she said, looking bored.

‘What about?’

‘Is there somewhere private we can talk?’

‘Come through to my office.’

Once we were sat down, she set up her tablet on her lap in preparation. I waited in anticipation.

‘Professor, could you tell me about your whereabouts during the afternoon of last Monday,’ she said in a monotone as if using a standard phrase she had said many times before.

‘Yes, I held my psychiatric clinic at Dunwick Park General Hospital.’

‘What did you do after your clinic?’

‘I took a walk through Dunwick, went on for a stroll in the countryside, and after, that I ordered an Autocab to take me home.’

‘Whereabouts in the countryside?’

‘There is a footpath that skirts past a caravan park and into some woods. I like it there.’

DS Travers peered at a map displayed on her tablet. ‘That would be Lakeside Caravan Park?’

‘Yes, that’s right.’

‘Did you observe anything unusual as you walked through Dunwick?’

This was getting into difficult terrain. ‘Nothing in particular,’ I answered cautiously.

‘Whom did you see?’

‘Nobody I knew.’

‘Did you speak to anyone?’

‘I don’t really recall.’

DS Travers sighed. ‘Professor, please think. It wasn’t long ago, was it? You must remember whom you talked to.’

‘I’m not sure I spoke with anyone.’

‘Professor, think some more,’ said DS Travers in an exasperated tone. ‘We have you on CCTV.’

‘There was a woman who came up to me for a chat at one point.’

‘Did you notice anything about this woman?’

‘Not particularly.’

‘Such as any special characteristics?’

‘Such as?’

‘Disability, ethnic group, sexuality.’

'Nothing like that. She was white, local accent, not disabled as far as I could tell.'

'Sexuality?'

'Straight, I would have thought.'

'How could you know that?'

'From the way she approached me.'

'What did you chat about?'

'This and that, nothing important.'

'Professor, if you are obstructive, we'll have to have this conversation down at the police station. What did you talk about?'

'Look, why do I have to tell you this stuff?'

'This is a serious matter. A murder enquiry. It really would be better for you to be candid with me.'

'Murder?' I queried, trying to appear innocent. 'What murder would that be?'

'We are investigating the murder of a young man that took place last Monday.'

'Oh, dear. Sorry to hear about that. Why are you interested in me?'

'You were reported to have been in the vicinity at the time.'

'You don't think I had anything to do with it?'

'You may have witnessed something. We need you to tell us everything you know. Now, about your conversation with the woman you mentioned, what was it about?'

'Alright. She thought I might be interested in having sex with her. She was mistaken, by the way. I told her that.'

DS Traver's air of boredom lifted and her eyes brightened and widened. 'What did you do to give her the impression you were interested in having sex with her?'

'Nothing at all.'

'Professor, I don't believe you,' snapped DS Travers. 'I put it to you that you must have sexually harassed her.'

'Certainly not.'

'We may want to talk to you some more on the matter of sexual harassment, Professor, but for now, I will leave that to one side. What happened after that?'

'There was a gang of youths who shouted and chased after her.'

'Didn't you think she might need help?'

'I told the youths to leave her alone.'

‘And what then?’

‘They were pretty threatening. I left it at that.’

‘Can you describe any of these youths?’

‘Well, sort of rowdy hooligan types, I’d say.’

‘Any particular distinguishing features?’

‘I may be wrong, but I sensed one of them may have been trans.’

DS Travers sat up straight and her eyes flashed. ‘How did you perceive that?’

‘Just something I sensed.’

‘You don’t have anything against trans people, do you, Professor?’

‘No, not at all.’

‘Why did you feel the need to mention it?’

‘You asked if any of the youths had distinguishing features.’

‘Trans people have the right to carry on with their lives without being stigmatised. We may want to talk some more to you later on the question of trans-exclusionary behaviour, which I have to inform you is an offence.’

‘I can’t help what I observed. I didn’t do anything to show it.’

‘Did you talk to anyone else?’

‘A gentleman wanted to borrow my mobile phone.’

‘Was that all he wanted?’

‘Yes, that’s all. He took it away with him and then brought it back.’

‘You didn’t think that was suspicious?’

‘No, he seemed to be a polite and trustworthy gentleman.’

‘What made you think he was polite and trustworthy?’

‘His manner and demeanour.’

‘Can you describe the man?’

‘Large build, about six feet four, seventeen or eighteen stone.’

‘Race, dress, distinguishing features?’

‘Black, smart-looking, formally dressed in a dark suit.’

DS Travers pondered for a moment, a slight frown of disappointment on her face from being unable to identify any transgression on my part. ‘You didn’t observe any disturbance during the time he had your phone.’

‘I heard some noises, but I kept away. I didn’t want to get involved.’

‘And you didn’t do or see anything else?’

‘No, I don’t think so.’

DS Travers did not seem convinced. ‘Could we just go over it again and pin down the timings of what happened?’

By the time we had re-examined every detail three times over, in addition to the already identified sexual harassment and trans-exclusionist transgressions, DS Travers also had me down on suspicion of loitering with intent of sexual predation outside a nursery school, and my entire morning had gone.

Rushing to catch up on the backlog of irritating problems building up, before I knew where I was, it was four o'clock, and I still hadn't collated the material I had promised for Robin Smith. A message informed me that there was a shortage of test tubes in the laboratories. Not having time to call in advance, I made my way straight down to Kyle's lair, a windowless room in the basement. It would have been polite to knock, I suppose, but being in a hurry, I went straight in.

Kyle was jumping up and down in excitement in front of a laptop screen on which I could see two muscled and blooded men crouched and circling each other within an octagonal ring lit by spotlights, around which a crowd of baying spectators could barely be made out in the surrounding gloom. In a sudden flurry of activity, the men exchanged bone-crunching kicks and fisticuffs. After sustaining four or five heavy blows in succession, one of the men toppled over onto the floor with an ominous thud, to be landed upon heavily by the other bulky man crashing down upon him with all his weight.

'Go on, kill him,' shouted Kyle shrilly, waving his weedy fist down into the air.

'Ahem,' I said. 'Not interrupting anything, am I?'

'Oh, sorry,' said Kyle, quickly closing the lid of his laptop.

'Test tubes. We're running short.'

'I'll take them up later.'

'We need them now. Where are they?'

'We've got some over here? Any particular size?'

'20 ml.'

'Here's a couple of boxes. Want me to bring them up?'

'Don't bother,' I said. 'I'll take them up myself.'

'Thanks…er…about, you know, the fight…you won't say anything, will you?'

'Don't worry. I won't be saying anything.'

'Thanks.'

By the time I rushed into the Earth Temple vegan restaurant in Datchet forty minutes late, Liz was already ensconced at our table, in a businesslike pose, scrolling down through something on her mobile phone, clearly of more importance than my arrival on the scene.

'Oh, so you're here,' she observed coldly after a minute or so. 'Just in time for dessert and coffee.'

'Look, I'm sorry. It's been a hell of a day.'

'Really? Do you have any other kind of a day?'

'So sorry, lots of bother to contend with today.'

'There always is, as far as you're concerned.'

'Things seem to just come out of left field.'

'Such as?'

'Er…um…' I stutter, realising that I can't really talk about any of it, not Robin Smith's officially secret project, not the murder, not the police accusing me of paedophilia for loitering near a kindergarten. 'Laboratory problems.'

'So, your damned laboratory is more important than us.'

'You know it isn't.'

'Could have fooled me.'

'Wish I could convince you.'

'We'll see. I took the liberty of ordering a bottle, which you're paying for, by the way. Here, have a drink.'

Liz poured me out a glass from an already half-empty bottle of the Earth Temple's most expensive vintage champagne.

I blanched slightly at the expense, then shrugged. 'Thanks, on a day like today, I need a drink.'

The waiter came round. 'Ready to order, sir?'

'Give me a moment,' I replied, hastily picking up the menu.

'I'll have the roasted harissa cauliflower with warm coriander hummus,' said Liz decisively, 'and to follow the broccoli, asparagus with hoisin sauce.'

I hurriedly chose something at random.

Over the next hour, the frostiness in the atmosphere between us thawed, enlivened by my amusing anecdotes of the happenings at the WRLP conference and lubricated by a second bottle of Earth Temple's extortionately expensive champagne.

'What should we do now?' I enquired as put my now heavily indebted credit card back in my wallet.

Liz looked back at me, defying me to make an indecent proposal for her to take offence about. I waited for her to say something.

'I suppose we could come back to my place for a coffee,' she conceded eventually.

'That'll be nice,' I said, avoiding the trap of insinuating that there could be more than coffee involved.

'I can manage, thank you,' said Liz as I tried to take her arm for us to walk the few steps from the Autocab to the front door of Liz's modern mock-Georgian-style apartment block in Windsor. The decorative brickwork edgings, Juliet balconies and slate effect roof tiles gave the place a certain elegance.

Liz's flat was decorated in a spare minimalist fashion designed for clean lines rather than comfort, with Scandinavian-style furniture formed into spindly curves combined with sharp angles and strictly functional lighting giving out a cold white light.

'Coffee?' suggested Liz.

She popped a couple of pods into a machine, which hissed and gurgled to produce a strong expresso-style brew.

As she waited for the machine to do its business, I came up close and put my arms around her from behind.

She grabbed my hands and forcefully pulled them away. Turning to face me, she gave me a piece of her mind.

'Let's get one thing clear. We work on a *Yes means Yes* basis. You do not put your hands on me like that without getting my express permission.'

'I'm sorry,' I said sheepishly, retreating out of the kitchen.

Presently, Liz joined me in the living room with the coffee. She had a coy look on her face, glancing at me sideways and flashing her eyelashes playfully. She set the coffee down on the marble-topped low table in front of the white slimline sofa. I was standing in the background, chastened by her earlier reprimand. She stepped over towards me, slowly, swaying her body slinkily, cat-like, emphasising her body's smooth curves, and came up on one side, very close, almost touching me but not quite.

'You know, you could always ask me,' she purred.

'Ask you?'

'Yes, ask. The answer could be yes.'

I stood for a moment or two, my mouth opening and closing in indecision about what I could dare to ask. 'Would you like it if I were to kiss you?'

'Yes, I think I would like that.'

I put my arms around her. She snuggled herself up close. I stroked her chin gently with my fingertips. She lifted up her head towards me. I brought my lips down slowly into contact with hers. All was well. We stood snogging for a minute or so.

Eventually, she pulled away, gently, not with any anger or hostility.

'Perhaps, we should sit down,' she suggested. 'The coffee will be getting cold.'

Damn the coffee, I thought, as we set ourselves down onto the severely firm cushions of the flat slab-like sofa. We sipped our coffee. She looked at me in a playfully challenging way, as if to say, 'Now what?'

'Would you like to kiss some more?' I suggested.

'Yes, why not?' she answered, as if to say, 'What have you been waiting for?'

We kissed some more on the sofa, bent over slightly awkwardly because it didn't seem quite right to lay out flat. She was enthusiastic, wrapping her arms around me and holding me tight, squashing her soft sensuous body against my muscly torso. I reached down and gently stroked her thigh. She lurched backwards, grabbing my hand and contemptuously thrusting it aside.

'I already told you. *Yes means Yes*. Don't you understand the meaning of consent?'

'Sorry, I got carried away,' I stammered as I edged away to one end of the sofa.

'Like many men, you just don't know how to control yourself.'

'Sorry, I guess you're right.'

In the uneasy silence, I swigged the dregs of my coffee.

'How did you get on with your underprivileged balance statistics?' I enquired after an awkward interval to break the silence.

'I don't give a damn about underprivileged balance statistics,' responded Liz. 'Isn't there something you want to ask me?'

I wondered what it might be that I should be asking her.

'Well, go on,' persisted Liz, looking me straight in the eye.

'Would you mind if I stroked your thigh?' I asked, finally taking the hint.

'Of course not,' she said, grabbing my hand and placing it on her thigh. 'I thought you'd never ask.'

We were off again, fondling and petting enthusiastically. We persisted for several minutes but keeping within the established parameters and kissing, holding and thigh stroking. Thigh stroking left some ambiguity, but I dared not let my fingers creep up too far lest I make another dreadful faux pas. Liz slid down in my direction, easing her crutch closer to my fingers. I pulled my hand back a little to compensate, so as to avoid straying close to her private areas. Liz thrust her pert breasts up towards my face as if inviting me to touch, but I dared not do so for fear of committing yet another heinous sexual assault.

'Do you like what you see?' Liz enquired.

I hurriedly looked away from her boobs out into the middle distance. 'Well, er,' I began. What was the right answer? I suppose she meant her bust. If I liked her breasts, I must have been leering at them, but I couldn't say I didn't like them. 'Yes, I like what I see.'

'Is that all?'

There's more? What could she mean? 'Not sure,' I say, confused.

'We might take something off,' I suggested tentatively. 'To see more, I mean.'

'What should we take off?'

'Our tops, perhaps.'

Liz slipped off her blouse and undid her bra, allowing her well-formed breasts to drop free. 'Like this?'

'Yes, very nice,' I said.

'Aren't you going to take yours off too?'

'Oh, right.' I hurriedly pulled off my shirt.

We got down to some more heavy petting, more passionate now. We were stretched out flat now, but it still wasn't comfortable. The upholstery was hardly plumptious, and the vertically set arms of the sofa were hard and unforgiving. I sensed Liz getting impatient.

'Is this all that's going happen?' she inquired at last in exasperation.

'I don't know, should there be more?'

'Well, this isn't very comfortable, like this, is it?'

'I suppose not. Should be go somewhere more comfortable, do you think?'

'I would have thought so.'

'Do you mean…' I hesitated.

'Well?'

'…in bed?' I said, at last, bracing myself to be lambasted for making an indecent suggestion.

'Of course in bed! About time.'

She led the way into the bedroom. We flung off our remaining clothing. There was only one problem. Instead of a horny rampant phallus between my legs was an incapably limp worm.

'I'm sorry,' I said after Liz's sexiness had failed to restore my virility. 'That *Yes means Yes* protocol has exhausted my passion juices.'

Chapter 9
Artisan Skills

"Let Us Work" said one of the placards outside Slough University's Willow Brook entrance. Another demanded "Vehicles for All". On this occasion, my entry onto campus was unimpeded by the weatherbeaten handful of shaven-headed Forward England protesters.

I arrived in my office to find a message from my boss, head of the Life Sciences Faculty, Professor William Englebirt. Could I please pop around for a chat when I had a moment?

'Jim, take a seat,' said Professor Englebirt in the manner of a kindly uncle, as I stepped into his office in the neighbouring building.

'What can I do for you, Bill?'

'Just a catch-up, really. Did you notice the protesters this morning?'

'Yes, usual noise about something or other. Nothing about their Jezza, though. They seem to have forgotten about our Mr Fitzregal.'

'People have short memories.'

'They are back onto their grievance about vehicle ownership rights, I notice.'

'Not sure why they want one, personally,' said Bill. 'I haven't had a car for years.'

'I had one myself,' I reflected, 'way back. It was a Mini, one of the last models still requiring a human driver. I drove it myself, but only up to a point. I remember it was like a busybody mother-in-law of a backseat driver. I couldn't start it up without my blowing into a built-in breathalyser, which would have grounded me if I'd had more than a half of shandy. Then, there was the barrage of bleeping if I came within ten feet of a bit of foliage and the speed restriction that I could have overridden, except that it would have reported me to my insurance company.'

'I don't think it's for the most part cars they want but rather more work vehicles, small vans for their plumbing and window cleaning businesses.'

'But they can have a van if they need it for their business, can't they?'

'Only if their business is legitimate.'

'Oh, right,' I acknowledged. 'I get it. They'd be Educationally Unsuitable, wouldn't they?'

'Exactly. Educationally Unsuitable means they can't get themselves qualified, so no legitimate work.'

'No proper bank account either, to stop money laundering and no credit.'

'They can't get legitimate credit,' said Bill, 'but there are unofficial sources.'

'You mean from folk like Mr Sharmoni.'

'Yes, he would see them right, at a price.'

'No, qualifications, no work, no credit. I'm surprised that social media isn't erupting in protest about it.'

'They can't get on social media, remember?'

'Of course. Unsuitables and Toxic Influences, blocked because they can't be trusted to use the facilities ethically.'

'"No Free Speech for Hate", remember?' Bill reminded me.

'Which explains why they have to take their protest out onto the streets, and why they complain about lack of work.'

'They work, anyway, but can't get a van because their work isn't official.'

'I expect Mr Sharmoni takes care of that for them, too.'

'He probably does,' Bill concurred. 'Anyway, talking of work, this brings me to what I wanted to talk to you about.'

'Okay, what's that?'

'I need you to do some interviews for the Artisan Skills intake.'

'Must I?'

'Someone has to do it, and it's your turn.'

'I've never really understood why occupations like waste disposal operatives, firefighters, security officers and cleaners need to be graduate careers.'

'Supposedly, it is about equality and respect for the working classes,' Bill explained. 'Why should only middle-class professions get the respect arising from graduate status? Shouldn't traditional working-class occupations have the same status?'

'Well, okay. Waste disposal operatives do a great job that's really important for society, but surely what they do doesn't justify spending three years in university to qualify? What do we have to teach them?'

'Well, they might encounter hazardous materials; asbestos, for example, and noxious chemicals. They need to know about those. They need to be able to identify accurately the various recycling categories. Then, there is the first aid medical training for accidents at work. Carrying out risk assessments. There is a lot to learn.'

The Artisan Skills faculty was a purpose-built annexe situated about a mile from the main university and accessible using the campus tram service. It consisted of a cluster of industrial-looking buildings like a distribution centre for a major corporation, with some swirling shapes fashioned out of concrete providing the modern art flourishes expected from a modern educational establishment. It contained communal areas, a canteen, meeting rooms, classrooms and practical training facilities to accommodate the fourteen thousand students learning the variety of artisan trades offered by the university.

I was surprised to see the slight frame of Kyle skulking in the cavernous central lobby next to a pillar. A young man in stained dayglo orange overalls slipped past and a package of something changed hands.

I wandered through into one of the echoing impersonal meeting rooms with white-painted walls, under cold white overhead lighting, where I joined the other twenty or so university academic staff drafted in to carry out the interviews for the new intake. We were seated on stackable moulded plastic chairs.

In due course, our interviewing coordinator took her place at the front to conduct our briefing.

'For those who don't know me, I am Cheryl Biggetty, the university's academic accuracy officer, and my pronouns are she/her.'

Ms Biggetty, in smart business attire, impeccably ironed and creased as if she was on a military parade, had an air of authority about her that left nobody in any doubt about who was in command.

'Today, we are conducting final screening interviews for admission into the Artisan Skills undergraduate courses.'

'You will not be assessing the skills or aptitudes of the candidates in their fields of study. For artisan roles, the faculty will provide whatever training is required, so prior knowledge and experience of the trade aren't required. What is essential is ensuring the protection of both the university and the wider community from contamination by hateful influences.'

'By the time you see them, all the candidates will have achieved a good pass in the Ethics and Society examination. To be eligible for taking the examination, candidates would have needed a Correct Ethical Attitude Certificate from their school, or a mandatory Ethics and Society remedial training course before the exam if not certified by the school. Possession of hateful material on their devices, phones or laptops, or on their personal cloud storage would have automatically disqualified them from the exam.'

'Additionally, the candidates' social media usage will have been vetted before they arrive today for any hateful associations.

'However, passing an examination demonstrates knowledge, but it does not demonstrate a correct attitude. Today, your job is to ensure both—that the candidates have absorbed more than the words and actually understand the concepts behind them as well as having a firm commitment to the ethos. It is no good just being able to list out the 72 defined gender categories. They need to be able to explain what they actually are.'

'We know from experience that there are those who cheat in the exam or have learned things by rote without gaining a proper understanding. By way of example, only last week, we had a candidate with a strong pass in the Ethics and Society exam and an otherwise unblemished record. When asked what problems arise from cisnormativity at the interview, she answered that we would get cancer and glow in the dark.'

There were sniggers of amusement from around the room.

'Finally, please be sure to check carefully the credentials of each applicant. Although these should already have been checked by security at the gates of the campus, we do sometimes get unauthorised people slipping through.'

My first candidate was a pretty well-groomed young woman, eighteen years of age.

'I'm Professor Hubbings, pronouns he/him, but you can call me Jim. Could I just check your details, please?'

'Details? Yer what?'

'Name, pronouns, address, date of birth, course of study.'

'Sarah Jones, she/her, the other stuff is on the paper here.'

'So, you're here for the Cosmetic Expression Studies course.'

'Yeah, I want to be a hairdresser and nail stylist.'

'If someone came into your salon asking for hair extensions, what is the first thing you ask them?'

'Yeah, well, I'd ask for her pronouns, wouldn't I?'

'But you wouldn't know they were her until they had told you their pronouns.'

'Well, I'm not blind, am I? I'd know if it was her by looking, wouldn't I?'

'But they might not want to be a her, even when they look like one.'

'Why would they be coming in asking for their hair done, if they didn't want to be a her?'

'Aren't you stereotyping?'

'Yeah, I'd put a stereo in the salon, and all. I like music, I do.'

'I meant, by assuming that only female persons want their hair done.'

'Nah, there's men too, gays and trans and that, but they want to be her with their pronouns and all, don't they?'

'If they say they want her for their pronoun, what does that make them, a man or a woman?'

'Dunno,' she looked at me puzzled. 'If they're a man, they're a man, if they're a woman they're a woman, ain't they?'

'But didn't they tell you what they were, by saying that their pronoun was her?'

'But I can see what they are. I'm not blind, am I?'

I sighed. 'Sarah, look, I don't want to stand in your way of becoming a hairdresser, I really don't, but this hasn't gone well so far.'

'How do you mean? What do you know about how I'd be as a hairdresser?'

'That's not the point. You have to pass on the Ethics and Society, otherwise you won't be on the course.'

'But I passed the exam, didn't I?'

'You also have to pass this interview.'

'Why, what's the matter?'

'I really shouldn't be doing this, but I'm going to give you another chance. I'll forget everything you've said so far. It's on tape, but I'll rewind to make it a fresh start. Before I do that, here are a couple of hints.'

'Oh, right, what are the hints?'

'You don't know someone's gender until they tell you their pronouns, okay?'

'Okay.'

'Anybody can have their hair done. It doesn't make them female.'

'Right.'

'Transwomen are women.'

'What, you mean when they've had their boobs chopped off and grown a beard, they're still women.'

'No, that's transmen.'

'I don't get it. It's all so confusing.'

'Never mind. I'll restart now, alright?'

'Alright.'

'If someone came into your salon asking for hair extensions, what is the first thing you ask them?'

'Erm…'

'Go on.'

'I'd ask for her pronouns.'

'Don't you mean, "I'd ask for *their* pronouns"?'

'Why, was they a group, or something?'

'No, just one person.'

'Why would it be their then?'

I put my hands to my forehead and shook my head. 'I'm sorry, Sarah, but I'm going to have to fail you on this interview.'

'Why, what have I done?'

'You have failed to show that you understand the principles of Ethics and Society.'

'What do you know about it? You stuck-up git.'

'I'm sorry, Sarah, you'd probably make a very good hairdresser and nail stylist, but without demonstrating you understand Ethics and Society, it's no go.'

I already recognised the next candidate from my clinic, but for reasons of confidentiality I couldn't let that show. They were wearing a pair of gloves, which was odd, because it wasn't particularly cold, even outdoors and especially not indoors.

'I'm Professor Hubbings, pronouns he/him, but you can call me Jim. Could I just check your details, please?'

'Hello, Prof, nice to see you.'

They were well-turned-out, much smarter than the last time I had seen them at the clinic, clean-shaven, clean, new looking trousers and shirt and brand-new trainers.

'Could you tell me your name, pronouns, address, date of birth, course of study?'

'You know who I am.'

'Yes, but I do have to check.'

'Surely you haven't forgotten, have you?'

'No, but I still have to check.'

'Carl Gellsten,' said Carl, then hesitating. 'Pronouns, dunno.'

'You can have any pronouns you like.'

'Not sure, really. Well, you know, I already told you what I'd really like, the other day at the clinic.'

'Anything said at the clinic is confidential and doesn't apply here. You need to think about what you would like to be for other people here at the university. It could be different to what you shared privately with a therapist.'

'Alright, he/him.'

'And your course?'

'Home Appliances Installation.'

'I see you were previously classified as Educationally Unsuitable. How did that change?'

'Saw this social worker, told her I was trans. She didn't know until I told her.'

'I see. She probably wouldn't. It's not obvious.'

'She said I was in a disadvantaged category. She could get my case reviewed.'

'Then what?'

'Got sent on this course, Ethics and Society remedial training. I did the course, but I didn't think anything of it. Then, just the other day, I got this letter saying that I wasn't Educationally Unsuitable no more and could apply for university if I wanted. So here I am.'

'Well, it's good to see you here.'

'Yeah, it was good. Before I got the letter, I was going to top myself, wasn't I?'

'Better not talk about that here. Save it for the clinic.'

'Right you are, Prof.'

‘Alright. Carl, imagine you have come to make an installation in someone’s home, and the owner comes to the door. What do you need to ask them?’

‘Their pronouns, so I can address them right.’

‘What would it be called if you didn’t address them right?’

‘Misgendering.’

‘Why would misgendering be a problem?’

‘It would be disrespecting them and make them feel like they cannot be who they want to be.’

‘If you had to come back to the same house later on and meet the same person, what would you do?’

‘I’d still ask for their pronouns.’

‘But you’d already know their pronouns, so why would you do that?’

‘They might have changed their mind.’

‘Well, Carl, as I said, it’s great to see you here and I hope you do really well on your course.’

‘Does that mean I’ve passed?’

‘Yes, absolutely.’

‘Thanks, Prof. I feel great now. Way better than from that Complianx stuff you gave me last time.’

‘Carl, I put in that referral to the Tavidown Clinic for you transitioning back to female. Do you still want to go ahead with that?’

‘No, thanks all the same, Professor. I think I’ll stay as I am, at least for now.’

My third candidate wasn’t present when I went to bring them in. I called the admin line to enquire. They had been barred access by security because they were showing a visible lightning flash tattoo, a banned hate symbol. I took my hat off to Carl for having had the nous to wear gloves.

Chapter 10
The Love Nest

I had the Autocab drop me off in the drizzly rain on the outskirts of Dunwick.

On the street corner, an elderly man wearing a blazer adorned with medals was selling paper Remembrance poppies. Such an emblem of jingoistic celebration of military exploits was not something I could dare be seen with around the university, I reflected.

It was only a couple of hundred yards from where poor Johnie Dorritt had met his end. That episode was not something that I wished to dwell on, so I set my sights in the opposite direction, out of the urban area.

Although it wasn't really very far, in the sullen grey rainy conditions, it felt like an arduous trek, trudging over spongy sodden turf on the roadside.

Had anyone asked, I would have assured them I enjoyed walking, regardless of the weather, allowing the fresh air to clear both my head and lungs. In reality, it would have been explainable for me to be in Dunwick, whereas I preferred not to have my presence at my actual destination recorded.

I continued alongside the broken concrete paving surfacing the cleared derelict site of a long-gone factory, upon which were parked an assortment of vehicles. There was a single building, a decrepit storage shed, from which I could hear the sound of an enthusiastic crowd cheering and jeering some kind of highly competitive sporting activity, probably violent in nature.

By the time I reached the tall fence topped with razor wire, the surface of my clothing was damp from the relentless drizzle, and wetness was oozing down my neck. I ignored my bleeping phone, presumably informing me of the dire peril I was in from being so close to the Toxic Influence Containment Area.

As usual, I avoided the main entrance of the Lakeside Caravan Park, instead taking the nearby public footpath leading to the adjacent woods. I tried in vain to avoid the mud by placing my feet onto the fallen leaves piled up alongside the path. About a hundred yards along, I scrambled up a slippery bank where I could squeeze through the scratchy hedge and onto the paved driveway of the caravan park.

A group of three disreputable-looking individuals observed me suspiciously as I walked past. I could see drug-related litter at the base of the hedge, some hypodermic needles and scrunched-up pieces of foil.

The reception hut looked forlorn in the grey gloom, its paintwork flecked with green lichen and a slimy bloom of mould. A little bell clanked as I opened the door. The caretaker, a man visibly worn down by his sixty-odd years of existence, was sitting in a stained dusty armchair he had probably rescued from a skip.

'Hello, Sid,' I greeted him. 'How are things?'

'Can't complain. You alright?'

'I'm good, thanks. You got the caravan for us?'

'Yes, all set up for you. Hundred quid, like we said, alright?'

'Yes, that's fine. We'll do crypto, yeah?' I pulled out my phone, selected the Crypto Cash app and entered the amount. Sid pulled out his phone and held it next to mine. It bleeped. Sid pulled back his phone and checked his screen.

'Yes, all gone through,' Sid confirmed. 'It's plot number 47. Kate's already in there, waiting for you.'

'Thanks, Sid. See you later.'

The park was relatively unused at this inclement time of year, with the few remaining people lurking in the shadows like woodland wolves and trolls poised to pounce on passers-by. A shabbily dressed man, huddled under a damp awning, watched me furtively as I counted along the plots.

Light shone from the dusty windows of the small, shabby-looking caravan set up on plot 47. I was obviously in a poor state of repair, not one which could normally have been rented out. I suspected that Sid was renting it out illicitly on a no-questions-asked basis without the knowledge of the park's owners.

I opened the door.

'Kate, are you there?'

Kate, still slim and lithe in her middle years, jumped up from the banquette seat and flung her arms around my neck. 'Jim, oh Jim, it's so good to see you.'

'And you, Kate.'

Our lips met and we hugged and kissed, passionately and lovingly for a good minute or so.

'Are you keeping okay?' I enquired when we broke off for a moment.

'Yes, jogging along, you know.'

'It must be awful, cut off from everything.'

'It's alright. There's some good people around. I'll tell you about it later.'

'Good to hear. Anything you need?'

'Nothing immediate. Let you know if anything crops up.'

'It's been too long. I need you. I really do.'

'I need you too,' said Kate with feeling, grasping her arms around me tight.

We stumbled over towards the end of the caravan, tipping over onto the raised platform laid out as a double bed. Our fingers grappled with the buttons and zips of each other's clothing, flinging garments aside as they became free.

The atmosphere inside was damp and musty, but we didn't care. For us, this sanctuary could have been the most luxurious of scented boudoirs. It was bliss to be together, the sordidness of our surroundings only adding to our ardour.

There was an earthy farmyard quality to our lovemaking, our sweaty bodies entwined in a squirming embrace, frantically bringing ourselves to an overpowering climax, for a few all too brief seconds of blissful moaning ecstasy banishing all worries and concerns.

Temporarily sated, we held each other tight, enjoying our togetherness, our feeling of oneness against adversity.

'Would you like a cup of tea?' said Kate, eventually.

'Yes, that would be lovely.'

'It's all here. I checked earlier—kettle, water, teabags, sugar, long-life milk in little sachets.'

'Great. Sid said he'd see us right.'

Kate squirmed apart from me and got to work making the tea. I admired her naked form, sagging just a little here and there, but still well-proportioned for someone in her late forties. She had her hair cut quite short, in a simple but professional style. Her face retained a youthful look, but etched lines showed the stress she had been under in recent years.

'How is Amelia?' Kate enquired.

I hesitated for a moment, deciding quickly not to mention her difficulties at school.

'She is insisting that I buy her a new smartphone.'

'What's wrong with the one you already bought for at Christmas?'

'It doesn't have all the latest features.'

'But it's just a phone with an Internet connection. What more does she want?'

'She says she feels ashamed of it when she is with her friends.'

'But money is short. She can't just have whatever she wants to keep up with the Joneses.'

'She claims that the one she has is unusable.'

'In what way?'

'It doesn't have multiconnection,' I explained.

'What on Earth is multiconnection?'

'It lets you have multiple video feeds coming through at the same time.'

'Why would you want to do that? You can only watch them one at a time.'

'It's to get around the new DVQ regulations.'

'What is DVQ?'

'Diversity Viewing Quota,' I spelled out.

'Ha, it would be something like that. What has that got to do with phone features?'

'The regulations require people to view all ethnic groups, genders, sexual orientations, physically and mentally challenged and so on in equal proportion. So, say, if you are watching a male football, the feed has to switch you over to a female or a disabled football game every five minutes or so.'

'So how does this multiconnection thing help with that?'

'The phone arranges it so that each time the feed switches to something you don't really want to see, you can go back to the original game via another connection.'

Kate brought us our mugs of tea. We lay quietly up on the bed, sipping our tea while we propped ourselves up against the back wall. Kate reached out and squeezed my hand. I squeezed back.

'How have you been keeping?' she asked.

'For a moment, I didn't say anything. 'Not too good, really, if I'm honest.'

'What's the matter?'

'Somebody was murdered.'

'Good grief! Who?'

'A young lad by the name of Johnie I knew from the clinic.'

'Where was it?'

'Dunwick.'

'How did it happen?'

'He had it coming. He and his mates had just been doing a gangrape on a young woman.'

'That's terrible. Who was she?'

'A prostitute. The youths thought that if she could sell herself, she should give herself to them, too.'

'How come the young lad got murdered?'

'She comes under Mr Sharmoni's protection. I guess he gets a cut from all the girls on the game in Dunwick like he gets from everything else that goes on.'

'What happened?'

'Some of Mr Sharmoni's minders saw what was happening and intervened. Johnie paid the price, to serve as an example to others, I suppose.'

'What did they do to him?'

'Beat him to a pulp, then just left him dead on the ground for all to see.'

'And you saw it?'

'Yes, I saw the whole thing.'

'You were over there for your clinic, I suppose.'

'Yes, on my way over here, actually, to leave you a message.'

'It must have been horrible.'

'It was. Gruesome.'

'Did you go to the police?'

'Mr Sharmoni's minder warned me off.'

'What made them do it?'

'Who, the youths, the woman or Mr Sharmoni's boys?'

'The youths, to start with.'

'They're Unsuitables. No hopers. No woman is interested in them. Incels, I think they're referred to. It turns them into feral creatures who don't care what they do anymore.'

'You must have nightmares.'

'Not only nightmares. The police did eventually follow up on it. They were asking me questions.'

'What did you say?'

'Acted dumb. Pretended I didn't see anything.'

'And all the time, I suppose you just have to carry on as if nothing had happened.'

'That's about the size of it.'

'Shocking. I'm sorry.' She gave me a hug.

‘By the way,’ I said after a pause. ‘I saw your old boss, Harvey Bentling.’

‘Oh, how was he?’

‘He didn’t look too happy. He was on his way into Lupton Tower at the time.’

‘Oh, the Star Chamber. I know that building only too well.’

‘Yes, it probably wasn’t good news for him, being there.’

‘I shouldn’t think it was.’

‘Well, enough about me,’ I said with feeling. ‘What have you been up to?’

‘I’ve been doing some interesting research.’

‘Is anyone going to get to see it?’

‘No, probably not. Not anytime soon, anyway. Doesn’t matter. It’s worth it just for the pleasure of figuring things out.’

‘Crying shame, that.’

‘The funny thing is, now that I am not in the mainstream anymore, I am free to discuss things much more freely than I ever could before. I’ve been having some rather interesting discussions, as a matter of fact.’

‘What about?’

‘Well, for example, is it possible to resolve questions relying on logical deduction?’

‘That is rather a deep question.’

‘These days, I have the time for pondering deep questions.’

‘Which you didn’t when you were at the university?’

‘Well, no, I didn’t.’

‘Funny that, when you consider that universities were invented specifically to ponder such deep questions.’

‘You know what it’s like. For one thing, there is all the administration, but it isn’t only that. You always have to be so careful about what you say, in case you offend someone, make them feel unsafe or something.’

‘Yes, I know only too well,’ I concurred. ‘So, did you reach any conclusion about the power of logical deduction?’

‘Yes, logic is only as good as the axioms that underpin it. Change the axioms, and you change the conclusions.’

‘So, what constitutes an axiom?’

‘Something that is self-evidently true.’

‘Or, might it be something that people dare not challenge? Like a religious belief.’

‘Yes, exactly. Things get stated as irrefutable facts, which are not necessarily irrefutable, just things that could get you burned at the stake for heresy if you were rash enough to do so.’

‘We have to skirt around a lot of such articles of unchallengeable doctrine these days. It gets me into trouble, now and again.’

‘You bloody well be careful,’ said Kate with feeling. ‘Amelia needs you, so don’t you go rocking the boat. You need to keep out of trouble for her sake.’

‘I know. Don’t worry, I am being careful and keeping in with the right people.’

‘You had better be.’

‘On the point about logic, did you conclude that logic was useless at the end of the day?’

‘No, it does have a purpose, even when axioms are questionable.’

‘How so?’

‘It gives you consistency. So long as the axioms remain unchanged, the logical conclusions remain the same, so you know where you are.’

I mused for some seconds. ‘Not necessarily. You can reach different logical conclusions depending upon which axioms you deploy and in what sequence.’

‘Then I suggest logical deduction still has a purpose, by uncovering incompatibilities between the axioms.’

‘That sounds dangerous. If you suggest incompatibility between axioms, are you not questioning the axioms and therefore committing heresy?’

‘Yes, that is all too true, unfortunately.’

‘Whom are you having these interesting discussions with, if I might ask?’

‘I have some very strange bedfellows, where I am.’

‘What do you mean, bedfellows?’

Kate smacked me playfully on the head. ‘Not literally. You’re the only one for me.’

‘Glad to hear it.’

‘So, you’re keeping positive, that’s good.’

‘Oh, yes. I’m keeping my spirits up.’

‘I’m glad your mental well-being is okay, but how are you for more tangible needs?’

‘I’m trying to do some research on 20th-century culture, but most of the material I need is banned these days.’

‘Does that mean you’re stuck?’

‘Not necessarily. Mr Sharmoni says he can get me what I need.’

‘Mr Sharmoni?’ I exclaimed with surprise. ‘So, you’re in touch with him.’

‘Oh, yes. We can go through Gordon, who is always in close contact with him.’

‘So, with Mr Sharmoni’s help, you’ll be able to make progress on your work?’

‘There is a problem actually.’

‘What’s that?’

‘Money. Mr Sharmoni wants paying if he is going to get me banned material.’

‘And you don’t have the cash?’

‘Well, no, at least not to hand. I did have some investments, but they’re unreachable now since I haven’t had proper banking facilities.’

‘Don’t worry, I can see you right, financially speaking. How much do you need?’

‘Five thousand should cover it.’

‘Alright, we’ll do it with crypto, okay?’

We pulled out our mobile phones, my relatively up-to-date model and Kate’s more rudimentary one, and I transferred the cash.

‘Anybody would think that I was on the game,’ Kate remarked, ‘taking money like this.’

I reached over and kissed her on the lips. ‘You know what? For me, that sordidness just adds to the experience.’

‘At this rate, Mr Sharmoni and his minders will be taking me under his wing.’

Chapter 11
Trials and Tribulations

Outside the Willow Brook entrance to the Slough University campus, the usual rough-looking Forward England supporters were wearing Remembrance Day poppies, their breath making smoke in the cold morning air as they held their placards saying, "God save the King" and "Long live His Majesty".

I didn't get the opportunity to enquire what had energised the protesters to agitate for the restoration of the monarchy, because no sooner had my Autocab driven off than a sleek black limousine pulled up into its place.

The loomingly large figure of Nelson, Mr Sharmoni's chief minder, stepped out from the front passenger side and deftly held open the back door.

'Professor, I wonder if you would mind coming with us,' said Nelson in a tone that suggested I would be coming anyway, whether I minded or not.

'Where would we be going?' I enquired.

'Mr Sharmoni would like to have a talk.'

'What about?'

'A private and confidential matter.'

'I've got things to do.'

'It won't take long.'

'Well, I don't know,' I prevaricated.

'Professor, Mr Sharmoni really needs to talk to you. Step in the car, please.'

Nelson had spread himself out, leaving me in no doubt that, were I to be uncooperative, he would bundle me into the car whether I liked it or not. I slid over onto the back seat, and Nelson closed the door behind me.

We drove north, passing through Dunwick, but we didn't stop there, cruising on further, a couple more miles into the countryside. Before reaching the rural village of Stoke Poges, we turned into a long driveway leading up to an old manor house, a confusing-looking building with multiple gables, mullioned windows and a forest of soaring ornate brick chimneys, originally Tudor with Georgian and Victorian additions.

The moment the limousine came to a halt in front of the impressive entranceway, Nelson promptly stepped out and held open the back door for me to exit as smartly as if I had been royalty.

'This way, please,' he said, indicating towards the mansion's front door.

Nelson led the way through and knocked on a dark, wooden, classically panelled double-door at the far end of the spacious oak-panelled hallway.

'Come in,' said a voice from within.

'Ah, Professor, welcome,' said the gentleman of Mediterranean extraction who met me as I came into the room. 'I'm Aldo Sharmoni. Good of you to come. Not putting you in any trouble, I hope.'

Mr Sharmoni was impeccably turned out in beautifully tailored trousers, a bowtie, a dress shirt and a sumptuous, burgundy-coloured, velvet smoking jacket.

'No trouble,' I assured him.

'Good, could I offer you a drink?'

'Bit early for me, but perhaps a coffee.'

Mr Sharmoni nodded slightly towards Nelson, who had remained hovering discreetly in the background. Nelson slipped away to the back of the room, and I heard his deep voice faintly talking into an intercom before returning to attend in case anything further was required.

'Please take a seat,' said Mr Sharmoni, indicating an antique Chesterfield-style leather armchair.

I settled myself in, enjoying the warm cosiness of the room in contrast to the cold dampness of outside.

'Professor, I understand the police wanted to talk to you about something that happened recently in Dunwick.'

'Well, yes, they did.'

'May I enquire what you told them?'

I sensed it would not be well received, were I to say it wasn't really any of Mr Sharmoni's business. 'Well, I said I was there.'

'Was that really necessary?'

'They already knew that. Said they had me on CCTV, so I couldn't really deny it.'

'No, I suppose you couldn't. Did you tell them anything else?'

'They wanted to know about the murder of Johnie Dorritt.'

'What did you tell them about it?'

'Nothing. I said I didn't see anything.'

'Good. Anything else?'

'I mentioned that I'd seen the young lady, Fenn.'

'Why?'

'I think they already knew that.'

'I see. What did you say about her?'

'That we had a brief conversation, and then some youths came and chased after her.'

'Nothing else about her?'

'No. I had to tell them about Nelson, though.'

'What about him?'

'He borrowed my phone, that's all.'

'Professor, I have certain business interests in Dunwick, which I would prefer were not shared with the police or anyone else. I could get unhappy were anyone to reveal them.'

'Yes, I understand what you're saying.'

'I'm glad to hear it, Professor.'

'Was there anything else?'

'Yes, I understand you are a friend of Kate Stillworthy.'

I was shaken by this, gripping the seat of my armchair. 'Well, not exactly a friend.'

'Oh, I think you are a very close friend. You were certainly very friendly with her at the Lakeside Caravan Park, in the caravan in plot 47.'

'So, you know about that.'

'Oh yes, we know. Ms Stillworthy is not very popular within the university, is she?'

'You could say that.'

'A trans-exclusionist, a "Toxic Influence".'

'Well, yes.'

'Were it to be known within the university that you had a close and intimate relationship with Ms Stillworthy, what effect do you think that would have on your position there?'

'I probably wouldn't have a position there for very long.'

'I guess, therefore, Professor, you would prefer if this wasn't made known to anybody.'

'I would prefer that.'

'Now then, about the police…is there anything you told them that you haven't already mentioned?'

'No, I can't think of anything.'

'Good. I take it, Professor, on the understanding that the information the police already have is all they are going to get, the university will hear nothing of your liaison with Ms Stillworthy. Can we be agreed on that?'

'Yes, Mr Sharmoni, it can be agreed.'

'Well, lovely to meet you, Professor. Nelson will see you safely back to the university.'

The first item on my agenda when I was back in my office in the Asima Shankar Laboratory Complex was a message from Dolphins, requesting that I call back to discuss an important matter. It would almost certainly be bothersome, but I decided, rather than leave it preying on my mind, it would be best to grasp the nettle right away.

'Professor, thanks for calling back,' said a male-sounding voice in an Estuary English accent. 'I am Fred Glibbins, pronouns ve/ver.'

'Mine are he/him.'

'At Dolphins, we advocate for gender-diverse young people.'

'Yes, I know. What can I do for you?'

'It relates to a case you referred to the Tavidown Clinic.'

'These matters are confidential, so I can't really discuss it except with the client themself.'

'You subsequently withdrew the referral. This is what concerns us.'

'If I did, it would have been because the patient requested me to do so.'

'Our concern is why your patient requested it.'

'Isn't that solely the patient's own concern?'

'We suspect the patient has been influenced against the affirmation of their chosen gender.'

'Do you have grounds for this suspicion?'

'The patient wished to affirm their chosen gender and was persuaded out of it. That constitutes conversion therapy, which is illegal.'

'The patient decided for their own reasons. We have nothing further to discuss.'

'If that is your attitude, it leaves us no alternative but to refer this matter to the appropriate authorities.'

As if I hadn't had enough bother for one day, I had a request from Celia Englebury, the School Safety Officer, to call in at Amelia's school in the afternoon.

I also had a lunch date with Liz. I was ridiculously busy, and I wasn't really in the mood, but after standing her up so often, I daren't call it off.

On this occasion, anxious to avoid being late, I arrived first in the Cloister Cafeteria in Seacole Square. I took a moment to reflect.

This place had history, right back to the reign of Henry VI in the fifteenth century. There had been a few changes over that time, not least in recent years with the transition into a university and the severing of the college's royal connections. The protesters at the entrance were calling for the restoration of the monarchy. I wondered in what other ways they might want to turn back the clock.

Liz, the epitome of unattainable blonde desirability as always, arrived, and I stood up to greet her. We briefly kissed and took our seats on the environmentally friendly recycled plastic chairs.

'What sort of a day have you been having?' Liz enquired.

I shook my head. 'Don't ask.'

'That bad?'

'Yes, that bad.'

We went to choose and collect our food from the cafeteria. Liz chose the spicy Chinese aubergine with Szechuan sauce and black rice. I needed comfort food, so it was vegetarian shepherd's pie for me.

'My own day has been, well, interesting,' said Liz when we resumed our seats. 'Possibly quite good.'

'Oh, how so?'

'I could be in line for a professorship, not guaranteed, but looking probable.'

'Oh, is there a vacancy?'

'Yes, actually, now that Harvey Bentling is leaving us.'

'Harvey leaving, how come?'

'Not quite sure of the details, but he has left his post.'

'Oh, dear. Did he jump or was he pushed?'

‘Pushed, I think. Officially, he resigned, but I think he was obliged to resign.’

‘What is he supposed to have done to be obliged to resign?’

‘I don’t know for sure. The rumour mill says something to do with racism, sexism and trigger warnings.’

‘That’s a shame for him.’

‘I know, I feel bad about that. But it is an opportunity for me, though.’

‘Won’t it leave a bad taste in your mouth, profiting from Harvey’s misfortunes?’

‘It’s his own fault. He would get into areas that are politically charged. It’s things like this which convince me to keep strictly away from anything political.’

‘Easier said than done. Almost everything seems to have a political dimension these days.’

‘Yes, I know. I find the way to manage the situation is to learn the politically approved terminology so you can reel out the right phrases as the situation arises.’

‘A bit like magic incantations.’

‘Exactly. They don’t have to mean anything particularly, just say the right words, and the danger recedes.’

‘You must have had a run-in with the powers-that-be at some point,’ I insisted. ‘I mean, doesn’t everybody?’

‘Yes, going back at bit now, before I knew better, I had a bit of bother with Rockface.’

‘What happened?’

‘I referred to Queen Elizabeth the first as she.’

‘What’s wrong with that?’

‘He announced in a speech to his troops that he had the heart and stomach of a king, by which he declared his gender as male, so he should be referred to as he/him and his title should have been King Elizabeth.’

‘I am glad I am in pharmacology. It has fewer hazards of that kind.’

The grounds of Slough Comprehensive Academy were surrounded by a high fence topped with razor wire. CCTV cameras were mounted in poles positioned at intervals along the perimeter. At the main entrance, I pressed a button to request access. The school receptionist appeared on a video screen.

‘Mr Hubbings to see Celia Englebury,’ I announced.

The receptionist referred to their computer screen and nodded.

‘Yes, Mr Hubbings, please come on through.’

There was a click and buzzing sound. I pushed on the cold, dew-covered metal of the turnstile gate, which moved around with a clunking sound to allow me onto the premises.

The central building of Slough Comprehensive Academy, now empty and covered in scaffolding, was a large concrete rectangular block originally built in the late twentieth century, currently being refurbished due to the presence of dangerous asbestos and the aerated concrete construction that was liable to collapse.

Spread around the site was a miscellany of newer buildings and temporary portacabins, stacked into two storeys and, in one case, a three-storey, now-semi-permanent fixture. On a couple of the blank walls, I could still make out imperfectly painted-out lightning flash graffiti.

Ms Englebury’s manner was cold and impersonal when she met me in the cramped entrance lobby of the makeshift temporary main school building, which still carried signs of its former purpose as a military field hospital, at one time briefly deployed as a Nightingale hospital during the Covid pandemic. Ms Englebury’s practical, unglamorous attire and businesslike authority instantly dispelled any notion of friendliness or informality.

‘Professor, please come this way.’

She showed me into a partitioned meeting area in one of the Portacabins, where we sat down on moulded plastic chairs on either side of a desk.

‘As you may remember, I am Celia Englebury, School Safety Officer, and my pronouns are she/her.’

‘And mine remain he/him.’

‘I’ve asked to see you today because we have seen some disturbing influences in Amelia’s schoolwork.’

‘Oh, I’m sorry to hear that. What are they?’

Ms Englebury pulled out some sheets of paper. ‘Here, she has written: *Gordon Garage and Forward England are demanding things that many people want, such as the restoration of the monarchy. If we are a democracy, shouldn’t this be put to the vote?* She goes on to say: *In a democracy, shouldn’t all the people have voting rights? How can denying the Educationally Unsuitable the right to vote be justified?*’

I pursed my lips in thought. I could have defended these ideas, or at least championed Amelia’s right to voice them, but I quickly put those thoughts aside.

'Yes, I can see that those are shocking ideas for some people,' I concurred.

'Where do you imagine she got these ideas from?' enquired Ms Englebury, looking at me accusingly.

'I wouldn't know. Other girls or boys in her class?'

Ms Englebury looked at me with a look of shock on her face. 'We don't use words like that here.'

'Sorry, what did I say?'

'*Boy* and *girl* are not words we allow to be used in school.'

'Oh, I'm sorry. I didn't realise.'

'Words like that suggest an inferior status to adult people and a false binary of genders, causing distress.'

'Fellow students, would that be acceptable?'

'That's better, though I think I would have noticed if these ideas were being expressed by other students. She can only have got them from outside the school.'

'Forward England put out leaflets saying that sort of thing, so it was probably from those.'

'If we were to suspect she was getting these ideas from within her home environment, her current domestic arrangements could be called into question.'

'When you say her current domestic arrangements, what do you have in mind?'

'It could become necessary to take Amelia into care for her own safety, to protect her from Toxic Influence.'

'So, if a child thinks for themself, it must be the parent's fault.'

'For now, I am prepared to accept your explanation about Forward England leaflets being the inspiration for this, but we will be keeping this under review.'

'Well, thanks for that.'

'Amelia is sailing close to the wind. If her current attitude persists, the school would not be able to issue her with a Correct Ethical Attitude Certificate, without which, she will not be eligible to take the Ethics and Society examination.'

'I see.'

'I am sure that you realise the implications of this. Without a good pass in Ethics and Society, entry into university will not be possible, and she could end up classified as Educationally Unsuitable.'

'Yes, that would be really bad for her.'

'It would, which is why I am looking for your cooperation in turning her attitude around.'

My phone rang. It was Bill Englebirt. 'Jim, the reason I'm calling is, you've been out of circulation a lot recently. I was wondering if there was anything the matter.'

'Sorry, Bill. A few things have cropped up.'

'Would you like to talk about it? Come over to mine for a drink if you like.'

Bill had a modest grace and favour bachelor pad on the university campus, a suite of rooms within Godolphin House, a Georgian building situated a short distance from the Oppressed Peoples Memorial Complex.

He showed me into his lounge-cum-study, a comfortable conglomeration of old dusty furniture and books. Bill mixed us both a stiff gin and tonic.

'So, Jim,' said Bill amiably. 'What are these things that have cropped up for you?'

'Mainly, it's Amelia, trouble at school.'

'Boyfriend issues?'

'Nothing like that. Worse, really. She has ideas about democracy.'

'That's alright, isn't it? We're all in favour of democracy, aren't we?'

'If it applies to Gordon Garage, not necessarily.'

'Ah, I see. We may like democracy, but Gordon Garage is beyond the pale. What did the school say?'

'The wretched School Safety Officer woman threatened to have Amelia taken away into care because of the Toxic Influence in her home, to have her Correct Ethical Attitude Certificate withheld and classified as Educationally Unsuitable.'

'Ouch. I can see why you're troubled.'

'Yes, I'm troubled alright,' I said with feeling.

'How are things with Liz?'

'Oh, they're fine.'

Bill looked at me with a disbelieving expression. 'She's alright, I suppose.'

'Yes, she thinks she might get a professorship.'

'Oh, where? Is she going away?'

'No. Did you hear about Harvey Bentling?'

'What about him?'

'It seems he has been turned out, leaving a vacancy.'

'Turfed out? Why?'

‘I don’t really know. Racism, sexism or some other ism.’

‘Goodness. Nobody is safe these days.’

‘Tell me about it!’

The doorbell rang. Bill stood up. ‘Excuse me a moment.’

It was Kyle, furtive like a naughty schoolboy. He handed over a small package to Bill, who nonchalantly slipped it into his pocket, typed something into his phone and held it close to Kyle’s phone. Kyle having departed, he came back into the lounge.

‘Do you like those old movies and TV shows from way back?’ Bill enquired.

‘Yes, I did enjoy them back in the day, but most of them are banned these days.’

‘It’s one of my weaknesses,’ said Bill. ‘One of the things that keeps me sane in the mad world we live in today.’

‘How do you get hold of them? Nearly all the old stuff has been stamped out, hasn’t it?’

‘There are ways. That was Kyle.’ Bill took out his packet, tore it open and tipped out a small object onto the coffee table. ‘Just brought me over *Last Tango in Paris*.’

‘You mean, you’ve got *Last Tango in Paris* on that memory card?’

‘Yes, at least I hope so. That’s what I ordered.’

‘But if you copy it anywhere or play it, wouldn’t the university electronic surveillance pick it up?’

‘Not if you’re careful.’

‘It monitors everything, doesn’t it?’

‘Here’s what you do.’ Bill took out his laptop and slid it under a small transparent plastic tent. ‘This here is a Faraday cage. It blocks all radio signals so the surveillance system can’t see the laptop. Now you slip in the memory card…and voila.’

The opening credits of the movie appeared on the laptop screen.

‘Well, I’m damned,’ I exclaimed.

‘Eddie Donagal, one of my PhD students, got himself into trouble looking at an old film recently. Do you think he got that from Kyle, too?’

‘I would think so.’

‘But Eddie was found out.’

‘He must have got careless,’ said Bill.

‘You know, I’d noticed Kyle handing out little packets of something. I assumed they were drugs.’

‘In a way, he is distributing a sort of a drug.’

‘How do you mean?’

‘None of the so-called entertainment around today is either sexy or funny, in case it might upset someone. The only humorous or amusing material available is the old classic stuff, now banned. Well, I for one need my occasional fix of fun and sexiness, lest I go insane.’

I didn’t stay to watch Bill’s movie. Back at home, I took a shower. There was a crack in the shower tray, and water was leaking through onto the joists below. That would explain the staining I’d seen on the ceiling downstairs, I realised.

I put a call into a home services installation engineer, formerly known as a plumber. He might be able to fit me in about three weeks’ time. His minimum charge would be £500.

Amelia was making an effort to be as nonchalant as she could when she let herself in, but I could see through her pretence.

‘I had to go into the school today,’ I informed her.

Her face betrayed a hint of concern. ‘What about?’

‘You. What do you think? Ms Englebury says there have been disturbing influences in your schoolwork.’

‘What disturbing influences?’ said Amelia with a note of defiance in her voice.

‘I think you know. Gordon Garage, the monarchy, democracy, votes for Unsuitables. That sort of thing.’

‘Ah, yes,’ she said as if dismissing a mere trifle. ‘I did get shouted at for that.’

‘It could be more than shouting. A lot more. It could get you into some real trouble.’

‘Oh.’

‘Yes, oh. So don’t do it anymore, please.’

I felt in my pocket and pulled out my packet of Complianx. I had rarely felt more tempted to take one than right now.

Chapter 12
Rockface Audit

I had, so I thought, *cleared the decks of all possible distractions from giving our annual Rockface audit my undivided attention, when my phone rang.*

'Robin Smith, Health Security Agency. Is it convenient to talk about our project?'

It wasn't, but wouldn't have been wise to say so. 'What do you want to talk about?'

'We're facing some challenges with homeostasis.'

'What sort of problems?'

'Our drug dosage levels are fluctuating wildly. We're getting either levels that are way above the therapeutic dose to the point of toxicity, or the inhibitor kicks in and we're left with next to no dose at all.'

'Well, yes, homeostasis isn't easy to set up; that's true.'

'Can you give us any pointers?'

'Without knowing rather more about the technical specifics, there isn't a lot more I can do.'

'I'm sorry, but the details of the project are classified.'

'Then I don't see what I can do for you.'

'We would like you to come over to Porton Down to help us.'

'I am rather busy.'

'This is a matter of national security. We really need you down there.'

'What if it isn't convenient?'

'It would be in your best interests to cooperate, Professor. Believe me, it really would.'

I believed him. 'Very well. When would you like me to come over?'

‘I am Shamina Chakrabarti, pronouns ze/zir,’ announced our Rockface auditor, zir commanding presence instantly making my office visitor’s chair the room’s centre of gravity.

‘Professor Jim Hubbings, pronouns he/him.’

‘Professor, as you know, this audit is to provide an assessment of the university as a whole and each department individually for “Diversity, Equity and Inclusion”, based on defined assessment criteria.’

‘Yes, of course, we will provide you with everything you need.’

‘First I need to assess your openness to all disadvantaged groups and provisions for their needs.’

‘We have complied with all the policies the university has put out.’

‘Second, we need to check the success of these policies in terms of the diversity of your workforce and students.’

‘We always endeavour to promote diversity whenever we can.’

‘Finally, I will be seeking out any hateful influences.’

‘When you say “hateful influences”, what do you have in mind?’

‘Inappropriate or demeaning comments being made, nostalgic fetishism of the past, militarism and imperialistic grandiosity, promotion of hateful ideologies such as from incels or trans-exclusionists. We need to root out any such tendencies before they get embedded.’

‘How do you propose to identify these things?’

‘I have already seen some disturbing items in email and text correspondence that I need to review with you.’

‘I see. As a matter of interest, how were these identified?’

‘As you probably know, all devices, smartphones, laptops and so on, are connected to the university’s communications network, which ensures that all email and text correspondence is recorded and scanned. The built-in artificial intelligence picks up any potentially hateful use of words and inappropriate pictures.’

‘And you have some of this, picked up by the system?’

‘Oh, yes, I do,’ said Mz Chakrabarti, with some relish. ‘I will also be conducting interviews of selected staff and students to explore for potential microaggressions and unconscious bias they may have experienced.’

‘Where would you like to start?’

‘Before I talk to other members of the faculty, there is a matter I need to talk to you about, Professor.’

‘Oh, right, what would that be?’

‘It concerns a patient of yours whom you referred to the Tavidown Clinic for potential gender affirmation but then withdrew the referral.’

‘If true, this would relate to my practice in psychiatry at the Dunwick Park General Hospital. How is this relevant to the pharmacology department?’

‘Hateful attitudes pervade the learning environment regardless of where they originate, so we explore the entire person.’

‘Apart from anything else, this question relates to the patient/doctor relationship, which is confidential.’

‘We have to consider any matter that could be illegal, Professor, and conversion therapy, very definitely, is illegal.’

‘There hasn’t been any conversion therapy. The patient changed their mind, that’s all.’

‘But what influenced them to change their mind, that is what we need to ascertain.’

‘Well, whatever it was, it wasn’t anything that I said.’

‘It will need further investigation. There is also another matter. What is your relationship with Kate Stillworthy?’

‘She is my ex-wife. Otherwise, I don’t have a relationship with her.’

‘I have checked the records, and I have found no record of you getting divorced.’

‘Alright, technically, she is still my wife. We haven’t actually gone through with the divorce yet.’

‘Any reason why not?’

‘We just haven’t got around to it.’

‘I suggest you do get around to it, Professor. It isn’t a good look, being married to Kate Stillworthy.’

‘I’ll call my solicitor and get the matter progressed.’

‘You do that. Now, perhaps you could take me over to the toilets, cafeteria, rest areas and other general facilities.’

With Mz Chakrabarti engaged elsewhere, I put in a call to Kyle concerning a shortage of clean lab coats. I went to meet him on his territory, a windowless storage room in the basement serving as his office.

Stepping around boxes of various cleaning products and washing implements, I sat down on a swivel chair in front of his cluttered desk, a utilitarian, steel, framed object surfaced in wipe-down white melamine. Kyle had his hands tucked into the pockets of the oversized baggy overalls draping over his slight frame like a tent, with his elbows spread sideways to give an impression of bulk.

'About these lab coats,' I began. 'It is causing us problems because they are mandatory in the laboratories, and we are resorting to using ones that are still soiled from previous use.'

'Our laundry provider can't get the qualified staff.'

'There must be plenty of people who can operate washing machines, surely.'

'Possibly, but there is a shortage of graduates.'

'What do they need to be qualified in?'

'Fabric treatment and maintenance. They need a thorough grounding in all the various types of fibres—cotton, polyester, nylon, et cetera, all the various mixtures, the dyes used, cleaning materials, water temperatures and so on.'

'Is there anything we can do to alleviate the problem?'

'Take on more fabric treatment students into the Artisan Skills faculty.'

'But that way, it would take years to solve the problem.'

Kyle shrugged. I raised my eyebrows and tipped my head in recognition and acceptance of this unresolvable situation.

'Well, okay. I don't suppose we can do much,' I conceded. 'How is life treating you in general?'

Kyle shrugged again. 'Can't complain.'

'I couldn't help noticing you popping around to Bill Englebirt's place the other day.'

'What of it? Who wants to know?' Kyle's demeanour changed to that of a nervous rabbit suddenly illuminated by headlights.

'I was wondering about where I might get some entertainment, not the preachy politically correct stuff we're allowed these days. Something actually funny.'

'What could I do about that?'

'What Bill had, that looked interesting.'

'Why should I have anything to do with what Bill had?'

'He got it from you, didn't he?'

'Did he say that?'

'Yes. Look, it's alright. I'll keep my mouth shut. I was just wondering whether there was anything that I might enjoy.'

Kyle relaxed somewhat. 'Alright, what sort of things are you interested in?'

'I don't really know. What have you got?'

'TV shows, *Dad's Army*, *Till Death Us Do Part*.'

'Hmm, perhaps. What else?'

'Classic British films: *Carry On* series, like *Carry On Camping* where Barbara Windsor's top flies off, *Confessions of a Window Cleaner*, where he sees all sorts going on through the windows, the *Doctor* series with strict matrons and sisters in those old nurses uniforms.'

'Okay, that's comedy. Any more serious subjects?'

'Classic British war films are banned now because they are militaristic. Like *Battle of Britain*, *Dam Busters*, *A Bridge Too Far*, *Bridge over the River Kwai*, *Lawrence of Arabia*.'

'Any other topics?'

'Are you into sport?'

'Some sports, yes, but there isn't much left of sport these days since it all became non-competitive.'

'I don't mean that rubbish. I mean proper sport.'

'What did you have in mind?'

'Cage fighting is very popular.'

'Is that what you were watching when I popped in the other day?'

'Yes, but please keep stumm about that.'

'Alright, but how do you get to see it?'

'Mr Sharmoni takes care of it. You can get it on the dark web if you have the code.'

'Gosh, that's quite a range. If I want something, what should I do?'

'Just find me and let me know. Not over the phone, messaging or anything, because they listen in on that.'

'Right, I'll do that. By the way, I've got some trouble at home, which you might be able to advise on.'

'I don't do therapy.'

'Not that. It's my shower tray. It's cracked and letting water through the floor.'

'I don't do plumbing either.'

'I called a plumber, and they told me it would take three weeks and cost at least five hundred quid, and it doesn't even include the materials.'

‘As it happens, I do know someone who might help.’ Kyle scribbled down a name and phone number. ‘Say I recommended you call.’

I called the number.

‘Hello,’ said a gruff male voice.

‘Is that Jeff?’

‘Who wants to know?’

‘I’m Jim Hubbings. I’ve got a plumbing problem.’

‘What’s that got to do with me?’

‘Kyle gave me your number; said you might be able to help out.’

‘Oh, alright. What’s your problem?’

‘Cracked shower tray, letting water leak through.’

‘Alright, I’ll come round to take a look. Tomorrow okay?’

Having made zir initial assessments, Mz Chakrabarti was back in my office.

‘There were no tampon dispensers in the All-Genders toilets,’ ze reported.

‘I believe we do have them in the Gender Safe toilets,’ I replied.

‘That isn’t any use for men with vaginas, is it?’

‘Couldn’t they go into the Gender Safe toilet if they want a tampon?’

‘The Gender Safe toilets are for genders that could feel unsafe, at risk of rape, in the company of people with penises.’

‘But if the men concerned have vaginas, wouldn’t the risk of rape from those men be rather low?’

‘That isn’t the point,’ Mz Chakrabarti insisted. ‘Transmen are men. Currently, men with vaginas are not being properly provided for.’

‘On the matter of safety, we do in fact permit women with penises to use the Gender Safe toilets. Isn’t that a threat to people with vaginas?’

‘Transwomen are women. We must respect that.’

I sighed. This discussion was never going to make any sense. ‘Very well, I’ll see to it that all the toilets, Gender Safe and All Genders, get tampon dispensers.’

‘Moving on,’ said Mz Chakrabarti, looking at me meaningfully, ‘I am concerned about the lack of representation of disadvantaged groups within the senior leadership of the pharmacology department.’

‘You mean me.’

‘Well, yes. Is there any disadvantaged group that you represent?’

‘Supposing I was Jewish, would that count?’

Mz Chakrabarti shook zir head. 'No, a group that is a colonial oppressor certainly doesn't count.'

'But if I was a Muslim?'

'Yes, that qualifies. Are you a Muslim?'

'No. My mother came from the Falkland Islands, which was a colony. Does that count?'

'No, sorry. The Malvinas are part of Argentina and those people of British extraction who used to live there are classified as colonial oppressors.'

'Well, in that case, I guess I'm not in any disadvantaged group.'

'I'm going to need to interview someone who has transitioned, is in the process of transitioning or is otherwise of non-binary gender. Whom have you got for me to talk to?'

'You may speak to Eddie Donagal, one of my PhD students. I can call him in.'

Eddie came in to join us. Mz Chakrabarti frowned, zir eyes fixated on the Remembrance Day poppy he had pinned to his sweater.

'Eddie, this is Mz Chakrabarti, our Rockface auditor, who would like to talk to you about your experience as a non-binary person.'

'Oh, yes, we've met,' said Eddie, with a truculent look of defiance on his cherubic face.

'Did you? When was that?' I enquired.

'Recently, about me having a banned movie on my phone.'

'Full of jingoistic militarism with a word used that is offensive to people of colour,' said Mz Chakrabarti with disgust in zir voice.

'The word concerned was the name of a pet dog.'

'Even worse, comparing people of colour to an animal.'

'Well, alright. What do you want to ask about?'

'We'll start with our pronouns,' said Mz Chakrabarti. 'Mine are ze/zir.'

'He/him,' said Eddie. I facepalmed.

'I thought you were transitioning or non-binary,' said Mz Chakrabarti.

Eddie looked confused for a couple of seconds, his countenance now childlike and confused. 'Sorry, force of habit,' he stammered.

'So, what are your pronouns?' Mz Chakrabarti insisted.

'Er…' Eddie hesitated. 'Ze/zir.'

'Why do you think that it is acceptable to wear that jingoistic symbol within the university?' Mz Chakrabarti asked, nodding towards Eddie's poppy.

‘They had them outside the entrance as I came in. Thought it was okay to commemorate people who died in wars,’ retorted Eddie, his chin jutting out combatively.

‘Like you thought it was alright to watch that militaristic film.’

‘We shouldn’t forget these things, should we?’ said Eddie, his voice now plaintive, glancing in my direction for support.

Whose damned fool idea had it been to put Eddie up for this? I asked myself, metaphorically kicking myself for my stupidity.

Mz Chakrabarti was making copious notes, none of which were going to be in our favour, I figured.

I find a stroll in the fresh air is a therapeutic way of dealing with a build-up of stress, at least as effective as a dose of Complianx, so as soon as I could divert Mz Chakrabarti onto harassing someone else, I stepped out of the pharmacology faculty building and caught the tram. Alighting at the stop for the Oppressed Peoples Memorial Complex, I emerged strolling into a misty drizzle on the high street of small shops serving the needs of the university community, quaint emporiums established centuries ago in the style of the Georgian era, their swirly glass window panes misted up, once selling school uniforms and fine wines, since changed over to modern trainers, T-shirts and multipack cans of beer.

At the far end, the high street barriers with electronic turnstile gates stood in front of a bridge leading over the Thames across to Windsor. Directly in front of the bridge, the dark grey soaring walls of Windsor Castle rose up with the LGBTQ+ Pride standard providing a flash of rainbow colour against the lighter grey of the cloudy sky behind the untidy assortment of riverfront properties.

Turning right before the bridge, I wandered along a back alley of terraced houses now serving as student accommodation before emerging onto a green space along the riverbank. On my right, a large new building with great views across towards Windsor housed the Social Science faculty.

Later on, Mz Chakrabarti was back in my office to discuss what ze claimed to be an important matter.

‘During my inspection of the basement administrative area, I found a case hidden away in an alcove containing a number of memory cards,’ ze informed me. ‘Do you have any knowledge of what these might be?’

‘No, I’m sorry, I don’t.’

‘Or who might have put them there?’

‘I have no idea. What is so special about these memory cards?’

‘I have good reason to believe these contain material of a hateful nature.’

‘What has it got to do with me or the pharmacology department?’

‘You were seen in the area earlier today talking to Kyle Fichner.’

‘I had to talk to him about a laboratory administrative matter.’

Mz Chakrabarti looked at me sceptically. ‘What laboratory administrative matter exactly?’

‘Concerning the shortage of clean lab coats.’

‘I shall be making enquiries. Rest assured; I will get to the bottom of this.’

Chapter 13
Rebellious Rumblings

'God Save the King!' and 'Lest We Forget,' said the placards held by the rough-looking poppy-wearing Forward England supporters outside the university's Willow Brook entrance. A folding trestle table was laid out with poppies for sale, protected from the drizzly rain by a large Union Jack umbrella.

As I approached the entrance from my Autocab, Cheryl Biggetty, the academic accuracy officer, was haranguing the portly chief security guard in a raised voice.

'These people are distributing militaristic emblems right here in front of the university. It is your job to put a stop to it,' she insisted.

'It is not within our remit,' explained the long-suffering security man.

'These jingoistic symbols are being taken into the university. It's not acceptable.'

'We only cover the grounds of the university, and these poppies are being sold from outside of the premises.'

'You should call the police.'

'We already did. What they said was, it is not clear whether they are breaking any laws, and anyway, with the current shortage of police resources due to de-funding, they would be unable to respond for forty-eight hours at least.'

'You could at least refuse admittance to anyone wearing one of those things.'

'There are no instructions for us to enforce the university dress code.'

'But these are symbols of hateful militarism.'

'Sorry, that's not for us to say. The university authorities would have to give us specific instructions about that.'

'Well, I'm telling you as academic accuracy officer,' pronounced Ms Biggetty, her well-tailored business outfit projecting authority.

'Sorry, but our instructions need to be in writing, signed by the university vice chancellor.'

'I'll see that those instructions are given. You can count on it.'

Ms Biggetty swept away imperiously back onto the campus.

'Those poppies are causing quite a stir,' I observed to the steadfast security guard.

'Certainly are. Don't see what's wrong with them, myself. Supposed to commemorate those who died in war. That's good, I'd have thought.'

'What they say is, it's soldiers they're commemorating. Soldiers fight and kill people, which is hateful.'

'The soldiers defended us from tyranny,' the guard said indignantly. 'We'd have been taken over by Hitler if they hadn't fought for our freedom.'

'It isn't me you need to convince. I'm just saying how people like Ms Biggetty see it. I don't necessarily agree with her.'

'You're not wearing a poppy, though, are you?'

'I value my job too much, truth be said.'

'What's more important, your job or standing up for what's right?'

'I have a young daughter who depends on me, so my job matters more.'

'I can understand that,' the security guard acknowledged. 'I'd do the same.'

'If Ms Biggetty gets that edict passed about poppies being banned, are you going to enforce it?'

'Can't see the point myself. They could just put the poppies into their pockets as they come in and put them back on again once they're through.'

Waiting for me in the Asima Shankar Laboratory Complex reception was Detective Sergeant Travers of Thames Valley Police.

'Professor, I need to talk to you on a few matters.'

'Very well, come up to my office.'

She declined my offer of a coffee, but I took the opportunity to get myself one before we took our seats. DS Travers assumed a serious authoritative persona as she opened our conversation.

'Professor, you will no doubt be pleased to know that we will be taking no further action in relation to the death of Johnie Dorritt.'

'I'm not sure I am pleased about it, actually. It was a homicide. Surely you can't just let it drop.'

'You are not under investigation on that matter. I would have thought you would have been pleased.'

'I wasn't a suspect, was I?'

'You were in the vicinity, and your account does not fully explain your presence there or your actions.'

'So, if you're not satisfied, why are you dropping the investigation?'

'The deceased, Mr Dorritt, did not fall into any of the disadvantaged categories we require to justify the use of police resources.'

'He was classified as Educationally Unsuitable. Wasn't that a disadvantage?'

'Being Educationally Unsuitable is not one of the statutory disadvantage categories. It would be different if he had been a person of colour or had a sexual orientation falling within an LGBTQ+ category.'

'So, you have to be gay or black to get justice if you are murdered.'

DS Travers shuffled in her seat, before moving on with her agenda. 'Professor, arising from our earlier interview, there were some other matters I need to raise with you.'

'Which are?'

'The first relates to sexual harassment of a woman who was later sexually assaulted in Dunwick.'

'I haven't carried out either sexual harassment or sexual assault.'

'I have you on record as stating that you thought that the victim was interested in having sex with you. You could not have known that without having first sexually harassed her.'

'It was her who did the sexual harassment, not me.'

'In any sexual encounter, it is the one in the disadvantaged category who is designated as the victim of harassment or assault.'

'That really is nonsense.'

'That constitutes disrespecting a police officer, Professor. Kindly mind your language.'

I let out a sigh. I realised I could not win. 'Look, I'm sorry.'

'Apology accepted. Now, the next matter concerns loitering in the vicinity of a kindergarten for the purposes of sexual gratification.'

'I have done no such thing.'

'We have evidence of you standing around loitering in the vicinity of Dunwick Park Infant School. How do you explain that?'

‘I lent my mobile phone to a gentleman, and I was waiting until he returned it to me.’

‘Doesn’t sound very plausible, does it? The law is that any man lingering near a school premises without reasonable excuse is presumed to be doing so for sexual voyeuristic purposes. I doubt whether you could convince a jury that your story about a borrowed mobile phone was a reasonable excuse.’

‘Even if it is the truth?’

‘Not for me to decide. All I do is collate the evidence. Now, there is also the matter of trans-exclusionism.’

‘How so?’

‘When I asked you whether any of the youths had any distinguishing features, you identified one of them as being trans.’

‘Well, yes, that was something I noticed.’

‘Singling out a transperson as differing from the fellow members of their gender is trans-shaming, a trans-exclusionary act.’

‘So, you are saying I shouldn’t have mentioned it all.’

‘Of course you shouldn’t have.’

‘Even if such information might have been useful to the police in identifying the individual involved.’

‘You need to use features other than discriminatory ones.’

‘I’ll certainly be less forthcoming about such matters in future.’

‘There has since been a further matter, which has been reported to us concerning suspected conversion therapy on your part in your capacity as a psychiatrist.’

‘Don’t tell me the Dolphins have been onto you about the withdrawal of the referral to the Tavidown Clinic.’

‘Yes, that is correct.’

‘I am not going to discuss any of these matters any further with you until I have consulted my solicitor.’

I had a message from Jenny Colepepper asking me to pop over to see her in the Oppressed Peoples Memorial Complex, but beforehand, I would need a moment or two to unwind after my encounter with DS Travers.

I took out my packet of Complianx and turned it around in my hand. I needed to keep my wits about me, so it wasn’t the answer. In truth, it was rarely the answer, but having it there reassured me. If needs must, I could numb the pain.

A stiff gin and tonic might have helped, too, but I settled for a slice of the gooiest cake available in the cafeteria washed down by an extra-large cappuccino coffee.

As the comfort food did its job, I couldn't help noticing several staff and students were wearing poppies.

Jenny Colepepper's office was within the vice chancellor's suite on a corner of the top floor of the modernist central administration building with double-aspect views over towards Runnymede.

Despite being a woman of advanced middle age, she showed no signs of letting herself go, presenting herself impeccably, immaculately coiffured and made up, the controlled athleticism of her body governed as strictly as she ran the administrative affairs of the university.

'Professor, thanks for coming over,' she said as I came in. 'Usual pronouns, I assume.'

'Yes, I'm still a man, at least for now.'

'Good, good. Now, about the laboratory administration. I'm afraid to say that Kyle Fichner has had to leave his post.'

'Oh, that was sudden.'

'Yes, it has been rather abrupt. As I understand it, he is in police custody.'

'Goodness. What is he supposed to have done?'

'Well, I can't go into the details of that, but I thought that it was only fair to warn you that the police may want to talk to you about it.'

'Why me?'

'You were in the vicinity in communication with Kyle shortly before some hateful entertainment material and pornographic violence was found in the vicinity. You were also with Kyle on an earlier occasion when what is thought to be some of this material was delivered to him.'

'The only times I have met Kyle were relating to issues concerning the laboratories.'

'From now on, until such time as we can appoint a replacement, I will be personally handling laboratory administration.'

I was just standing up to leave when there was a knock on the door. Without waiting for a reply, the door opened and Shamina Chakrabarti's head leaned into the room like an attractive black hole sucking in our attention.

'Sorry to interrupt, Ms Colepepper, but something has arisen that needs to be attended to urgently.'

‘Well, I think we have finished, haven’t we, Professor?’ said Ms Colepepper. ‘What is this urgent matter?’

‘Poppies,’ said Mz Chakrabarti in a voice suggesting ze was uttering an obscenity. ‘People wearing poppies all over campus.’

‘Professor, have you noticed this?’ Dr Colepepper asked me.

‘Yes, as a matter of fact. It seems to be quite widespread.’

‘Why didn’t you mention it?’ enquired Dr Colepepper accusingly.

‘We were discussing other things.’

‘Come in, Shamina. We obviously need to get this dealt with.’

Back in the Asima Shankar Laboratory Complex, I went over to find Eddie Donagal to discuss his research into homeostasis. When I found him, I couldn’t help noticing the poppy still ostentatiously pinned to his sweater.

‘Do you have a problem?’ Eddie enquired, tossing his curly mop of hair as he turned to confront me.

‘One or two, I have to admit.’

‘I meant, with this,’ Eddie explained, pointing at the poppy.

‘Why do you ask?’

‘You were staring at it.’

‘Those poppies are controversial at the moment.’

‘In what way?’

‘Some consider them to be militaristic, jingoistic, that sort of thing.’

‘We aren’t allowed to commemorate those who died in wars then?’

‘Some say it glorifies those wars.’

‘That’s their opinion,’ said Eddie defiantly.

‘Problem is, if their opinion is correct, it would make the poppies symbols of hate, which is against university rules and possibly also against the law.’

‘What are you going to do about it?’

I shrugged. ‘Me? Nothing. But others probably will. It could cause you a lot of bother.’

‘It won’t just be me they will have to deal with,’ Eddie declared, casting his eye around the room and taking in several other poppy wearers.

‘Alright, enough about poppies. Let’s do some real work. What can you tell me about those issues you were having with inhibitory over-compensation?’

‘Okay, I found that was due to the inhibitor bonding with fat molecules, delaying its release.’

'So, what is the solution?'

'Adding an oleophobic radical to the inhibitor molecule.'

As I scanned my eyes around, looking for Liz in the Cloister Cafeteria, one of the social hubs within the rambling rabbit warren that formed the Oppressed Peoples Memorial Complex, I couldn't help noticing the poppied, bright-red emblems of rebellion on some of folk around the place.

Liz, smoothly and glamorously turned out as always, had found us a quiet niche within one of the archways. She was beaming with the self-satisfied look of a cat that had got the cream.

'You're looking happy today,' I remarked.

'It's confirmed. I've got my professorship. Head of the history faculty.'

'That's brilliant. Well done.'

I may have said the right thing, but my voice must have been flat, failing to convey sufficient enthusiasm.

'Aren't you pleased for me?' Liz enquired.

'Of course I am.'

'So, why the long face?'

I flopped my arms and shoulders forward. My body language had given me away, but I couldn't share the full picture with her. 'Laboratory problems,' I offered lamely, by way of explanation.

'What sort of laboratory problems?'

'They've got rid of Kyle.'

'He's the one kept the labs in working order, isn't he?'

'Yes.'

'Why is that such a catastrophe?'

'You wouldn't believe the hassles we get with the labs. I could rely on Kyle to sort things.'

'Whom do you have to rely on now, with Kyle gone?'

'Ha,' I snorted. 'Jenny Colepepper.'

'What? The deputy vice chancellor herself, dealing with the labs?'

'Yes.'

'Why did they get rid of Kyle?'

'Supposedly trafficking illegal entertainment material.'

'What, pornography or something?'

'Well, yes, they said something about pornography, but I think they were probably referring to sporting events.'

'How are sporting events pornographic?'

'Competitive for one thing, which isn't allowed these days, but I think it was probably fighting that they were referring to.'

'But fighting isn't exactly pornographic, is it?'

'Well, it's violent, and these days, I think violence counts as being pornographic.'

'How come you know so much about it?'

'Well, it isn't so much knowing, more inferring. I get to go over to Dunwick for my clinic, so I see and hear things.'

'So, it was just the dodgy sports then?'

'No, other things as well. I think they would say it was hateful stereotypes, racial jokes, that sort of thing.'

'Is anyone making stuff like that anymore? I wouldn't have thought it was possible.'

'Not current stuff. I don't really know, but I'm guessing it's old stuff from the 1960s and 70s, *Carry On* films, *Dad's Army*, that sort of thing.'

Liz made a face. 'I wouldn't call that entertainment. Hateful. Needs to be stamped out.'

'People do find it amusing, though.'

'Why can't they look at something more wholesome?'

'The problem is, many people aren't amused by what is put out today as entertainment.'

'What's wrong with it?'

'Let's take an example, I turned on the television the other day to be offered *Pride in my two daddies*. Does that sound like fun?'

'Oh yes, I know it. An inspiring story of a teenager discovering their true gender identity while attending Pride with their gay parents.'

'It didn't impress Amelia. Within two minutes of it starting, she made some excuse to leave the room to do her homework, wash her hair or something.'

'Why didn't she like it, do you think?'

'My guess is that it felt like she was being preached at, not entertained.'

'It doesn't need to be entertaining,' Liz pronounced grandly. 'It's important, that's what matters.'

Before we could explore the importance of the very worthy media output of the current age, we were diverted by a commotion.

'Why are you wearing this militaristic rubbish?' a young person of female appearance screamed out in a shrill voice as they grabbed at a poppy another person of female appearance was wearing, wrenching it off the other person's clothing, hurling it to the floor and stamping on it.

'None of your business what I wear,' they shrieked back. 'And keep your hands off me.' They swung a punch, hitting the poppy-grabber in the face.

Two more young people intervened to defend the assaulted vigilante of public morals, whereupon three other poppy wearers joined the fray. A fracas of shouting, pushing and slapping ensued before order was restored by the arrival of the university security guards.

'You've been looking out of sorts recently,' Bill Englebirt observed as he handed me a gin and tonic. He had invited me back for a drink in his apartment in Godolphin House. 'What's the matter?'

'You know Kyle got arrested?'

'Yes, I heard.'

'They found what they are saying was his stash of banned entertainment material.'

'But why would that upset you?'

'They're making out I had something to do with it.'

'But you don't, do you?'

'No.'

'Do they have anything to substantiate this?'

'No, nothing at all, as far as I can see. I got to see and talk to Kyle sometimes, that's all.'

'Which of course, you would, in your position.'

'Quite.'

'That couldn't be all there is to it. There must be something else.' Bill leaned back, gazing at me benevolently and expectantly, his hands held over his chest, fingers enmeshed.

'Well, there is, actually. I've got the Dolphins on my back.'

'What are they onto you about?'

'I shouldn't really tell you, patient confidentiality and all that.'

'Of course. Keep it in general terms. You can rely on me to be discreet.'

‘I referred a patient to the Tavidown Clinic for gender affirmation, but the patient subsequently changed their mind. Now, the Dolphins are making out that I talked them out of it, making me guilty of conversion therapy.’

‘Oh dear. Ugly.’

‘I know. The thing is, their changing their mind had nothing to do with me. Their situation changed, that’s all. The ridiculous thing is, in this case, the patient has already transitioned once, so it would have been a transition back to what they were in the first place.’

‘Sort sad irony there, somehow.’

‘The problem is, you can’t just flip back willy-nilly. The original transition will have made irreversible changes that can’t be put back now. Once bits have been chopped off, there’s no putting them back on, and the hormones have permanent effects.’

‘What made them change their mind?’

‘They had been depressed due to being an Unsuitable. That’s what made them want to transition back, but since then, things have changed. Their Unsuitable classification was removed, and they have a place on a degree course, so they aren’t depressed anymore and happy as they are.’

‘Wow, that’s rare. Once you’re an Unsuitable, you’re usually stuck with it.’

‘Being trans helped. The powers-that-be bend over backwards to be nice to trans folk.’

‘I can see why you’re worried,’ Bill commiserated. ‘Once Dolphins have you in their sights, they don’t let up. They’re like the Inquisition on a witch hunt. Keep me informed, and I’ll support you in any way I can.’

‘Thanks, Bill. I appreciate it.’

‘I’m on the Social Cohesion Advisory Committee, so I’ve got some contacts.’

‘Nice to know. What does this committee do?’

‘It concerns itself with influences in the community that could disrupt the social order, providing advice to the government about how they might be kept under control.’

‘Is it particularly concerned about anything at the moment?’

‘As a matter of fact, it is. The level of discontent from within the Unsuitables has been increasing in recent months, as you have probably seen for yourself from the demonstrations we see outside the university.’

‘Not only outside the university,’ I remarked. ‘You must have seen how many have been wearing poppies. There are clearly sympathies for them among our own ranks.’

‘Yes, we might seek to isolate the university from the Unsuitables, but the connections still remain.’

‘What is the committee advising, if that isn’t a secret?’

‘It is, but I’m sure I can rely on your discretion.’

‘You can.’

‘Obviously, means are being sought to dampen down the unrest among the Unsuitables.’

‘Such as?’

‘The use of Complianx has been identified as beneficial, but it has been only partially successful. Suggestions are being made for widening its use.’

‘As a practising psychiatrist, I am already encouraged to prescribe Complianx for practically everything. I can’t imagine what scope there could be to spread it out wider.’

‘Toxic influences are a major concern, especially how they are fomenting disorder within the Unsuitable community.’

‘That isn’t a secret. I heard about that on the news. Gordon Garage seems to be hitting a nerve there.’

‘Don’t be surprised if there are measures to rein in Toxic Influences.’

‘I wouldn’t be. They’re already confined to TICAs, which are almost like Soviet Gulags.’

‘Your former wife, Kate, could be affected. She’s in a TICA, isn’t she?’

‘Yes.’

‘How is she doing?’

‘I wouldn’t know.’

‘You haven’t been in touch?’

‘No,’ I lied.

‘You have a daughter, though; wouldn’t that require some contact?’

‘Everything is dealt with through solicitors,’ I said, lying again.

‘There is talk about the “No Free Speech for Hate” policy being ineffective, requiring tougher enforcement.’

‘What sort of tougher enforcement?’

‘Tightening up on their freedom of movement and communication, among other things.’

'Disenfranchisement and other suppression of "undesirables". Didn't we see that in the fascist regimes of the 1930s?'

'There are some more drastic and permanent measures being considered.'

'It sounds chillingly like some kind of Nazi-style Final Solution to me.'

'But it's the Toxic Influences who are considered to be the Nazis.'

'So Nazi-style measures are justified so long as those they are applied against are Nazis.'

Kyle's plumbing contact came around in an old vintage van, something of an antique, to assess the problem with my shower. 'I could sort it for £200.'

'When could you do it?'

'Now, if you like. I've got a shower tray in the van. Recycled. Got it off a building demolition job.'

I took a look at the item. A little scuffed here and there and smeared with mud, but serviceable. 'Yes, please go ahead. Crypto cash okay?'

The man got stuck into his work while I kept him well-stocked with builder's tea and biscuits.

'I like that van of yours,' I remarked, once the job was complete. 'How did you get it?'

'Mr Sharmoni sorted me out.'

'It's quite distinctive. Don't you need to have an identity check and permit?'

'Nah. It's a classic vehicle, see? Exempt.'

'How did you get hold of a classic?'

'It's one from Mr Sharmoni's collection. He has me as a driver.'

'It looks quite old.'

'It is. Mr Sharmoni lets them out for films, TV shows, that sort of thing. When they need to show the 1950s or 60s, telling us how bad things were in those times.'

'Do you think things were as bad as they say?' I enquired.

'Well, there's other films, made at the time that say otherwise.'

'You're not supposed to be able to see those these days.'

The man tapped his nose. 'There are ways.'

'How come you get to have the van, if it's for film and TV work.'

'Mr Sharmoni lets me use it between times. If anyone asks, I'm taking it out on a test drive.'

I called to cancel my visit from the legitimate plumber.

'Why are you cancelling, if I may ask?'

'I made alternative arrangements.'

'I wouldn't advise doing it yourself, sir, or using unqualified personnel.'

'Why not?'

'Imagine pipework being fitted without the necessary health and safety protocols and with no risk assessment. The possibilities don't bear thinking about.'

Chapter 14
Joining the Sharmoni Enterprise

"Militaristic or Jingoistic Symbols Prohibited" stated the large new notice at Slough University's Willow Brook entrance.

'The wearing of militaristic or jingoistic symbols, such as poppies as a glorification of war, contravenes the university's zero-tolerance-for-hate policy and accordingly is banned on university premises,' explained the text below in smaller print.

Despite this order, poppies were still being sold by a bedraggled man wearing a damp blazer and soggy beret from a trestle table prominently decorated with a Union Jack. Placards proclaimed, "God save the King" and "God Bless King William".

When a student approached the entrance wearing a poppy, a vigilant security guard stepped in front of them, shaking his head and indicating with his hand that the poppy should come off. The student pulled off the poppy and shoved it in their pocket. The dutiful security guard stood aside to let them through.

More than likely, they'll put it back on again later, I mused.

As I made the short walk to the Asima Shankar Laboratory Complex, my mobile rang.

'Is that Professor Hubbings?' enquired a male-sounding voice.

'Yes, speaking.'

'I am Charlotte Grenger from *The Daily Truth*, pronouns she/her.'

'Mine are he/him. What can I do for you?'

'Do you have anything to say about your wife fomenting gender hate?'

I sighed. Yet more bother to deal with. 'I don't know what you're talking about.'

'Kate Stillworthy is your wife, isn't she?'

'We're not together anymore.'

'But you are still married, aren't you?'

What should I say? If St Peter could be forgiven for denying Christ, perhaps I could be for denying Kate. 'In name only. We've been apart for over three years.'

'Why aren't you divorced?'

'Legal complications. It's in the hands of the solicitors.'

'It wouldn't be because you sympathise with her trans-exclusionary views, would it?'

'What she believes is entirely her business. It has nothing to do with me.'

'Even though you are still married?'

'We haven't been together for years. I don't even know what her views are, nor do I care.'

'So, you don't care that someone close to you is actively fomenting gender hatred.'

'I don't know anything about it, so I don't know whether I care.'

'If she is fomenting gender hatred, you couldn't approve of it, could you?'

'What is it that she is supposed to have done?'

'She is conspiring with Gordon Garage in making hateful and unfounded accusations against transwomen.'

'I know nothing about it, and I have no comment to make,' I said, as I ended the call.

The caretaker Sid answered when I called the Lakeside Caravan Park.

'Lakeside Caravan Park.'

'Sid, it's Jim.'

'Ah, Professor, what can I do for you?'

'Can you get through to Kate?'

'Sure, what should I tell her?'

'Could she come and meet me this evening, say, around 6:30, in one of the caravans, if you could see to that?'

'Yes, Professor, that'll be fine. Hundred quid, as usual, okay?'

'Professor Hubbings,' said a deep voice on the phone.

'Yes.'

'It's Nelson. I'm calling on Mr Sharmoni's behalf.'

'Oh, right.'

‘Mr Sharmoni would like you to join him for lunch at his club if that’s convenient.’

‘That’s nice of him. When did he have in mind?’

‘Today, if you wouldn’t mind.’

‘I was planning to lunch with someone else today.’

‘Mr Sharmoni would be much obliged if you would reschedule your other engagement.’

‘Of course, it is very nice of Mr Sharmoni to invite me, but it would cause me a bit of bother to rearrange things.’

‘Mr Sharmoni would make it worth your while,’ said Nelson, putting a bit of menace in his voice. ‘Trust me, it doesn’t pay to disappoint Mr Sharmoni.’

He was right. Mr Sharmoni was not someone whom it was wise to say no to. ‘Very well. I’ll come over.’

‘I’ll pick you up in the motor at 12:30, from the Willow Brook entrance.’

Damn, now I would have to put off my lunch date with Liz again!

As promised, Nelson was waiting for me at 12:30 with the black limousine, long, sumptuous and prestigious but a little too reminiscent of a hearse for my taste.

Minutes later, we drew up in front of the Bulldog Club, situated in a narrow back alley off Dunwick’s main shopping street. What had once been the loading bay for a sweatshop business premise was faced with dark marble, set out with an awning, blacked-out windows and dark, heavy doors picked out with shiny chrome and stainless steel.

A large muscular man with close-cropped hair, a broken nose and a square, stubbly jaw, dressed formally in a dark suit, white shirt and black bowtie stood by the doorway. I recognised him as one of Nelson’s fellow participants in the killing of Johnie Dorritt.

Nelson led me through the reception area, patchily illuminated with little pools of light against a dark background, like lanterns spread around over a deep dark lake, through into the club’s main entertainment area, now almost empty, a central arena for dancing, lit by twinkly spots of light reflected from rotating mirror balls with a stage at one end illuminated by spotlights.

‘Mr Sharmoni will be with you presently,’ said Nelson. ‘If you care to come over to the bar, I’ll get you a drink.’

He led me to the opposite end of the stage where there was a large bar with coloured LED strip lights illuminating downwards onto the floor, surrounded by bar stools upholstered in red velvet. A barman caught my eye, formally dressed in a white shirt glowing purple under the light, set off with a black bowtie.

'What can I get you, sir?'

'Gin and tonic would be nice.' I felt my pocket for my wallet.

'On the house,' said the barman. 'Mr Sharmoni's guest.'

He served the drink and a little dish of savoury nibbles. I turned towards Nelson, who was hovering in the background.

'Any idea what Mr Sharmoni wants to discuss with me?'

'I'll leave that to Mr Sharmoni.'

I shrugged. Figuring I wasn't going to get any conversation from these gentlemen, I sipped my drink in silence.

A door at one end of the bar opened. Looking over, I did a double take. A man emerged, who was either Gordon Garage or his doppelgänger, followed by Mr Sharmoni.

Gordon, or his lookalike, was wearing a tweed suit, checked shirt, a striped tie with a motif, brown brogue shoes and his signature velvet-collared jacket. *From his outfit, he really is Gordon Garage*, I concluded.

Mr Sharmoni was impeccably turned out in a navy-blue velvet tuxedo set off with gold embroidery and a dress shirt with a matching bowtie.

'The police won't do anything,' said Gordon.

'What if they send in the Army?' said Mr Sharmoni.

'The Army will come over to us, you'll see.'

'We'll talk it some more later on. Nelson will see you back.'

They shook hands. Nelson indicated for Gordon to follow him out of the club.

'Professor, good of you to come over,' said Mr Sharmoni, coming over to shake me firmly by the hand. 'Come on through.'

He led the way into a private room set out with a dining table. The wall was lined with Victorian-style wood panelling upon which were patriotic pictures and decorative items, a painting of a Battle of Britain spitfire flying in bright blue sky with a flaming German plane behind, a battleship firing a broadside on a choppy grey sea amidst huge shell splashes from incoming fire, a cavalry sword mounted on a wooden panel.

'Please take a seat,' invited Mr Sharmoni.

I settled into one of the opulent buttoned leather upholstered carver-style dining chairs.

'Thank you.'

'Do you like steak?'

My mouth watered at the prospect. 'Well, yes, I do.'

'Good. Pomme frites, that's posh for chips, red cabbage, with a pepper sauce. Sound all right?'

'Sounds lovely. Really nice, actually.'

'Not your usual fare, I imagine,' remarked Mr Sharmoni, observing my enthusiasm.

'You're right; not my usual fare.'

'Let me guess, that would be vegan cuisine, generally speaking.'

'Yes, it tends to be. These days eating animal products is frowned upon.'

'Not frowned upon by me,' assured Mr Sharmoni. 'I like a bit of meat. I've selected a nice bottle of Saint-Émilion to go with it.'

'Really good, thanks.'

Mr Sharmoni pressed a bellpush and the barman came in to pour out the wine.

'Professor, the reason I've asked you over is that I have a vacancy in my organisation that I think you could fill.'

'Oh, I see. What was it you had in mind?'

'I provide certain entertainment material aimed at those who like something rather more exciting and amusing than is offered by the powers-that-be.'

'Where would I come in?'

'I need a distributor within Slough University.'

'To replace the one you lost recently?'

'You know about that?'

'Yes, that would have been Kyle, wouldn't it?'

'Are you already a customer then?'

'Not me personally, but I know one or two who were.'

'Will you take on the role?'

'I would rather not, if you wouldn't mind.'

'It would be worth your while, financially. Twenty per cent of sales.'

'I don't really need the money, and I'm already pretty busy in my role as professor and running my psychiatric clinic at Dunwick Park.'

Mr Sharmoni gave me a look, not exactly angry. His face was impassive apart from a slight frown; displeasure, which, his eyes told me, ran deep.

'I really need someone, and you would be ideal.'

'Look, I'm flattered, but I would really rather not.'

'You'd need the money if you were to lose your job as Professor, wouldn't you?' he observed, with menace in his voice and penetrating eyes.

'Why would that happen?'

'When it comes out about your very intimate relationship with Kate Stillworthy, I can't imagine the university keeping you on.'

'When it comes out, what do you mean?'

'There is photographic evidence. A video was taken in Lakeside Caravan Park, in the caravan on plot 47. You gave her quite a rogering. I was well impressed. She seemed to like it, too.'

'You bastard. You mean you filmed us, while we were, you know, doing it.'

'Sid owed me a favour.'

'What do you plan to do with it?'

'Nothing if you help me out.'

'If I don't?'

'The evidence goes anonymously to Jenny Colepepper. She is the deputy vice chancellor, I think, isn't she?'

'You really are a bastard.'

'If you think that's bad, I might arrange for a copy to go to Liz Entworthy too. I don't imagine she would be so friendly with you after she has seen you giving Kate Stillworthy a good seeing to.'

'You wouldn't.'

'Trust me, I would.'

'What if I just said, stuff you, do your worst?'

'It seems likely you would end up joining Ms Stillworthy in the TICA. You might like that. You could shag her all you like there. But think what would happen to Amelia. She would end up in care, wouldn't she?'

He had me cornered. 'Alright, what do you want me to do?'

'Don't look at me like that. If you look out for me, I'll look after you. I could be very good for you.'

The barman brought in our meal, set it out in front of us and refilled our glasses.

‘Well, this looks good, doesn’t it?’ said Mr Sharmoni. ‘Go on, Professor, dig in.’

I looked at the food but didn’t start on it. ‘I don’t like it. It’s blackmail.’

‘Tell you what I’ll do. I’ll up your commission to twenty-five percent. Can’t say fairer than that.’

When I saw Sid later on in his ramshackle reception hut at the Lakeside Caravan Park, I felt like punching him extremely hard. I looked at him, skinny, bent, and weedy, wheezing as he breathed. Had I punched him, I could have done him some serious damage. I don’t know what leverage Mr Sharmoni had on him. Like me, he probably didn’t have an option other than to cooperate. I restrained myself, but I couldn’t bring myself to be friendly.

‘Got the caravan then?’ I asked.

‘Yes, same one as before, number 47. Kate’s there, waiting for you.’

‘Good. Shall we settle up?’

‘Like we said, hundred quid.’

‘Alright. Crypto.’ I pulled out my phone and entered the amount then held it out next to Sid’s.

‘I’ll be off then,’ I said as I stepped out of the reception hut into the damp evening mist, filling my nose with musty autumnal scents of soggy decaying leaves, mud and bonfires.

It is Mr Sharmoni I should be annoyed with, I reflected. Sid was just a pawn in Mr Sharmoni’s game. Still, filming us making love? That was disgusting. I would always view Sid with distaste from this point on.

The funny thing is, I couldn’t bring myself to hate Mr Sharmoni. He had charming manners and was clearly a very smooth operator. He was ruthless, but I couldn’t help admiring him. Besides, I certainly wasn’t going to be punching him. I’d seen what Nelson and his other minders could do, and I didn’t fancy my chances.

‘Kate?’ I said as I opened the weatherbeaten door of the dilapidated caravan on plot 47.

She leapt up and grabbed me in a fond hug. ‘Jim, it’s lovely to see you.’

‘And you, too,’ I assured her, holding her tight, but restraining my passion in view of the surveillance I now knew we were under.

Kate moved her lips to mine. I kissed her briefly but held back from a full-on snog.

‘What’s the matter?’ Kate enquired.

‘I got a call today from *The Daily Truth.*’

‘What did they want?’

‘They’re on your trail, saying you’re fomenting gender hate, ganging up with Gordon Garage to oppress transwomen, or some such.’

‘Oh dear. I wonder who has been talking.’

‘Is there something in it, then?’

‘Only that with us all being in the TICA, we get to talk about things, sometimes saying things that would outrage some folk out in the mainstream world such as the readership of *The Daily Truth.*’

‘They know we’re still married, too, which is why they got onto me about it.’

‘They don’t know about us being here, do they?’

‘I don’t think so. Not yet, anyway.’

‘Did they say what they had about me?’

‘The only thing mentioned was conspiring with Gordon Garage about oppressing trans people. What is that about, do you think?’

‘Gordon wants to make it illegal to change gender.’

‘Ouch. That would inflame some people, for sure. How are you involved?’

‘Being shut up together in the TICA, we get to talk, that’s all.’

‘I got to see Gordon Garage today,’ I remarked.

‘How was that?’

‘I was in the Bulldog Club in Dunwick.’

‘I wouldn’t have thought the Bulldog Club was your thing. You’re not a member, are you?’

‘No, first time I’d been there. Mr Sharmoni invited me.’

‘Mr Sharmoni? You’re full of surprises. How come you know him?’

‘Long story. He isn’t someone you want to say no to if he invites you.’

‘What did you think of Gordon then, in the flesh?’

‘We didn’t get a chance to talk. He was leaving just as I arrived.’

‘I can see why Gordon might have to get away. He isn’t supposed to be there at all. It breaks his curfew conditions.’

Kate snuggled up to me, putting her arms around me. I reciprocated tentatively, holding my hands against her back, pressing only softly as if she was an egg and I might break her if applied any pressure.

‘What’s the matter? You’re holding back today?’ said Kate.

I didn't want to tell her about the surveillance, so I would need another excuse. 'There is something that Mr Sharmoni wants me to do for him.'

'What thing?'

'Acting as his distributor for entertainment material within the university.'

'Why you?'

'He knows about us. If I don't do his bidding, he will inform the university authorities.'

'So what? Everyone already knows about us being married.'

'But not about us still being married and seeing each other like this.'

'What does he want you to do for him?'

'People want entertainment material that isn't allowed anymore.'

'You mean pornography.'

'Yes, but there are a lot of other things as well.'

'Such as?'

'Stand-up comedians, people like Bernard Manning and Jeremy Clarkson, James Bond films, competitive sports.'

'How does it work?'

'People have an encryption program on their phone. They give an order for what they want on an encrypted memory card and pay with crypto. I pass it on to Mr Sharmoni's people, they get me the card back with what the client ordered, and I pass it on.'

'But why you? Didn't Mr Sharmoni have someone already?'

'He did. It was Kyle, but Kyle got discovered.'

'You might get discovered, too.'

'I might, but I can't really say no to Mr Sharmoni.'

'I suppose not,' Kate agreed.

'Anyway, enough about me. What dastardly schemes have you been plotting in your TICA?'

'I've been working with Harvey Bentling, you know, my old professor, on his research into the religious doctrines of the Reformation.'

'Oh, yes, he was cancelled recently, but I never got to hear exactly what for.'

'Islamophobia is what they said,' said Kate. 'In a discussion about past British prime ministers, he quoted Boris Johnson referring to Muslim women as letterboxes, without having first given a trigger warning.'

'Well, you couldn't expect Boris to give a trigger warning.'

‘It wasn’t Boris they were fussed about. It was Harvey who should have given the trigger warning when he referred to it.’

‘Who could reasonably expect any discussion of Boris Johnson not mentioning his politically incorrect utterances? He came out with remarks like that almost every day of the week. It was why people voted for him.’

‘This is the basic contradiction we have in educating people in history these days. Bad things happened, but people can opt out of learning about the bad things if they want.’

‘Surely, Harvey could have been forgiven for his lack of a trigger warning if he had grovelled and apologised enough.’

Kate shook her head. ‘I don’t think so. Once those in control have it in for you, they are going to get you for something, even if they have to cook up an accusation.’

I nodded. ‘I would say that is what happened to you.’

‘Yes,’ Kate concurred. ‘It was. Once I had contradicted the *Transwomen Are Women* dogma, I was done for.’

‘Ouch, yes. That is heresy for sure.’

‘There is an inherent contradiction, we all say that sexual violence against women is a bad thing, yet the very same people who demand women-only safe spaces for their protection, with their *Transwomen Are Women* ethos, are quite happy to allow people with penises into those safe spaces, making them safe spaces in name only.’

‘I tried to make this point recently, but I was shut down because I lacked the lived experience of being a woman.’

‘Lucky for you. As a woman, I found myself classified as a Toxic Influence and banished to a TICA.’

‘Had I identified as a woman, then under the *Transwomen Are Women* rule, I should have been allowed to speak.’

‘Perhaps not. To have the lived experience, you would have had to be a woman with a vagina.’

‘It’s quite mad.’

‘It wasn’t only the *Transwomen Are Women* dogma that I breached. I had the temerity to suggest that there were only two biological sexes.’

‘Yes, that doesn’t go down well. The myriad of gender categories we must recognise these days are a fundamental article of faith that we dare not contradict.’

'Yet, to the uneducated masses, not to mention every species of animal from a mouse to a crocodile, it is blindingly obvious that there are only two biological sexes and it is self-evident which is which.'

'Just being the devil's advocate for a moment, it is arguable that there are more biological sexes than that. I mean, if you take into account intersex conditions. I've seen it suggested that there could be twenty or so if you allow for all the possible combinations of X and Y chromosomes, hormone insensitivity, chimaeras and so on.'

Kate's eyes fired up for the challenge. Bounce and energy sprang into her slim frame. 'This argument about the existence of intersex conditions is misleading and distorting because it takes no account of the numbers involved. Intersex conditions exist in around one per cent of the population, but of those one per cent, in around nine out of ten clearly present as either male or female in appearance. Thus, only about one in a thousand have a genuinely ambiguous biological sex.'

'Being the devil's advocate again, just because they are a minority doesn't mean we should ignore their needs.'

'Much better to help them fit into the two-gender world as best as possible than to invent spurious new gender categories, in my opinion.'

'They would say, by force fitting them into a two-gender world, you are denying their right to be what they are.'

'Let's be realistic here. For 99.9% of the population, their day-to-day lived experience is that they are one or the other of two clearly identifiable biological sexes. Extrapolating the experience of 0.1% of the population to claim that sex is spectrum rather than essentially binary is plain wrong and driven by ideology, not reason.'

'But trans people should have their rights, shouldn't they, even if they are only 0.1% of the population.'

'We're talking about intersex conditions here, not transsexuals. They have almost nothing to do with one another.'

'How do you mean?'

'Intersex conditions have almost no relevance to transsexual expression in reality because the overwhelming majority of those who become transsexuals are not intersex at all, being unambiguously one particular biological sex. The overwhelming majority are transsexual because of gender dysphoria, a mental not a physical condition.'

‘As a psychiatrist, I would concur. But shouldn’t we accommodate those who wish to transition, if that is what they want and feel they need to be themselves?’

‘Transitioning is a brutal process involving drastic and irreversible mutilation of body parts and body changes arising from opposite sex hormones. It is not something to be done lightly.’

‘But if the person understands these consequences and still wants to proceed, they should be allowed to do so, shouldn’t they?’

‘You mean, even if they are children? Can children be expected to have a full understanding of what is involved?’

‘But if you leave it until they are adults, they will have already been through puberty and acquired the body form opposite to the gender they aspire to.’

‘There are huge concerns with this. We have the unrealistic expectation of prepubescent children being able to make an informed choice, the motivation of adults who influence them or make decisions on their behalf, peer influence and social contagion.’

‘What do you mean by social contagion?’

‘Following fashion, what’s trendy, following the lead of friends and fellow pupils who have come out as trans.’

‘Devil’s advocate again, wouldn’t this social influence simply be enabling children better to discover who they really are?’

‘Not if what the children are exposed to is propaganda rather than unbiased information. We see educational materials for children equating non-conformity to gender stereotypes with being trans, which is a dangerous distortion.’

‘Right, equating boys liking feminine style clothing or girls playing with machines as indicative of being trans.’

‘What is more, once a child displays any behaviour that is non-gender conforming and gets labelled as trans, no adult is allowed to discuss this with the child, lest they be accused of conversion therapy.’

‘Happened to me just the other day. One of my patients changed their mind about a referral for transition, and now, I’m being accused of conversion therapy for no other reason than they changed their mind.’

‘The puberty blockers and social pressure from the myriad gender ideas could just be blocking the developmental process, whereby gender dysphoria would normally resolve, leading to people making some very bad choices.’

‘I agree, although, for Amelia’s sake, if nothing else, I couldn’t possibly say so publicly.’

'No, you had better not.'

'*The Daily Truth* suggested that you had teamed up with Gordon Garage about this. What's that about?'

'Through his Forward England party, he is going to combat the prevailing gender ideology.'

'How does that concern you?'

'He wants to use me as an academic authority to support what he is saying.'

'I suppose it's that *The Daily Truth* has got wind of.'

'I'd guess so.'

'You're going to get hated for it.'

'Hated for being hateful, supposedly. There is an irony there somewhere.'

'Doesn't it worry you?'

'Not really. I've already been de-platformed, cancelled, classified as a Toxic Influence, separated from my family and confined in a TICA. What more can they do to me?'

Chapter 15
Cesspit of Hate

"Cesspit of Hate" said the headline in *The Daily Truth*, going on to say:

Far from containing hate, our Toxic Influence Containment Areas have become a hotbed of persecution against trans people. From their TICA in the Dunwick area, notorious trans-exclusionist Kate Stillworthy and Gordon Garage, far-right leader of Forward England, are conspiring to deny the rights of non-binary people, reversion to a false binary of genders and exclusion of trans people from expressing their preferred gender. This is a blatant infringement of the principle of "No Free Speech for Hate". The government must act!

I was in my Autocab on my way to my clinic at Dunwick Park General Hospital as I caught up on the news. I sensed a shedload of grief coming in Kate's direction.

There was a small group of demonstrators standing on the damp pavement in front of the hospital entrance as I came in, chanting, 'No to Conversion Therapy.' One of them recognised me as I approached, blocking my way.

'Why are you carrying out illegal conversion therapy, Professor?' shouted the protester, a bulky individual in feminine clothing, with a deep voice and a stubbly chin not entirely disguised by heavy facial makeup.

'You are misinformed,' I asserted. 'I don't do conversion therapy, never have.'

'You're a liar. We know you are,' they shouted back, continuing to block my way.

'Kindly get out of my way.'

'Not until you explain why you are carrying out conversion therapy.'

‘Stop causing an obstruction, please,’ said the security guard, after I had looked over pleadingly and caught his eye.

The security guard stood his ground, leaving me a small gap to squeeze through to the gate.

My first patient was Fenn Holby, the prostitute who had been raped by Johnie Dorritt before he was slain in retribution by Nelson and his fellow minders of Mr Sharmoni’s business interests. Wearing a baggy tracksuit, she wasn’t looking for any trade today. With her face devoid of makeup, she revealed a fragility she normally kept well disguised.

‘So, Fenn, what brings you in today?’ I enquired.

‘Last few days, I haven’t been able to work.’

‘Why is that?’

‘It’s me nerves, see. When I’m near a punter, a guy who wants a bit, you know, I gets all nervous. I want to get away. Frightened like. I can’t bring meself to do it.’

‘When did this come about?’

‘Just the last week or so, really. I forced meself to go through with it a couple of times, but then it just got too much, and I couldn’t do it no more. Not for the last three days. If I don’t work, I’ll have nothing.’

‘It isn’t all of a sudden this has happened then; it’s been getting worse as time goes on. Am I right?’

‘Yes, it’s got worse. I was feeling frightened, you know, but I thought I’d get over it and put it out of me mind. But I didn’t get over it. It got worse each time, ’til I couldn’t do it no more.’

‘When did you start to feel frightened?’

‘It started after that time when Johnie and his mates did what they did and then Johnie got killed.’

‘It must have been horrible for you.’

‘I can’t get it out of me mind. When I’m with a punter, it comes back to me. I can’t stand it. It’s not the punter, it’s the thoughts that come with it.’

‘It’ll be the post-traumatic stress triggered by the sexual situation.’

‘What can you do, doctor?’

‘We would have to work through a sexual situation with you, getting you through the fear and relaxed, gradually one step at a time. There is a drug we can use for relaxation. It should work, but it’ll take some time. A few sessions, I would think.’

'How long would it take?'

'The sessions could be stressful, so I wouldn't want to do more than one a week to give you time to get over it. I'd start with about eight to ten sessions and then see how we go.'

'But that would be months. I don't have time for all that. I've got to earn a living.'

'These things do take time. Post-traumatic stress takes some working through.'

'You know that Complianx stuff you gave me last time?'

'Yes.'

'That did the job. I didn't get so frightened when I'd had one of those.'

'I could give you a prescription, but we should really do the therapy as well.'

After I had finished with Fenn, there was a message on my phone from Nelson, Mr Sharmoni's minder. I called him back.

'Professor, I have some things for you to give out. Orders to be fulfilled. Could I come round with them when you finish your clinic?'

'That would be alright, except for one thing. There's a group of demonstrators at the hospital entrance who have it in for me. There could be some bother.'

'Don't worry, we'll sort them out. They won't be there later on.'

I had a video call scheduled with Dr Ezra Bengold from the Tavidown Clinic. He was a keen-looking young man in his thirties, with short, slightly curly brown hair and a sparse beard trimmed short, his heavy-framed glasses giving him an air of serious intent. I couldn't tell whether the smile on his face indicated friendliness or was akin to a thug relishing the prospect of giving someone a good kicking.

'Professor, thanks for coming on this call,' said Dr Bengold. 'If you wouldn't mind, I would like to explore the background of a referral you made to us, Carl Gellsten, for affirmation of their female identity.'

'Carl has chosen to withdraw from the referral, so I'm not sure what there is to discuss.'

'We need to explore this to make sure that the patient's needs are being met.'

'They are. He now wishes to remain in his male identity.'

‘We have had unfortunate cases of self-harm and tragically sometimes, suicide, when patients have been denied the gender affirmation they need. It is incumbent on us to ensure that remaining in his male identity genuinely represents Carl’s aspirations.’

‘In my judgement, they do.’

‘Professor, do you see yourself as a gatekeeper to gender affirmation treatment?’

‘In a sense, yes. I would need to be assured that the patient had the mental capacity to make an informed decision about their gender.’

‘Are you saying that you would refuse to refer someone on the grounds of them being mentally challenged?’

‘I might. It depends on the circumstances.’

‘If someone was mentally challenged, autistic let’s say, would you stand in their way to gender affirmation?’

‘I would need to be convinced that they fully understood the implications.’

‘You would therefore deny the rights of someone for affirmation of their chosen gender on the basis of their neurodiversity.’

‘I didn’t say that at all. All I said was, I would need to be sure they knew what they would be getting into.’

‘If someone who was suffering from a mental illness, psychosis or depression, say, would that stand in the way of you making a referral?’

‘It might. I would need to be convinced they had a good understanding of what would be involved and their desire for transition would remain subsequently when their mental health improved.’

‘Hasn’t it occurred to you that misgendering of the patient would probably be the root cause of their mental illness?’

‘Yes, of course, it could be.’

‘You would thereby be blocking the treatment they needed, would you not?’

‘I would need to be assured that such treatment was in the patient’s best interest.’

‘Wouldn’t affirmation of the patient’s chosen gender identity always be in their best interest?’

‘As it happens, Carl’s case demonstrates that perhaps, this is not always the case.’

‘How is that?’

'He was born female. While he was still a child, he had puberty blockers, then a hysterectomy and phalloplasty. Fortunately, due to the puberty blockers, he was spared the double mastectomy. Yet, now, he was exploring a retransition back to female.'

'What is your point?'

'His desire to transition back to female suggests that the original transition was not actually in his best interest.'

'So, you admit that they have requested to have their gender affirmed as female.'

'Yes, he did request that.'

'Why then did you cancel his referral?'

'He asked me to.'

'Tell me, Professor, how do you identify a person's gender?'

'I ask them about their pronouns.'

'When you last saw Carl, what did he tell you their pronouns were?'

'Initially, he said he wasn't sure.'

'Unsure until you influenced them to identify the way you wanted rather than what they wished for.'

'No, he told me himself that he wanted to remain identified as male.'

'You just told me they said they weren't sure.'

'Initially, yes.'

'So, their decision was made after you influenced them.'

'He was very clear that he now wanted to stay as he was.'

'But this was only a week after you had made the referral; what made them change their mind so quickly?'

'He didn't explain to me in detail, so I can only speculate; however, as I see it, it was due to a significant change in his life situation.'

'What was that?'

'His previous classification as Educationally Unsuitable was lifted and he became eligible for an artisan degree course.'

'Were you in any way responsible for enrolment on his course?'

'Yes, as it happens I was. I was doing some of the interviews.'

'So, you were responsible for the change in their circumstances that dissuaded them from their gender affirmation treatment.'

'The academic staff take it in turns to carry out interviews, and simply by chance, Carl was rostered to me. I didn't arrange for that to happen.'

'It could therefore have been getting their place on the course served as an inducement to abandon their gender affirmation.'

'There was no inducement involved. All the university's courses are open to all genders.'

'What was the course they were enrolled on?'

'Home appliances installation, as I recall.'

'A stereotypically male activity, wouldn't you agree? Obviously, this was an inducement to remain in the male gender.'

'There is no truth in this insinuation at all.'

'Professor, you should know that I will be putting in a report to the General Medical Council based upon what you have told me today.'

As I emerged from the hospital, the towering figures of Nelson and another of Mr Sharmoni's minders were waiting for me outside with Mr Sharmoni's black limousine. I don't know what they had done to intimidate the demonstrators, but now they were nowhere to be seen. Nelson held the door open for me to step into the plush and spacious rear interior of the vehicle.

'We'll drive to the university if you like,' said Nelson.

'Yes, thanks. It'll save me getting an Autocab.'

'Don't mention it. I'll fill you in about the gear on the way.'

Nelson took the front passenger seat, leaving his colleague to drive. Once we were underway, he leaned over to face me, handing me a small bag containing envelopes, discreetly numbered in pencil together with a loose memory card.

'This card contains an encrypted file with the numbers and the names of the people each number represents. Never let anyone see it and try to remember it. Best not to refer to it unless you have to. You'll need to put in that encryption key I gave you to see it. Okay?'

'Yes, okay.'

'You memorised that encryption key, didn't you?'

'Yes, I did.'

'You mustn't ever write it down. Without it, they'll have nothing on you. It'll just be noise on the card. But if they get that info, it'll blow the whole thing. You just need to call the clients and arrange for them to pick up their gear, yeah?'

'Yes, got it.'

Outside the university's Willow Brook entrance, the Forward England demonstrators had a new slogan, *Men are men, women are women, get used to it*, printed out onto placards and as a headline on leaflets they were handing out. *Time to sweep away the nonsense of gender ideology*, said the wording on the leaflet. *Time to get back to basic common sense, where there are two sexes and whichever way we were when we were born, that's how we are and always will be.*

At this point, the leaflets were still dry despite the drizzly dampness in the air, and there were as yet no counter demonstrators, but I had a feeling there soon would be, with such an inflammatory message, and some ugly scenes, too. My mood was as glum and unsettled as the billowing low grey clouds as I waited for the campus tram.

As I passed through the covered thoroughfare linking the assortment of buildings forming the Oppressed Peoples Memorial Complex, I noticed people wearing badges with the word *CENSORED* in prominent red capitals. Some wore additional stick-on paper badges with other slogans. Two, I noticed, were "God Save the King" and "Votes for Unsuitables".

The Cloister Cafeteria was bright and colourful in contrast to the sombre wintry outdoors. Liz, combining beauty with an air of calm, capable control, was waiting for me in a quiet corner of the Cloister Cafeteria.

'Jim, you look terrible.'

'Sorry, I probably do. A few problems to contend with.'

'What sort of problems?'

'Did you see the article in *The Daily Truth*?'

'You mean the one about Kate Stillworthy and Gordon Garage?'

'Yes, that's the one.'

'I know she was your wife, but she's history now, isn't she? Why should you care?'

'We're not actually divorced yet, and *The Daily Truth* is trying to make out that I'm implicated.'

'You mean you're still married?'

'Well, technically yes. There were some legal hiccups, so we just let things slide.'

Liz looked back at me with narrowed eyes. 'I think you had better get it finalised, don't you? If you want to avoid that sort of problem. It's bad enough being linked in people's minds with Kate, but now you'll be linked with Gordon Garage as well.'

'I guess you're right.'

'I am right. What made you drag it out, anyway? I would have thought you would have wanted to be free of her as quickly as possible, so you could move on.'

'I don't know really. There were other more pressing priorities.'

'Such as?' She gave me an intense look. 'It wouldn't be because you still have a soft spot for her, would it?'

'No, just inertia. A lot of messy details to be gone through with the solicitors that I didn't want to face up to.'

'If you want us to have a future, you had better face up to them now.'

'I've got something for you,' I said to Bill Englebirt on the phone. 'Mind if I drop it round at your place this evening?'

'I'm intrigued,' replied Bill. 'What is it?'

'I'll tell you later.'

It was evening standing in the doorway of Bill's Godolphin House apartment when I handed Bill his envelope containing an encrypted memory card.

'What's this?' he enquired.

'What you ordered. *Stable Yard Romp*, wasn't it?'

'Goodness. How come you've brought it over?'

'You know Kyle had to go. Well, I'm the new Kyle.'

Bill's eyes widened and his tousled hair appeared to stand up in amazement. 'Well, I'll be damned.'

'Afraid I need thirty quid off you.'

Bill pulled out his phone and we made the necessary Crypto cash handover.

'Is this wise?' asked Bill.

'Probably not.'

'Why then?'

'Mr Sharmoni could make life difficult for me if I don't.'

'Good God. What has he got on you?'

'Long story.'

'Better come on in and have a drink.'

'What on Earth made you join Mr Sharmoni's payroll?' Bill asked me as he handed me a stiff gin and tonic. We settled ourselves down into Bill's lived-in easy chairs, sagging under us as we all do when we get older.

'If I hadn't, he was going say things about me and Kate Stillworthy.'

'I saw she was mentioned in today's *Daily Truth*. Anything to do with that?'

'I have no doubt that *The Daily Truth* would have made a connection out of it, given half a chance.'

'These things from our past come back to haunt us, that's for sure.'

'It's not so much about me. It's Amelia that concerns me. If anything happened to me, she would be taken into care.'

'You did the right thing, distancing yourself from Kate.'

'I didn't have much choice. If I hadn't distanced myself from Kate, I might have been declared a Toxic Influence myself, and then I would have lost custody of Amelia.'

'I see that. Bad enough for her losing her mother but losing her dad as well…' Bill shook his head.

'Exactly. It would make her an orphan, which is why I daren't say no to Mr Sharmoni.'

'How did you even get on Mr Sharmoni's radar?'

'I witnessed the murder of that young lad in Dunwick, you know, Johnie Dorritt.'

'I heard about it. What has that got to do with Mr Sharmoni?'

'Quite a lot, though I'd rather not say any more.'

'Alright. Understood. I won't pry.' Bill remained silent for a few seconds. 'If it hadn't been for what Kate did, would you still be together, do you think?'

'Yes, I think we would.'

'It's good that you've been able to move on now, with Liz.'

'Actually, things aren't so good between us.'

'Anything you want to share?'

'She suspects that I still have feelings for Kate.'

'Do you?'

'Look, I've moved on from Kate.'

'Have you, really?'

I grimaced, uncomfortable with where we were going. 'Enough about me. How's your love life?'

'I haven't really got one,' Bill confessed, shaking his head.

'You must have some kind of a love life. I don't believe you've taken a vow of chastity.'

'It isn't as if I necessarily have a choice. I guess I'm one of those incels.'

'You and a lot of other guys. You're definitely not alone, being in that position.'

'Not something that one can admit, though.'

'Very true. People get suspicious. For my part, I'm glad to have Liz. If I didn't, I think people would talk.'

'You're lucky, having Liz. I don't have that cover.'

'Being older, they probably cut you more slack than they would for a younger guy.'

'Just because I'm older, doesn't mean I don't still have needs.'

'Yes, I know. It's a vicious circle. People look at you suspiciously for being a single man—there must be something strange about you, being single. Then, being this suspicious single guy, no woman wants to go near you, so you stay single.'

'Tell me about it.'

'The politics worsen the situation. Incels are designated as a hate group by those who make the rules about these things.'

'Rockface, you mean. They're the ones making the rules.'

'Yes, them. As a result, instead of giving sympathy to folk who are depressed and lonely in their singleness, being a designated hate group, it becomes everyone's duty to pour scorn and hatred on them.'

'It's rather difficult to do anything to change the situation, because these days, if we were to say anything even slightly suggestive to a woman, we instantly get accused of sexual harassment.'

I nodded in agreement. 'Yes, that's true. Not worth the risk.'

'I value my career too much for that. There are countless guys who are now languishing in TICAs because they said or did something they shouldn't.'

'You do take some risk. Like today for example, with that movie you got from me—something about romping in stables, wasn't it?'

'As you pointed out, I haven't taken a vow of chastity. A man needs some outlet, even if it isn't the real thing.'

'You could have tried online dating, I suppose.'

'Tried that. Hopeless. The dating apps don't let men approach the women, and over some years, I think I have only ever had two women contact me, neither of which came to anything.'

'Amazing there are any relationships at all, the way things are.'

'How did you get together with Liz?'

'I have an idea Jenny Colepepper put her up to approach me.'

'Why would she do that?'

'She was trying to protect me, I think. If I was with someone else, it would allay suspicion of me still being in league with Kate.'

'What makes you think that?'

'She had a quiet word with me, shortly before Liz suggested we have lunch together. Told me about rumours that were circulating, and how there were moves to have me classified as a Toxic Influence. If I knew what was good for me, I would publicly distance myself from Kate, and how it would be helpful for me to be seen with someone else.'

Bill nodded. 'Sounds like her, the way she fixes things. But what's in it for Liz?'

'Well, me, perhaps. I'm not such a bad catch.'

Bill looked me up and down. 'Got to be more to it than that.'

'Cheeky. Actually, there may be. Liz is ambitious, always angling for the professorship that has now come her way. Dr Colepepper probably dropped a few hints about that.'

'You're a lucky sod,' Bill remarked.

'How come?'

'Nobody's taking care of me like that.'

'Like what?'

'Like Jenny Colepepper did for you.'

'Not all it's cracked up to be.'

'You must be kidding. Liz is gorgeous. I'm well jealous.'

'That's true. She is lovely to look at.'

'Not half.'

I mused for a moment. 'You know, when I go over to the clinic at Dunwick, I often get accosted by prostitutes, some of whom are quite nice. That's one way of getting some sex that I wouldn't blame anybody for indulging in.'

Bill looked embarrassed, as well he might. 'Could be a temptation for some, I suppose,' he conceded.

Chapter 16
Permanently Toxic Influence

The chief security guard, a stout, middle-aged man with a round, friendly face and receding hairline, showed me into the office behind the reception desk of the university's Willow Brook security kiosk. I handed over an envelope containing a memory card.

'Thank you, Professor. We like to keep up to date with sport.'

'Cage fighting, isn't it? I've never actually seen it before.'

'Would you like to see it now?'

'Well, thanks, if only to satisfy my curiosity.'

The security guard loaded the memory card onto a tablet computer and used the secret code to access a site somewhere on the dark web. An octagonal ring surrounded by a high chain link steel mesh fence appeared on the screen. Within the ring, two rough muscular men faced off against each other. The ring was situated within a barnlike building, surrounded by a vociferous audience cheering and jeering in support of their favourite. In the front row of the crowd, my eye caught sight of a woman gesticulating with excitement, someone I recognised, Celia Englebury, the Safety Officer from Amelia's school.

The fighters circled around, landing heavy blows and kicks on each other. One went down onto the floor, whereupon the other slammed onto him with bone-crunching force. Blood poured out from a head wound, forming a slippery puddle on the floor surface.

'Enough blood sport for one day,' I remarked. 'I think I'll be getting along.'

As I made the short walk over to the nearby Asima Shankar Laboratory Complex, overcoming my revulsion at talking to him, I made an encrypted call to Sid at the Lakeside Caravan Park.

'Sid, it's Jim.'

'Hello, Professor.'

'Would you be able to set up for Kate and me to meet up this evening in one of the caravans?'

'I don't think that'll be possible.'

'Why not?'

'Haven't you heard? Kate won't be allowed out anymore. It was on the news.'

Arrived in my office, I called up the latest news:

Trans-exclusionist Kate Stillworthy and Gordon Garage, far-right leader of Forward England, following agitation denying non-binary gender identities and seeking to ban affirmation of non-birth gender identities, in accordance with the Government's "No Free Speech for Hate" policy, have been classified by the Department for Personal Freedom as Permanent Toxic Influences, requiring them, for the protection of the public, to remain within the precincts of their Toxic Influence Containment Area.

With my mind in turmoil, I couldn't focus on intellectual work, so I decided to make a couple of deliveries, starting with Jenny Colepepper, the university's deputy vice chancellor.

'Something for you,' I said as I put my head around her office door. I handed over the envelope containing an encrypted copy of *Monty Python's Life of Brian*.

'Thank you,' she acknowledged, her surprise betrayed by only a slight raising of her eyebrows. 'I wasn't expecting to see you bringing it, but nothing surprises me these days. But thanks, anyway.'

'Don't mention it!'

'I won't.'

'Well, I'll be off.'

'Before you go, take a seat for a moment.'

I sat down in the visitor's chair in front of her desk.

'It's about Eddie Donagal,' she continued. 'One of your PhD students, I believe.'

'Yes, that's right.'

'There has been a complaint about him.'

'What sort of complaint?'

'The allegation is, jingoistic triumphalism.'

'When and how is he supposed to have done this?'

'When he was required to remove the poppy he was wearing, in accordance with university policy about militarism, in a raised voice, he lauded the victory of the British empire in two world wars.'

'Is that so bad as to make an issue of it?'

'He said what he did very publicly in front of a lot of people who were clearly offended by it.'

'What happens now?'

'There will have to be a disciplinary hearing.'

As it happened, I already had something to give Eddie, so I sought him out right away.

'Something for you, Eddie,' I said as I passed him his envelope containing his encrypted copy of the film *Zulu*.

'Thanks, Jim.'

'Eddie, a little bird has told me you could be in trouble about something you said.'

'I always seem to be in trouble these days,' replied Eddie, his face glowing with defiance.

'Don't we all? Something about jingoistic triumphalism.'

'What, is that against the law?' asked Eddie, shaking his shoulders as if limbering up for a fight.

'It seems so.'

'They'll need to watch it, those folks with their witch hunts.'

'Why's that?'

'I've got quite a bit of support here within the university.'

'Really? I'm surprised anyone would speak in your support over this, lest the witch hunters come for them, too.'

'Take a look at this.' Eddie tapped away on his phone and brought up a social media site. I skimmed through what he showed me, with multiple people holding forth, complaining about contemporary politics and expressing similar points of view to the Forward England supporters who had been picketing the university's Willow Brook entrance over recent months.

'What is this site?' I enquired.

'*England Awake*, it calls itself. It's on the dark web. You need a special code to get into it.'

'From looking at this, there seem to be a lot of people who have this special code.'

'You bet. And quite a few of them are from amongst us here, in the university.'

'You could get yourself into even more trouble by going onto this site.'

'I'm past worrying about that now. We're going to be making some changes. When we do, we'll be doing the hunting, and the self-appointed witchfinders will be our prey.'

As I emerged from the Autocab dropping me outside Dunwick Park General Hospital, I could hear raised voices and cheering.

Out of curiosity, instead of going straight in, I made the short walk towards the sound, along a small street to reach a small park a couple of hundred yards away.

The source of the commotion was Gordon Garage, standing on a crate under the sullen grey sky, addressing a small crowd of Forward England supporters and curious bystanders. Standing alongside him, scanning the scene for possible trouble, were the imposing Nelson and others of similar stature.

'We, the English people, will never forget those who made the ultimate sacrifice for our freedom, our nation,' proclaimed Mr Garage in a thunderous tone.

The Forward England supporters cheered and clapped.

'We, the English people, will resist the traitorous metropolitan elite seeking to extinguish the flame of our national identity with a deluge of warped woke claptrap.'

'Never,' shouted someone, followed by cheering from the crowd.

'We, the English people, demand our rights, traditions and the restoration of our true sovereign, King William.'

'God save the King,' called the crowd, repeatedly.

How did he get to be here? I pondered as I made my way back towards the hospital. According to the news, along with my Kate, Gordon Garage had been classified as a Permanent Toxic Influence and confined to his TICA, yet there he was out in public speechifying. And how did Nelson and his colleagues come to be involved?

'Could we get together for a chat?' I enquired Mr Sharmoni by text message.

'It's girls, they frighten me,' said Carl Gellsten, when he visited me at my clinic. He was hugging his knees, his fingers clenched together.

'How do they frighten you?'

'By looking, you know, sexy.'

'Have they always frightened you?'

'No, it's come on recently. Since I started on my course in the university.'

'Was there anything that started it, that you can tell?'

'It was at the freshers' party. There was this girl there. We got chatting, friendly-like. We'd had a few drinks. She got up kind of close like she wanted me to kiss her or something. It was then.'

'What happened?'

'I got this vision of what Johnie was doing to that prostitute woman before he got topped by Mr Sharmoni's boys. I kind of panicked. Got all in a sweat, like, if I did anything with her, the one getting friendly-like, then Mr Sharmoni's boys would come and find me and do me in like they did Johnie.'

'What did you do?'

'I stood up, said I had to go to the toilet and legged it. She came up to me the next day and asked, "What was the matter?" I couldn't say anything, just panicked. Said, nothing, and got out of there quick.'

'So, you find you need to avoid her now, or else you get a panic attack. Is that right?'

'Not just her. It's any girl who looks sexy. I just need to get away from them. But I can't. Not when I'm in class and stuff.'

'It was different, what Johnie was doing. That was rape. You wouldn't get into any trouble if it was what they wanted. Also, nothing needs to happen, if you don't want it to.'

'I know that, but it doesn't make any difference. I still get panicked. I just need something to make me less nervous.'

'I could prescribe you some Complianx. That'll make you less anxious.'

'Would you, Professor? That would be great. Don't know if I could face college anymore without it.'

I typed in the relevant prescription details into the computer. 'While you're here, Carl, there is something else.'

'What's that?'

'You know I put in that referral to the Tavidown Clinic when you were thinking of transitioning back to being a girl.'

'Yes, but I don't want that now.'

'I know, but I'd already put in the referral before you told me. Did they get in touch?'

'Yes, they asked if I wanted to affirm my gender. Told them I didn't know what they were talking about. Then they said, did I want to be a woman? I said, no, I was alright as I was. Then they asked if that was after I'd talked to you. I said, yes, it was. They said, it didn't matter what you said, I could still transition if I wanted to. I said, no thanks.'

'They're coming after me about it.'

'How do you mean?'

'Saying that it was me that talked you out of it, which would be illegal if I'd done that.'

'Nah, it wasn't you. I changed me mind when I got that college place.'

'Would you be prepared to say that in court, if it comes to that?'

'Rather not. Don't like courts much.'

'I could get into quite a bit of trouble if you didn't.'

Carl looked at me and saw the concern in my eyes. 'Alright, I'll come into court, if you need me.'

'Thanks, Carl. That means a lot to me. I appreciate it.'

My next visitor was the mysterious Robin Smith from the Health Security Agency, bland and inscrutable as usual.

'Mr Smith, I'm surprised to see you here. I'm here in my capacity as a psychiatrist rather than the pharmacology matters we have been discussing.'

'Actually, it concerns your psychiatric practice, Professor.'

'In what way?'

'I imagine, from time to time, you get to prescribe Complianx.'

'Yes, I do, as a matter of fact. It has become one of our most commonly prescribed drugs.'

'How confident are you that your patients actually take what you prescribe?'

'To be honest, I haven't given it much thought.'

'Could there be consequences to patients not taking their medication?'

'Some patients may be more anxious and disturbed than they might have been.'

'Could that lead to them carrying out antisocial activities?'

I mused for a moment. 'Yes, I suppose it could, if they were inclined to act in that way. Complianx makes people less likely to act impulsively.'

'It would be fair to say then, that people not taking their prescribed Complianx leads to greater levels of antisocial behaviour.'

'Among other things, that could be true.'

'Are you not concerned, therefore, about people failing to take their prescribed Complianx?'

'I prescribe Complianx to help people to cope through difficult times. If they don't take it, that probably means they are already coping and perhaps don't need it.'

'But it isn't only about the individual, is it? We need to consider the needs of society as a whole.'

'That has never been a consideration for me. My concern is always what is best for the patient.'

'Do you check whether the patients are taking the medication?'

'Not as a rule.'

'It would be possible to check, wouldn't it?'

'Yes, a blood test would do it.'

'Another concern is, what happens to the prescribed medications that patients neglect to take? They could fall into the wrong hands.'

'I suppose they could.'

'It may be in the public interest to make sure that prescribed medications are taken.'

The formal attire of the man guarding the dark doorway of the Bulldog Club gave him a veneer of civility, only thinly disguising his towering-high octane testosterone muscular bulk.

'I'm Jim Hubbings,' I said as I approached.

'Come in, Professor,' replied the man mountain in a deep voice, reverberating in his barrel-like chest. 'Mr Sharmoni is expecting you.'

As I made my way through the reception area, with its brightly glowing lights shining like stars and galaxies against an infinite dark cosmic void, another club doorman indicated the way into the more brightly lit entertainment space. Mr Sharmoni, suave as always in his elegantly tailored tuxedo and perfectly pressed trousers, emerged to meet me from his bastion behind the bar.

'Professor, what can I do for you?'

'I'm hoping you can do me a favour.'

'Always happy to help if I can. What sort of a favour?'

'It concerns what was on the news today, concerning Kate Stillworthy.'

'You had better come on through,' said Mr Sharmoni, showing me the way into his private office. The walls were lined with dark wood panels and ornate bookshelves holding leather-bound volumes, not books that I figured Mr Sharmoni referred to frequently, rather designed to impress with an air of formal legality. There was a very large, dark, polished wooden desk upon which stood a pair of ornate marble table lamps. Mr Sharmoni indicated for me to sit in one of the buttoned leather visitor's chairs while he settled into the matching high-backed chair behind the desk.

'Tell me about it,' said Mr Sharmoni.

'Kate has been declared a Permanent Toxic Influence.'

'I was sorry to hear that. How can I help?'

'She isn't allowed to leave the TICA anymore.'

'How is that a problem?'

'You already know. We used to meet in the Lakeside Caravan Park, but she can't go there now.'

'It was a government decision. I can't change what they do.'

'It wasn't just her who was declared Permanently Toxic. Gordon Garage was too.'

'What has that got to do with it?'

'I happened to see Gordon in Dunwick today. He was giving a speech. And your blokes, Nelson and his mates were there, minding things.'

Mr Sharmoni looked at me knowingly. 'I see what you're saying. If Gordon can get out, why not Kate?'

'Exactly.'

'Mr Garage and I have an understanding. I help him out sometimes.'

'Perhaps you could do the same for Kate.'

'What's in it for me?'

'Is there anything I can do for you?' I said, pleadingly.

'Tell you what I'll do. You can owe me a favour.'

'I'd be very obliged.'

'Yes, you would. Now, listen up. When people owe me a favour and I call it in, I don't expect any arguments. You do what I ask, whatever it might be. Capiche?'

I let the implications sink in. 'You mean, anything you ask, whatever it is, I must do it. Sort of a blank cheque.'

‘You’ve got it. And remember, if you give me any problems, Nelson and his mates may come visiting, and they won’t be polite.’

‘Alright, if you can help get me to see Kate from time to time, I’ll owe you that favour.’

I found Sid, pasty-faced and shifty, in his decrepit reception hut at the Lakeside Caravan Park.

‘Hello Sid, I understand Kate is here already.’

‘Yes, Professor. Plot number 47, as usual.’

I pulled out my phone. ‘Shall we do the crypto as usual?’

‘No charge this time. Favour for Mr Sharmoni.’

‘Oh right, thanks.’ I put my phone away. ‘By the way, Sid. That surveillance you had in the caravan.’

Sid narrowed his eyes and looked shifty. ‘What surveillance would that be?’

‘The surveillance you had set up for Mr Sharmoni, which you used to spy on me and Kate, that’s what.’

Sid backed away, looking right and left for an escape. ‘I don’t know nothing about that.’

‘Don’t lie to me, Sid. You were the one who set it up, on Mr Sharmoni’s orders.’

Sid clenched his teeth, staring at me like a frightened rabbit. ‘Look, when Mr Sharmoni wants something, you can’t say no.’

‘Why not?’

‘He doesn’t like it, and when he doesn’t like it, people get hurt.’

‘Yes, I know that,’ I acknowledged.

Sid looked at me, tense as a violin string.

‘Look, Sid, don’t panic. I’m not bearing a grudge. I know what Mr Sharmoni is like.’

‘So, you’re not going to do nothing to me then.’

‘No. It’s water under the bridge.’

‘Thanks, Professor, I appreciate it. You’re a gent.’

‘One thing, though; it is switched off now, isn’t it? The surveillance, I mean.’

‘Yes, Professor. Definitely. I took it out, the camera and that, and gave it back to Mr Sharmoni. It’s not there no more.’

When I stepped into the caravan, Kate and I didn’t need any words. We were in each other’s arms right away, hugging and kissing with an unbridled passion, no longer inhibited by the sense of being watched.

'Kate, it's wonderful that you are here. When I read the news, I feared it wouldn't be possible.'

'I had thought it might be the end for us, too.'

'As a matter of interest, how did you manage it?'

'Mr Sharmoni arranged for me to come out in a delivery van.'

'Is that how you'll get back in again?'

'Yes, I'll sleep over here, then first thing in the morning there's another delivery that'll pick me up before it calls in at the TICA.'

'So, he's got it all organised then, Mr Sharmoni. I'll give him that.'

'Why, though?' asked Kate quizzically. 'Why would Mr Sharmoni be doing this for us?'

'I asked him to, as a favour.'

'How come he owed you a favour?'

'He didn't, but now I owe him one.'

'I don't get it.'

'He has me owing him a debt, which one day, he'll want repaid, and I will have to oblige him, whatever it is. It's how Mr Sharmoni gets things done, apparently.'

'I see. Sort of mafia-type arrangement.'

'I saw Gordon Garage today, out and about in Dunwick.'

'Can't say I'm surprised. Gordon and Mr Sharmoni work hand-in-hand all the time.'

'Yes, I already had that figured after I'd seen them together at the Bulldog Club and again, today, Gordon had some of Mr Sharmoni's boys looking after him.'

'Never mind about that now. We're together, and that's what matters.'

We made our way over to the bed and flopped down in each other's arms. Now, without the inhibition of being spied upon, we languidly made love. For a while, I held her tight, feeling my soul soothed by the proximity of her soft warm body.

'I can't bear the idea of us being separated,' I said.

'I can't bear it either.'

'What's it like in the TICA?'

'It's a prison in all but name.'

'But you're not locked up in cells or anything like that?'

'No, it's more like a prison camp. We can move around within the TICA, talk to each other and so on. It's just that we are not allowed out anymore.'

'They let you out before this Permanently Toxic thing happened.'

'Yes, but only to go out for exercise in the fresh air nearby, like the woods around here for example. We weren't allowed to go into Dunwick, for example, or even to come in here into the caravan park.'

'But you did come in here.'

'You can slip in easily without coming through the front gate.'

'I know. I do that.'

'But now they don't let me out of the TICA at all unless Mr Sharmoni arranges something.'

'I've been thinking. It wouldn't be so bad if we were both in the TICA. At least, then we could be together.'

'You can't do that. What would happen to Amelia?'

Chapter 17
Mounting Opposition

'That fight we were looking at, who won?' I asked the friendly chief security guard as I came through the university's Willow Brook entrance.

'Hammer Hudson.'

'Which one was he?'

'The bald one in the green trunks.'

'I've got another one here,' I said, handing him an envelope.

'Come on through, and I'll settle up.'

I followed him through from the damp outdoor chill into the warmth of the security back office.

'What is it this time?' I enquired.

'Why, don't you know?'

'Well, kind of. It just says *News Report*. Why do you want the news? Can't you just get that on the TV or radio?'

'Let's take a look, shall we?'

He slotted the memory card into his tablet computer. The unmistakable face of Gordon Garage filled the screen.

'I say this to the metropolitan elite. We, the English people, reject your nonsense of about 57 varieties of gender or whatever it is these days. I lose track. There are only two sexes, and that's how we like it. Men are men, women are women, get used to it.'

The security guard grinned. 'You wouldn't get that on the mainstream media, would you?'

'I see what you mean,' I conceded.

Later, when I wandered through into the postgraduate working area to find my PhD student, Eddie Donagal, I was shocked to see Gordon Garage again on his laptop screen. Despite seeing the consternation on my face, Eddie made no attempt to switch it off, leaving it playing blatantly for me to see.

'Wouldn't it be a good idea to turn that off when somebody might see it?' I said.

'Why should I? He tells it as it is,' replied Eddie, his curly heap of hair quivering, eyes narrowed and jaw set in defiance.

'It could get you into a lot of trouble, you chump.'

'Too late for that. I'm already up for a disciplinary hearing. May as well be hanged for a sheep as a lamb as the saying goes.'

'What's this about, a disciplinary hearing?'

Eddie finally switched off Gordon Garage and called up an official notification he had received, according to which, a report had been made about Eddie glorifying the British empire amounting to jingoistic triumphalism contrary to the university code of conduct, for which he was required to attend a disciplinary hearing in Lupton Tower.

'It's not just that,' said Eddie. 'Have you seen what's in *The Daily Truth*?' He called up the relevant article on the screen, under the headline *Jingoism in Academia*:

Slough University has seen an outbreak of denialism of the evils of the British empire. Following the scandalous claims of discredited academic Jeremy Fitzregal, another PhD student from the university, Eddie Donagal, has reiterated his outrageous militaristic triumphalism. Victims of colonialism are being gaslighted by these so-called academics seeking to whitewash imperialist atrocities.

'I'm going to be thrown out, aren't I? Like you did to Jeremy Fitzregal.'

'Not if I can help it.'

'How do you mean?'

'I value what you are doing, and I will do whatever I can to keep you here.'

'It's hopeless. The Rockface mafia have it all stitched up.'

'We'll see. I may have some leverage.'

A shortage of reagents in the laboratories provided me with a reason to visit Jenny Colepepper in her eyrie within the central administration building.

‘The usage must be predictable, so why haven’t we been ordering the stuff in time?’ Dr Colepepper enquired accusingly.

‘It’s not that we don’t have it, but it needs to be decanted into reagent bottles for the students to use.’

‘How hard can it be, decanting the material into the reagent bottles?’ she objected, her frown of irritation making hairline cracks on the edges of her smoothly made-up face.

‘It isn’t particularly hard, but we need hundreds of reagent bottles and we need to get the concentrations exactly right for consistent experimental results.’

‘That can’t be difficult, can it?’

‘Many of the reagents are potentially dangerous and need careful handling, so it has to be done by qualified lab technicians. It’s the technicians we are short of, not the bulk supplies.’

‘Why don’t we have the technicians?’

‘We can’t just recruit these folk off the streets. It takes a three-year degree course for them to become qualified and then some additional specific training.’

‘What is the answer?’

‘We’ll need to persuade them to do overtime.’

‘Alright, leave it with me. I’ll see what I can do.’

‘While I’m here, I’m concerned about the disciplinary process pending for Eddie Donagal.’

‘What are you concerned about?’

‘He is doing important work. I don’t want to lose him.’

‘He has been very foolish with the things he has been saying.’

‘That’s true, but his technical contribution is too valuable just to throw away.’

‘Nevertheless, I don’t see what I can do about it at this stage. Rockface are involved.’

‘Surely there must be something you could do.’

‘Things are dicey at the moment. The controversy about Gordon Garage, poppies, Kate Stillworthy…well, it’s winding people up and we’re under a lot of pressure to clamp down on undesirable influences.’

‘Eddie may be foolish and indiscreet, but I wouldn’t see him as an undesirable influence.’

‘We have a “No Free Speech for Hate” policy, which makes being foolish and indiscreet undesirable in itself.’

I stood up and looked out of the window, taking in the view over the river beyond Windsor towards the muddy fields of Runnymede. 'Magna Carta was signed over there, symbolising freedom and the rights of the individual over a tyrannical power. Wouldn't you say that this "No Free Speech for Hate" policy is a denial of freedom of expression, a restoration of the tyranny the people were fighting against all those centuries ago?'

Dr Colepepper joined me taking in the view. 'Unrestricted freedom of expression would deny people the freedom to live in safety from hate.'

'One of the problems we have these days is who gets to decide what is hateful and what isn't. As far as I can see, that is an unelected clique in Rockface.'

'Neither of us is in a position to change the situation.'

'One thing that hasn't changed is the power exerted from where we are currently standing.'

'How do you mean?'

'In days gone by, when this was Eton College, the battles were won on the playing fields of Eton. Here we are today, within academic institutions such as ours, still with dictatorial power to decide for the nation what it is allowed to think.'

'It is different. In those days, Eton College trained people to run the British empire, whereas these days, we deplore that legacy.'

'We're still imposing our values from here, even if those values have changed.'

'If we don't set society's values, who will? Gordon Garage?'

I sat back down on the visitor's chair. 'Back to the here and now. I'd appreciate it if would you think of something to save Eddie from being cast out into oblivion.'

Dr Colepepper resumed her seat behind the desk. 'As I say, I don't think there is anything I could do.'

'It was *Monty Python's Life of Brian* you were looking at, wasn't it?'

'Is this relevant?'

'Doesn't it contain a passage where John Cleese's character ridicules someone for wanting to change their gender?'

'What about it?'

'If our friend from Rockface, Shamina Chakrabarti, were to get to hear of it, I think ze might make some trouble, just as ze no doubt has about Eddie.'

'Who is going to tell zir?'

'I might if you don't do something to help Eddie.'

'That's blackmail.'

'Yes, it is. It isn't something I do lightly, but I need Eddie for the work that I'm doing.'

'You feel that strongly that you would make threats like this.'

'I do.'

'I see.'

'If it helps, right now, I'm doing some work that involves the Health Security Agency, you know, the secretive people in Porton Down. I need Eddie's contribution for that. A matter of national security.'

'National security. I see. That puts a different perspective on things. I'll put the disciplinary hearing on hold.'

I was surprised to see Carl Gellsten appear in my clinic at Dunwick Park General Hospital, wearing a pair of tight-fitting leggings and a flowery blouse.

'Hello Carl, how are you doing?' I enquired.

'Actually, I'm Carla now,' he said.

'Oh, I see. You're affirming your gender as female, is that right?'

'Yes.'

'What brought you to decide to take this step?'

'This doctor called me, Dr Bengold from that Tavidown place.'

'What did he say?'

'He said my true identity was female, and I must have been pressured to deny it. I said I didn't really know what my true identity was. He said I had wanted to be female, but must have been talked out of it.'

'What did you say to that?'

'I said, no, I'd decided to stay as I was when I got my place at the university. So, he said, it was the place at the university that decided it then. I said, yes.'

'Right, but after that, you changed your mind.'

'Well, see, he said that I'd been induced to change my mind by being offered that place. That made me an accessory to the denial of my true gender identity. That could get me classified as an Unsuitable again, and I'd lose my place. So, I say I need the place. I want to make something of meself. So, he says, if I affirm my true gender identity, I'll be alright. So, I says, all right then, what do I do? He says, come over to Tavidown.'

'So, you've been over there.'

'Yes, I'm on the hormones now, and I'll be going over later to have me bits changed back to female ones.'

'Is this what you really want?'

'Yes, I don't mind. That cock of mine isn't real, anyway, and the balls are plastic.'

'I meant, actually being female, does that feel right for you?'

'Don't really mind, to be honest. Won't make much difference. I'm neither one nor the other, really.'

'Well, if you're happy with the transition, that's good enough for me.'

'One other thing Dr Bengold said, if you get had up for anything, like he said you might, I shouldn't testify.'

'He did, did he? Why would that be?'

'He would have to bring up how I got the place at the university. If that had been an inducement, I'd lose it and be classified back as an Unsuitable.'

'So, you won't be testifying for me, then?'

'No, sorry. I can't.'

'I understand. I wouldn't either, if I were in your position.'

Emerging from the hospital, I heard military marching music. A band of pot-bellied middle-aged and elderly men in blazers advanced along the street, now free of traffic, playing an assortment of drums, brass instruments and a couple of flutes.

Behind the band, flanked by four or five of Mr Sharmoni's minders, Gordon Garage was at the head of a hundred or more Forward England supporters.

As I stood beside the kerb, watching them march past, I spotted a face I knew well—Harvey Bentling, Liz's disgraced predecessor as history professor. He had a certain serenity about him, as if not fighting the fates anymore, resigned to go wherever they might take him. I hesitated for a moment before throwing caution to the winds by joining the marching throng.

'Harvey, what are you doing here?' I said as I drew up alongside him.

'Oh Jim, I could ask the same thing.'

'I just happen to be here. I've been doing my clinic at Dunwick General.'

'You're taking a chance. One thing observing from the sidelines, another actually being in the march itself.'

'I'm getting tired of being cautious. But what about you?'

'As you probably know, I'm in the TICA now. They can't do much more to me there.'

'But you're not supposed to be this far away, are you, if you're in the TICA?'

'No, but Gordon has an arrangement with Mr Sharmoni to take care of things.'

'You and Gordon are close, then?'

'Oh yes, we get plenty of time to discuss things in the TICA.'

The march turned off the main thoroughfare into a small street. A loudspeaker blared loudly to make itself heard over the sound of the band.

'This is an illegal gathering. You are required to disperse immediately. If you persist, enforcement action will be taken.'

The crowd of marchers jeered their defiance and the band continued to play.

'Jim, hop it!' said Harvey.

'Why?'

'They'll be filming us, looking for people to arrest later.'

I considered for a moment. 'No, sod it! I'm not going anywhere.'

We continued into the same small park where I had seen Gordon Garage on the previous occasion.

'I don't see much enforcement going on,' I observed to Harvey.

'The police can't do much since they've been defunded. They'll be making recordings of who is here and then picking people off later, including you, if you're not careful.'

The band marched over to one side and ceased playing. Gordon Garage, clad in his trademark velvet-collared jacket and cloth cap, stepped up onto a makeshift podium. Mr Sharmoni's minders took up protective positions on either side.

'We've got them on the run,' announced Gordon, his voice booming out from a public address system. 'The arrogant metropolitan elite still rule in their ivory towers in the universities, indoctrinating and dominating gullible middle-class youth, but we, the real English people, control the streets. We are winning over the hearts and minds of real English people, English patriots, despite the stranglehold these despots have on the nation's cultural norms.'

I called around to Bill Englebirt's modest apartment in Godolphin House with a memory card containing his latest entertainment, *Frolics in the Hayloft*.

'Come in for a drink,' said Bill, beaming benevolently.

'Don't mind if I do.'

'How are things going?' Bill enquired as he handed me a stiff gin and tonic.

'Not brilliantly, to be honest.'

'What's the matter?' Bill enquired, with a look of kindly concern.

'Looks like I'm going to be reported to the General Medical Council.'

'Good heavens. What for?'

'I'm being accused of conversion therapy.'

'Doesn't sound like you.'

'Not me at all. I didn't do anything, not that it makes any difference these days.'

'How come they are accusing you?'

'The patient changed their mind, so I withdrew the referral I'd made to the Tavidown Clinic. They are making out that I talked the patient into withdrawing.'

'What made the patient withdraw?'

'They got a place in the university, having previously been classified as an Unsuitable.'

'The patient could explain, couldn't they? Straighten things out.'

'That's what I thought, but it's become more complicated.'

'In what way?'

'You know you had me go over to interview people for admission to the Artisan Skills faculty. The patient concerned was one of the ones I interviewed. Now, they're saying that I got them the place as an inducement to withdraw from the gender affirmation treatment.'

'The patient could still back you up, couldn't they?'

'Afraid not. The Tavidown got onto them and persuaded them to go ahead with the gender affirmation and not to testify on my behalf.'

'How did they manage that?'

'Threats. If the patient didn't do what they wanted, they would be reclassified as an Unsuitable and lose their university place.'

'Darn. That's dirty.'

'Yes, it is. And as a result, it looks as if my career is toast.'

'You need another drink, I think.' Bill prepared me a refill.

'You know,' I mused reflectively. 'What we have created here is a cult based upon a bizarre ideology with a doctrine driven by the quirks of a tiny minority with gender dysphoria.'

'This is a dangerous conversation to be having,' said Bill, shaking his head.

'I don't care anymore. You can turn me in if you want. It won't make any difference to me as things are.'

'I don't mean dangerous just for you. Being a party to the conversation puts me in danger, too.'

I stood up. 'Sorry, I'll leave and we can forget about it entirely if you would prefer.'

'No, sit down. I'm too old to get precious about things. I'll live dangerously for once.'

I sat myself back down.

'Although, as you know, I keep out of politics,' said Bill, 'for personal preservation and for a quiet life, it doesn't mean I am oblivious to how things are. You are right; it *is* a cult.'

'This little bit of difficulty I am facing illustrates an obsession to so-called gender affirm as many people as possible. I am being accused of conversion therapy because my patient changed their mind, but actually, it is the zealots who applied undue pressure on the patient to go through with it, probably against their better judgement.'

'Rank hypocrisy,' Bill concurred.

'There is worse. In my psychiatric practice, I have seen several mentally ill patients persuaded to undergo so-called gender affirmation. You would have thought that at the very least, people should be of sound mind before taking such a step, but I could never dare oppose it, lest I be accused of standing in the way of free expression of their chosen gender.'

'You mean people who have psychotic symptoms, manias or severe depression are being pumped full of hormones and having their body parts hacked about?'

'Exactly that. They play around with words. Mental health difficulties become mental health differences, and severe autism or having multiple personalities becomes neurodiversity. If I were to point to the symptoms these people experience, they would claim that they have arisen from being misgendered and gender affirmation is the cure.'

'As a matter of interest, what do these folk do if the chosen gender is non-binary?'

'There are drugs that block sex hormones normally used for treating either breast or prostate cancer as the case may be, which also block normal sexual function. Then there is so-called gender nullification surgery.'

'What does that involve?'

'Removing all external genitalia to create a smooth, doll-like appearance.'

'Ugh. I'm sorry I asked.'

'I have a concern that many who put themselves forward for gender reassignment do so as an act of self-harm. They hate their original selves and want to see what they hate, themselves, being hurt.'

'I suppose they imagine that by changing gender, they make a new, better version of who they are.'

'As I said, it's nothing but a bizarre cult. They have rejected the objective reality that, with only a tiny minority of exceptions, there are two biological sexes. According to them, all gender is socially constructed so you can affirm yourself as whatever gender you want, assisted by grotesque surgery and hormones people are persuaded they need.'

'It's a mess. I try to keep out of it.'

'As well you might because anyone who has the courage to question this orthodoxy is a heretic who is harangued, suppressed and thrown into outer darkness.'

'The ironic thing is, those supposedly against hate are the ones doing most of the hating,' Bill mused.

'It is a form of religion, supposed all about peace and love, except of course for witches and the devil. We are expected to hate them.'

'Yes, I can see parallels between Rockface and the Spanish Inquisition, now that you mention it.'

'I was thinking more of seventeenth-century Puritans.'

'Those Puritans certainly knew how to hate people, particularly anybody enjoying life.'

'Our present-day fanatics portray those who dissent as pantomime villains, figures who can be legitimately hated.'

'I see what you mean—scapegoats to take the blame for all that goes wrong.'

'A new establishment has displaced the old sufficiently recently that they can still blame the old establishment. There are parallels with post-revolutionary Russia and France.'

'There are a lot of people who don't believe this gender stuff, but they're more or less left alone.'

'Who do you have in mind?' I enquired.

'The folk wandering about in the streets of Dunwick, for example. I don't suppose even half of them would know what you're talking about if you mention gender affirmation.'

'You mean the Educationally Unsuitables. There is a difference between the as-yet-uninitiated and dissenters-from-within. The former, the Unsuitables, are the noble savages who haven't yet heard and understood, whereas the latter have the knowledge and have wilfully rejected it, which is unforgivable heresy.'

'So, the Unsuitables are treated as being mentally defective, unable to figure anything out for themselves.'

'Exactly, so when they misbehave, they are assumed to be doing so under the nefarious influence of the hated pantomime villains.'

'Possessed by the devil, as it were,' Bill observed.

'An arrogant intellectual elite is assuming swathes of the population are too stupid to be responsible for their own actions.'

'Mentally defective, except we wouldn't be allowed to call them that.'

'It is turned on its head because it is the self-appointed intellectual elite who have rejected reason in favour of warped ideology and beliefs, while their supposed inferiors often have grounded common sense based on real experience. If they aren't careful this despised underclass of university rejects, the so-called Unsuitables, will rise up and overthrow the new establishment.'

'I prefer to keep my head down and have a quiet life,' Bill admitted. 'Does that make me a coward?'

'No. Probably, you are the sensible one. Sure, my Kate is brave, no question about it, but I often wish she had been less outspoken.'

'You said, your Kate. Do you still feel like she is yours?'

'I do, as a matter of fact.'

'I guessed as much.'

'Why do you say that?'

'Whenever her name comes up, I sense that you have feelings for her.'

'Am I really that transparent?'

'You do have feelings for her?'

'Put it this way, it isn't an accident or oversight that we are still married.'

'I see. But you are separated.'

'Not exactly.'

'How do you mean?'

'We get to see each other now and again.'

Bill looked at me quizzically, weighing up what to say. 'When you say, seeing each other…no, none of my business.'

'It's alright. We're talking frankly. Yes, when I say see each other, I do mean, intimately.'

'But where? She's in the TICA and you're out here.'

'We have a place where we can meet discreetly.'

'Oh, I see. Well good for you.'

'It's bizarre, having to have a hole-in-a-corner love-nest in order to be together with my own wife.'

'Yes, that is kind of weird.'

'You know, there is one silver lining from this sorry situation—our love life has been way more passionate than it had ever been before Kate had her falling out with the powers-that-be.'

'Oo, too much information, mate.'

'You're right, I've said too much.'

'I hear that it isn't only Kate who has had a falling out with the authorities. Your Eddie Donagal has got himself into some trouble.'

'It concerns the British empire, that sort of thing. He sympathises with the Forward England fellows who we see hanging around Willow Brook.'

'I've seen more of them about than usual, those Forward England chaps. Something is stirring them up.'

'Gordon Garage. He's been out and about in Dunwick.'

'I thought he was confined in his TICA now, like Kate.'

I tapped my nose with my finger. 'There are ways and means.'

'It's one thing him getting out there, but he must have a following. What's he getting them fired up about.'

'We're not supposed to celebrate Remembrance Day anymore and the monarchy has been abolished. People don't like that.'

'Yes,' Bill mused. 'Remembrance Day and the monarchy—you tamper with those at your peril.'

Chapter 18
Pharmaceutical Plot

'Autocab waiting for you at the taxi rank,' said the message on my phone as I stepped off the train at Salisbury.

'Professor Hubbings,' said the small electronic display on the side of a rain-soaked cab, not for hire and lacking any corporate markings. I tried to open the door, but it remained locked.

'Please look at the red spot,' said a voice. I complied.

The door lock clicked and opened.

'Welcome, Professor. Please step in,' said the voice.

The cab took me out through the drab Salisbury suburbs into the autumnal countryside, through some villages, until we reached the high perimeter fence surrounding the rambling campus of the Porton Down government research facility. The barrier at the guarded main entrance raised automatically to admit us.

As we entered, I noticed in the distance some strange flat pyramid structures sunk into the ground, with grass-covered slops and vertical concrete faces, reminding me of ancient monuments in central America. Amongst the structures were roof lights set into the ground suggesting a vast underground space. We cruised up in front of a lowkey administrative building set within the untidy collection of dispersed office and industrial buildings.

'Please proceed to the security reception,' instructed the cab.

After looking at the red spot again at the front door, I was allowed into a waiting area. Within a minute or so, a door opened, and Robin Smith was there to meet me, smooth and impersonal as always.

'Good morning, Professor. Thanks for coming. You'll need to wear this,' he said as he handed me a badge on a lanyard. 'I'll escort you over to the laboratory. Please come this way.'

Mounted on the wall of the cramped reception area was a Rockface Audit Certificate rating the Health Security Agency as "good".

We took a lift which took us down what must have been the equivalent of several storeys below ground, to emerge into the hub of an electric monorail system, which in turn took us some distance along a tunnel, where we emerged into a cavernous, concrete-lined atrium topped out with one of the roof lights I had observed earlier among the semi-submerged pyramid structures.

We set off on foot along one of the plain, white-painted corridors radiating out of the central space, finally reaching an access door identifying itself as Laboratory C46.

We went into a small meeting room where an oriental woman in a white lab coat was waiting for us.

'Professor Hubbings, this is Jane Jones.'

'Hello, Professor, my pronouns are she/her,' she said with a slight Chinese accent. I believed the pronouns, but not her name.

'Hello, mine are he/him. What would you like me to help you with?'

'It's the process for regulating the dose.'

'You mean, holding back production of the primary agent when it reaches the desired level.'

'Yes, exactly. Our results are erratic. At times, our process shuts down the agent production completely, while at others, it doesn't seem to work at all, and we are into an overdose situation.'

'The homeostasis mechanism will necessarily need to be tailored for the specific drug involved. What exactly is it that we are talking about?'

'That's classified,' said Robin.

'That's a problem because without some more information, I won't be able to assist.'

Robin and Jane looked at each other. Jane widened her eyes and spread out her hands. Robin shrugged and nodded.

'It's a psycho-active agent,' said Jane.

'That's a very wide range,' I observed. 'I'll need more than that.'

Jane pulled out a piece of paper with a chemical formula on it. 'This is the marker we are targeting for regulating the dose.'

I examined the chemical structure. It looked familiar. I felt uneasy, but I couldn't quite pinpoint exactly why. 'Some sort of a sedative, by the look of it,' I observed. Jane and Robin looked back stony-faced.

'Any thoughts on where our problem might be?' Jane enquired.

'It mimics the naturally occurring gamma glutaphemerol molecule, which would mess up the homeostasis.' I pointed at the diagram. 'I would be inclined to insert a sulfonyl group just here, which would make the marker unique to the agent involved.'

Jane's eyes widened, and she nodded her head.

'What do you think, Jane?' Robin enquired. 'Would that resolve the issue?'

'I think it would,' said Jane. 'That would certainly fit with what we have seen in our experiments.'

'Well, thank you, Professor. Is there anything else we need Professor Hubbings for?'

'No, I think we have enough to make progress now.'

'In that case, thank you, Jane. I'll catch up with you later,' said Robin. Jane left the room.

'There was another matter I wanted to talk to you about, Professor,' Robin continued after she had left.

'What was that?'

'You have been seen at illegal street demonstrations organised by Forward England. It calls your security clearance into question.'

'Evidently not enough to prevent me from coming here today.'

Robin's face creased into a wry smile. 'We needed your expertise despite the security concerns.'

'What is your point in raising this?'

'Your position in the university depends upon your security clearance.'

'I see. What are you going to do about it?'

'Not me. As things stand, your security rating will be reviewed in the light of this information, and I would expect the Security Committee to withdraw your security clearance.'

'So, I'm going to lose my job; that's what you're saying.'

'Not necessarily. I could put in a word.'

'What sort of a word?'

'It's like this. We like to keep tabs on what Forward England are up to. If you could keep us informed, we would be very grateful.'

'How grateful?'

'I could inform the Security Committee that you were at the Forward England events on our behalf.'

‘Who is us?’

Robin smiled enigmatically. ‘Let’s just say, the Security Services.’

‘So, if you put a word in, my security clearance is safe.’

‘Exactly. But you need to keep us informed about Forward England.’

‘Doesn’t look as if I have any choice, does it?’

Back in my office at the Asima Shankar Laboratory Complex, I had an official communication from the General Medical Council summoning me to appear before the Investigation Committee for a review of my fitness to practice in the light of an allegation of conversion therapy on a patient seeking gender affirmation.

I don’t suppose that Robin Smith would be in a position to get me out of that one, I mused. Still, nothing to be done about that now. I wandered over to find Eddie Donagal.

‘I’ve got an uneasy feeling,’ I said to Eddie.

‘What about?’

I scribbled down a diagram with some chemical symbols on a scrap of paper. ‘Does this suggest anything to you?’ I enquired.

‘Yes, it looks like Complianx to me,’ said Eddie.

‘Of course; that’s why it looked familiar.’

‘Why do you ask?’

‘It was something I was looking at yesterday.’

‘Anything in particular?’

‘I’m not supposed to say.’

‘But you’re obviously concerned about it.’

‘Yes, I am. Very concerned.’

‘Anything I can do to help?’

I stroked my chin. Sworn to secrecy, I had already said too much. ‘No, not just now, thanks.’

The atmosphere was frosty when I met Liz for our lunch date in the Cloister Cafeteria. She was beautiful as always, but it was the sharp arctic beauty of an ice queen.

‘When is your divorce likely to go through?’ Liz enquired.

‘Trouble is, I can’t get in to see her because she is now permanently confined in the TICA.’

‘Can’t you just handle it through the solicitors?’

‘Yes, I suppose we’ll have to do it that way.’

Nelson called. ‘Mr Sharmoni would like to see you at the Bulldog Club.’

‘When?’

‘Right away, if that’s convenient.’

‘It’s not really convenient.’

‘Best not to disappoint Mr Sharmoni,’ said Nelson, his deep voice conveying a sense of menace.

‘I guess not.’

‘I’ll come round in the limo, then. I’ll be at the Willow Brook entrance in ten minutes.’

‘Professor, I need your help,’ said Mr Sharmoni, when I arrived in his inner sanctum behind the bar in the Bulldog Club. His tone conveyed this as a command rather than a request.

‘What do you need?’

‘Certain drugs have become hard to come by.’

‘What sort of drugs?’

‘Opioids, amphetamines, among other things. I’ll give you a list.’

‘How could I help with that?’

‘As a psychiatrist, you get to prescribe those things, don’t you?’

‘Yes, but only to meet the medical needs of patients.’

‘You could get some for me, couldn’t you?’

‘It would be completely illegal and unethical for me to do that.’

‘You haven’t forgotten you owe me a favour, have you?’

‘No, I’m very grateful.’

‘You realise I had to bend the law to get Kate over to see you, didn’t you?’

‘Yes, I realise that.’

‘So, you can bend the law a little for me, can’t you?’

‘Yes, I suppose so,’ I acquiesced, feeling uncertain.

‘Here is what we’ll do,’ said Mr Sharmoni, oozing confidence and reassurance. ‘I’ll send my people over to you. You take them on as patients and prescribe whatever is needed.’

Although I seemed to be beset from all angles, the question of the fiendish Porton Down plan remained uppermost in my mind. I wandered over to find Eddie again.

'Eddie, you know when we were talking earlier, you asked if there was anything you could do to help.'

'Yes, that's right.' Eddie's eyes twinkled with interest.

'Well, I think there might be.'

'What would you like me to do?'

'Can you keep a secret?'

'Yes, I think so.' Eddie leaned in close, his curly mop bouncing from the sudden movement.

'What I am going to tell you is top secret, but what I am going to ask of you is even more secret than that. There could even be some danger involved.'

'Sounds intriguing.' Eddie's eyes shone as if relishing this chance to live dangerously.

'Can I trust you?'

'Totally. Just between us. I won't breathe a word.'

'Alright. Yesterday, I was at Porton Down. I was helping them on one of their projects.'

'What, you mean the secret squirrel research place?' Eddie was almost licking his lips with the intrigue.

'That's the one.'

'What are they up to?'

'They wouldn't tell me exactly, but I think I've figured it out.'

'So, what are your conclusions?'

'I believe they are developing a vaccine that will permanently keep people dosed up on Complianx.'

'What would they be doing that for?'

'I suspect the intention is to vaccinate all the people the authorities consider to be a threat, in particular the population of the Unsuitables and Toxic Influences.'

Eddie's jaw dropped, and his eyes bulged in horror. 'You mean, they want to keep them quiet and placid, permanently, to crush all the protests.'

'Yes.'

'It's absolutely fiendish. Are you sure they would go that far?'

'It isn't only what they are doing at Porton Down. In my psychiatric practice in Dunwick, the Health Security Agency were asking about our use of Complianx, and there was talk about verifying that people were taking it. It was an odd thing for them to be taking an interest in.'

'What exactly is it that they are doing at Porton Down?'

'The idea is to insert DNA into people that both produces Complianx and also maintains the dose at a desired level. Just enough to keep them placid, but not enough to be toxic.'

'And you were helping them with this? What were you thinking of?'

'I didn't know it was Complianx, did I? I thought it might be something like insulin for Type-1 diabetics. It was only when they showed me the formula that I became uneasy.'

'So, what are we going to do?'

'I'd like you to help me develop an antidote to Porton Down's Complianx vaccine.'

'How would that work?'

'We would use the same technique to insert DNA to create an immune reaction to Complianx, antibodies that neutralise the substance.'

'Yes, that could work.'

'We don't have much time. It would mean dropping everything else we are doing and working around the clock.'

'We'd need access to the laboratories at night,' Eddie observed.

'I think I can arrange that.'

I made the trip up to the top floor of the central administration building within the Oppressed Peoples Memorial Complex to see Jenny Colepepper, who, as usual, got straight down to business.

'About the laboratories, then?'

'Yes,' I replied. 'I'll need use of the main pharmacology lab overnight for the next week or two.'

'What would that entail?'

'Security would have to be informed, the alarms switched off and with access in and out of the building as necessary.'

'It's against health and safety regulations to work alone in the laboratories. Who will you be working with?'

'Eddie Donagal.'

'What is this in aid of?'

'We're working on a classified project for the Health Security Agency.'

Dr Colepepper's eyes opened wide in surprise. 'So, you're involved in this?'

I pursed my lips and frowned. 'I'm not sure what you mean by, this?'

'Quite right. You shouldn't say anything. It's classified. I'm surprised though, you participating in it.'

'Why are you surprised?'

'I would have expected you might have some moral qualms about it.'

'Qualms about what?'

'Mass sedation as a means of suppressing dissent. I'm surprised that you would be comfortable with that.'

'I'm not comfortable.'

'I'm even more surprised that Eddie is involved, to be honest. I'm amazed he got security clearance.'

'He isn't fully in the picture.'

'He must have guessed what's happening by now.'

'He hasn't said anything yet to suggest he has.'

'You must have a good cover story,' remarked Dr Colepepper.

As I came in an Autocab for my clinic in Dunwick, reports of public disorder were prominent in the news reports.

Police struggled to maintain order as campaigners for the restoration of the monarchy and the British Union took to the streets across the nation under the umbrella of Forward England, the outlawed political party led by disgraced Toxic Influencer, Gordon Garage.

'We must stand firm against this outbreak of hate,' said a government spokesperson. 'There can be "No Free Speech for Hate".'

My heart sank as I saw about five demonstrators run forward as I stepped out of my Autocab, shrieking 'No to Conversion Therapy!' Within a couple of seconds, they were intercepted by Nelson and three more of Mr Sharmoni's minders. Fists flew, and within seconds, three of the demonstrators were on the ground, bleeding and groaning in pain while two others ran away, leaving smashed-up remnants of their placards trodden into the dirty puddles accumulated in the gutter after incessant overnight rain.

Benny, my charge nurse, greeted me as I arrived with a puzzled look on his face.

'Professor, there is something strange today. We suddenly have six new patients referred to the clinic by a doctor I haven't heard of. They have all turned up without appointments, saying they are urgent cases and you agreed to see them.'

'Six? That seems a lot. Could I see the referrals?'

I had a quick look at the paperwork. I recognised the doctor's name as the one Mr Sharmoni had told me would be making the referrals.

'Yes, I did say I would see them. It won't take long. Please show them through.'

I saw Nelson, followed by five more of Mr Sharmoni's minders in quick succession, furnishing them with prescriptions for the drugs they had informed me Mr Sharmoni required.

'Professor, it probably isn't my place,' said Benny after they had gone, 'but I have to say, those people coming in like that, it was more than a little odd.'

'Yes, I suppose it was,' I acknowledged.

'Forgive me, but some of those fellows work for Mr Sharmoni, don't they?'

'Yes, I believe they do.'

Benny looked at me with a concerned and anguished look on his face, struggling to find something to say.

'Benny,' I said. 'I can see what you must be thinking. Mr Sharmoni is up to no good, and now us being involved. I have only one question for you: do you want to make an issue of it?'

'I don't know. It doesn't feel right.'

'I know, it doesn't feel right to me, either. But it would be very unwise to stand in Mr Sharmoni's way.'

'Yes,' Benny acknowledged. 'He is a dangerous man.'

'So, what do you want to do?'

'I don't know.'

'May I suggest doing nothing? Best stay safe.'

'I suppose you're right,' said Benny with a resigned sigh. 'I do like to do the right thing, but I can see that can be difficult.'

'Even figuring out what is the right thing is hard, let alone doing it.'

'We should stand up for honesty, integrity, ethics, that sort of thing, shouldn't we?'

'Well, yes, but for example, what about when we are told that we should encourage patients to undergo brutal surgical mutilation in the name of supposedly affirming their preferred gender? Is that really ethical?'

Benny looked quizzical, casting his eyes from side to side as if looking for an escape route. 'I'd rather not say.'

'Very wise. Saying anything at all on that subject could get you into deep do-do.'

'Then there is labelling people who want to commemorate those who died in battle as hate-mongers. Is that right?'

Benny looked at the floor.

'Best not say anything on that subject either,' I continued.

'There was another strange thing that's come up,' said Benny.

'What was that?'

'I've got a notice here from the Health Security Agency telling us to prepare for a programme of mass vaccination.'

'Let's have a look.' I read the notice and blanched. The vaccinations were scheduled to commence on 12th November, only days away.

'Why ask us?' enquired Benny. 'We're psychiatry. We don't usually get involved in vaccinations. That's Public Health and general practice.'

'I think I know what this is,' I said through gritted teeth. 'I can see why we would be involved.'

I called in to see Bill Englebirt in his apartment, ostensibly to deliver the titillating delights of *Fun with the Fillies*, but also intending to pump him for some more insights into the Health Security Agency's fiendish plot.

'I'm going to be rather tied up with some urgent research work over the next week or two,' I said, as I settled down into a battered sofa with a stiff gin and tonic.

'Why's that?'

'Some stuff for the Health Security Agency, classified, secret and all that.'

'Oh, I see. They've got you working on it.'

'You seem to be aware of it, then.'

'Well, yes, I know about it in broad terms.'

'For something so secret, a lot of people are in the know.'

'How do you mean?'

'Earlier, I spoke to Jenny Colepepper about using the main pharmacology lab overnight, and she seemed to be in the picture.'

'She and I both sit on the Social Cohesion Advisory Committee.'

'So, the committee's involved, then?'

‘Yes. They are concerned about the growing unrest among the Unsuitables fomented by some of the Toxic Influences, like Gordon Garage and your Kate. A number of strategies for keeping a lid on it have been discussed.’

‘Among them being keeping everyone permanently pacified with Complianx, I suppose.’

‘They’ll be happier that way.’

Chapter 19
The Antidote

Focused on the task in hand, Eddie and I were only vaguely aware of the surge of disorder and rioting in the real world beyond the tranquil setting of the university campus. We battled through the night, figuring out the intricacies of harnessing the human immune system to neutralise Complianx, the DNA needed to build this capability and the vector for bringing it into the cells.

With no time for clinical trials, our vaccine would be unproven and potentially unsafe, but weighed against a lifetime of zombie-like existence, we figured it would be worth the risk.

According to the news, Gordon Garage was now at large from the TICA, fomenting the unrest and suspected of being under the protection of organised crime.

Jenny Colepepper put out a message to university staff and students, advising them to bring in an overnight bag and plan to remain on university premises during the current disturbances until such time as law and order could be re-established.

Having worked through the night, it was the first light as we checked the final details of our formulae, to be interrupted by a call from Amelia.

'Dad, I won't be going to school today.'

'Why not?'

'The school is shut. We've been told to stay at home.'

'Why?'

'A lot of people broke into the school grounds yesterday. A lot of windows were broken, they burned one of the classroom blocks, painted stuff on the walls, and some people got hurt. We all had to go home early.'

'Good God. Are you alright?'

‘Yes, I’m alright. I’d be scared to go out, though. There’s lots of people out there, shouting and breaking things. I heard noises all night.’

‘Stay there. I’m coming home myself. See you soon.’ I hung up and turned to Eddie.

‘I’m worried about Amelia. I need to get home to make sure she’s safe.’

‘That’s okay, Jim,’ Eddie reassured me. ‘Her safety has to come first.’

‘We’re almost there now, aren’t we? We just need to get the batch process going to get the vaccine churned out.’

‘Yes,’ said Eddie, smiling confidently. ‘Leave it to me. Go and see to Amelia. I know what to do.’

‘I wouldn’t go out there if I were you,’ said the concerned looking chief security guard on the Willow Brook entrance, now windswept and deserted. ‘It’s not safe. People are getting hurt.’

‘It’s my daughter,’ I explained. ‘I’ve got to see she’s alright.’

‘We’ve doubled the guard and been told to keep the gates shut. Security clampdown to keep the campus safe.’

‘How do I get out then?’

‘Don’t worry, I’ll just open up for a moment.’

He pressed the release button, and I slid out through the slightly open gate.

‘Well, do take care,’ he said as he secured the gate behind me.

At this particular time, all was quiet outside the entrance, the street deserted, but the now soggy debris strewn around suggested that it had been lively earlier on—several burnt-out vehicles, bricks and rocks and what appeared to be blood stains on the pavement.

Earlier, I had tried to book myself an Autocab, but the website informed me that the service was temporarily suspended, so I set off for home on foot.

There were stretches of road that appeared normal, although eerily quiet for what would ordinarily be the morning rush hour, then I would come upon a burnt-out shop or vehicle and sprayed on graffiti with Forward England slogans.

Seeing a group of men a few hundred yards along the street, I took a side road to avoid them.

When I reached home, there was graffiti sprayed onto the fence again, but otherwise, everything seemed to be in order.

‘Amelia,’ I called as I came in through the front door.

‘Oh Dad, so good to see you,’ Amelia replied as she bounded down the stairs.

'Thank goodness to see you're alright.' I put my arms around her and held her tight.

'Dad, things are scary out there.' There she was, no longer a cocksure teenager, but my frightened little girl.

'I know. I've seen what the streets are like.'

'What's going to happen, Dad?' She looked at me as if I was her hero who knew and could solve everything.

'I honestly don't know.'

'What do you think might happen?'

'The government will try to clamp down on things, I think.'

'Will people get killed?'

'Killed, locked up, drugged, all sorts, I wouldn't wonder.'

'Drugged?' Amelia looked at me questioningly.

'Given something to pacify them, make them more compliant.'

'Would they do that?'

'I'm afraid they would.'

'Are the people going to put up with it?'

'Perhaps not.'

'If they don't, what then?'

'In that case, we could be in for some very difficult times.'

'How difficult?'

'Some sort of coup. A change of government. Worst case, civil war.'

'What can we do about it?'

'Muddle through as best we can.'

We went through into the kitchen and fixed ourselves something to eat and drink, a sandwich, a pot of tea and some biscuits.

'Amelia, I'm sorry, but I've got to get back.'

'Must you? I'm scared here on my own.'

'I know. I wish I could stay, but I've got some things I must do.'

'You're looking tired, Dad, like you've been up all night.'

'I *was* up all night.'

'You should stay home and get some rest.' I could see her morphing from my little girl into my mother.

'Wish I could, but I really must get back.'

'Is it really that important?'

'I'm afraid so. There is something really nasty cooking at the moment and I need to do something about it.'

'What sort of thing?'

'Something that could ruin the lives of thousands of people if I can't head it off.'

'It won't take too long, will it?'

'No, I don't think so. Only a day or so. Then I'll be back.'

I put a call in to Mr Sharmoni, but it was a gruff-voiced Nelson who answered.

'It's Professor Hubbings. Could I speak to Mr Sharmoni, please?'

'Mr Sharmoni is busy at the moment. He isn't answering any calls.'

'It's important.'

'It always is, but Mr Sharmoni still isn't answering calls at present.'

'I've got information. It's about Mr Garage, Ms Stillworthy and the others in the TICA.'

'What sort of information?'

'What the authorities intend to do to them.'

'Hold the line a moment.'

A minute later, Nelson was back. 'Could you come into the Bulldog Club? Mr Sharmoni would like to talk to you.'

'I'll be there within the hour.'

Without any Autocabs or any other means of transportation, I had to make it to Dunwick on foot. As I came into the urban area, the signs of disorder increased, makeshift barricades, damp crumpled cardboard around looted shops and debris strewn around.

The huge ape of a doorman nodded an acknowledgement as I approached the Bulldog Club. 'Go on in, Professor. Mr Sharmoni is expecting you.'

The club's central entertainment space was a hive of activity. Trestle tables were laid out with stacks of leaflets, placards and some weapons such as knives, knuckledusters and batons. A mixed crowd of around twenty Forward England supporters, mostly pot-bellied men, and Mr Sharmoni's mountainous enforcers milled around the place. In the centre of it all, in the role of revolutionary guerilla leader, Mr Sharmoni was in deep conversation with Gordon Garage.

'Ah, Professor, have you met Gordon Garage?' said Mr Sharmoni.

'I've seen you around, but we've never actually met,' I replied, holding out my hand.

'Professor, likewise. Mr Sharmoni told me about you,' said a beaming Gordon Garage as he shook my hand firmly.

'What is this information you have?' enquired Mr Sharmoni.

'The Health Security Agency has developed a vaccine that will keep subjects permanently dosed up with Complianx. I believe the intention is to vaccinate everybody classified as a Toxic Influence and many of the Unsuitables, too.'

'What does that mean?' enquired Gordon.

'You know what Complianx is?'

'Enlighten me.'

'It pacifies people, calms them down and makes them passive and cooperative.'

'Is that so terrible?'

'The vaccine will get a person's body to produce the drug continuously, keeping them dosed up all the time.'

'How long does it last?'

'For life.'

'You mean turning people into zombies permanently.'

'Exactly.'

Mr Sharmoni and Gordon Garage looked at each other, their faces white with shock. 'That's diabolical,' said Mr Sharmoni.

'Most fiendish thing I've ever heard,' Gordon concurred.

'When is this due to happen?' enquired Mr Sharmoni.

'Very soon. I heard something about starting rollout in Dunwick from 12th November.'

'Good God. What can we do about it?' asked Gordon.

'I've been working on an antidote. Should have the first batch ready later on today.'

'How do you propose to get the antidote distributed?' asked Mr Sharmoni.

'I'd like to get it into the local TICA tonight.'

'How? They have the place locked up tight.'

'If you can get Kate Stillworthy into the Lakeside Caravan Park this evening, I'll give it to her to take back in with her.'

Mr Sharmoni shook his head. 'That's not so easy anymore. Security in the TICAs has been tightened right up.'

'You'll be able to find a way, though, I guess.'

'Leave it with me. I'll think of something. Nelson will be in touch to let you know.' said Mr Sharmoni. 'Another thing, though—how do you propose to get back into the university? That's been sealed up too.'

'I don't really know, to be honest. I know the chief security guard. He would let me in.'

'We're on our way there now,' said Gordon. 'Would you like to come with us?'

I mingled with the group of Gordon Garage's supporters as they spilled out of the club to join a larger crowd of some hundreds that had gathered outside in the street. Gordon Garage, strutting forth, with his jaw jutting out in the style of a 1930s dictator, addressed them before we moved off.

'Fellow patriots, we have taken control of the streets from the virtue-seeking cult that has mis-governed our country for too long, forcing them to retreat into their strongholds in the universities. Today we strike out to confront them in their academic bastion.'

We set off several hundred strong in an untidy marching formation behind the local brass band of elderly ex-military gentlemen in blazers.

As we emerged from Dunwick, two police vehicles blocked the road. A loudspeaker crackled out over the noise from the band.

'This is an illegal gathering. You are required to disperse immediately. If you persist, enforcement action will be taken.'

The brass band stood aside as the marchers behind jeered and surged forward. A dozen police officers tried to hold a line across the road but were brushed aside by the crowd. A dozen marchers surrounded each police vehicle and shoved and bounced them to the side of the road before smashing the windows. The band reformed and the march continued.

The mood was one of aggression and elation as we continued south towards Slough University. As we approached the locked-up Willow Brook entrance, we could hear shrill cries of "Fascist scum" coming from the other side of the campus boundary fence.

There were scuffles and shoving on the university side of the entrance gates as the security guards struggled to prevent people from breaking out. Presently, the gates burst open and a couple of dozen students led by a frantically hysterical Shamina Chakrabarti hustled their way through to confront the far more numerous forces behind Gordon Garage.

The students hesitated in the space between the gates and the Forward England mob, shrieking about fascists while simultaneously proclaiming, 'They shall not pass.'

A phalanx of the more muscular Forward England marchers ploughed into the few students with fists flying and boots stomping. There were screams of pain, and students ran or crawled back to the gates where security guards dragged their battered bodies back into the campus.

For a moment, it looked as if the Forward England crowd might surge on through after them into the university grounds. Nelson's authoritative voice boomed out over a loudspeaker, 'Leave it. We're not going in.'

The Forward England crowd might not be going in, I reflected, *but I need to.*

The situation stabilised as the Forward England mob stood around the gates, glaring inwards at student activists on the other side. I edged my way through towards the front, tapping people on the shoulder and saying, 'Excuse me.'

Reaching the front, I waved and caught the eye of the chief security guard, who nodded in my direction.

'Do you mind?' I said to my neighbour. 'I need to go and talk to him.'

'Be my guest,' said my neighbour gruffly.

I went up to the gate and gestured towards the chief security guard to come up close.

'What are you doing here, Professor?'

'Trying to get in.'

'With this mob?'

'No not really. Just trying to get through.'

'It's difficult. If I open the gate, that lot might surge in.'

'But you heard what he said; they're not going in.'

'I can't really count on that.'

I turned around to the front row of the crowd.

'Look, I need to go in and talk. If he opens the gate for me, you won't make any trouble, okay?'

They nodded in agreement. I turned back to the security guard. 'They'll be alright.'

'Tell them to back off a bit,' said the security guard.

I turned back to the crowd holding up the palms of my hand, gesturing backwards. 'Give us a bit of space, okay?' The crowd eased back a few feet. I went back to the gate, which the security guard opened slightly. I squeezed through and the security guard slammed it shut behind me.

Back in the Asima Shankar Laboratory Complex, it was clear that not all the student body were behind Shamina Chakrabarti in defying Forward England. Many were wearing poppies in defiance of university rules.

I found Eddie back in the lab, beaming with satisfaction.

'How's it going?' I enquired.

'Great! The first batch is all ready, over there,' replied Eddie, gesturing grandly towards some boxes containing vials of individual vaccine doses and disposable syringes.

'Fantastic work. Now I've just got to figure out how to get it out there, into the TICA.'

My phone rang. It was Nelson.

'Professor, we can get Kate Stillworthy out this evening, usual place.'

'The way things are, I'd struggle to get there myself.'

'Don't worry, I'll take you over in the limo. Be at the Willow Brook entrance at five.'

'What about the demonstrators?'

'Don't worry about that. They'll only be there for an hour or so. Mr Garage will make a speech, and then they're going back.'

As Nelson had promised, all was quiet again at the Willow Brook entrance.

'You're busy today,' said the security guard.

'Yes, things to see to.'

'What have you got in that case?' enquired the guard, indicating the large suitcase I was dragging behind me.

'Ask no questions and I'll tell no lies.'

'Alright, none of my business. You be careful out there.'

As promised, Nelson was waiting with the limo. He pulled over to the side of the road about a quarter of a mile short of the Lakeside Caravan Park.

'You'll need to walk the last bit, Professor. We need to be careful these days.'

I discreetly slipped into the caravan park from the side, scrabbling to get the suitcase over slippery wet tree roots and through the scratchy hedge.

'She's waiting for you in number 47 as usual,' wheezed Sid, looking shiftily from side to side.

'Anything wrong?' I enquired.

'It's all a bit dodgy, this. We'll have the law round soon, I wouldn't wonder.'

As I came in through the caravan door, Kate threw herself at me, holding me tight as if fearful someone would be pulling us apart at any moment.

'Oh Jim, I so glad you're here. I feared we might never see each other again.' She looked haggard, scared and tense.

'I would move heaven and Earth to get to see you, I promise you.'

'I know you would.'

'So, what's been happening with you?'

'The TICA is in complete lockdown. The authorities are everywhere, trying to hunt down Gordon Garage.'

'I saw him earlier today.'

'Where?'

'At the Bulldog Club and then leading a Forward England march.'

'That was brazen of him.'

'There is rebellion in the air, and people are quite open about it.'

'Gordon has really upset the powers-that-be,' Kate observed.

'But what about you? They seem almost as upset with you as they are with him.'

'Yes, I know. That's why I thought I'd never be able to get away.' She shivered, recollecting her recent experience.

'How did you manage it?'

'I was under guard, but a new guard turned up to relieve them, except it wasn't a guard; it was one of Mr Sharmoni's people. He got me out hidden in a delivery van, like before.'

'They'll find out what happened, won't they?'

'Yes, they would eventually, but there is a delivery van coming to take me back, hopefully before they discover I'm not there.'

'Well, look, you see all this lot,' I indicated the suitcase. 'I need you to get this back inside with you and distributed around.'

'Why, what is it?'

'An antidote.'

'Antidote to what?'

'They're planning to vaccinate you all with something that'll keep you permanently dosed up with Complianx.'

'Complianx? What would that do?'

'It pacifies people. Makes people compliant, as the name suggests. So you won't cause the authorities any trouble.'

'You mean, make us into zombies.'

'Exactly.'

'What does the antidote do?'

'Neutralises the Complianx.'

'Is it safe?'

'I can't guarantee that because we haven't had a chance to do any clinical trials or anything. But better than being turned into a zombie, I'd say.'

'It's despicable.'

'I know. Look, I'd better give you the antidote now, so at least you're safe.'

'You mean right now?'

'Yes, let's get your sleeve rolled up.' I opened the case and took out one of the vials and a syringe. 'Sharp scratch.'

We sat down side by side on the caravan's padded bench, holding hands.

'I'm relieved to have got that done,' I said.

'I need to get back,' said Kate after a short while.

'Must you go so soon?'

'Yes, the delivery van is due.'

'Okay, but you need to get this case back in with you and then get the antidote out there among the inmates to make them safe too.'

'Yes, I'll do that. Not sure how because there is so much surveillance now.'

'I wish I could come in with you.'

'But you can't. Amelia needs you.'

'I know.'

Kate stood up, clenching her fists in determination to do what must be done. She took hold of the case. 'Better be going.' She let in a chill draught as she opened the caravan door. I stood up, making to come out with her. She waved me away. 'Better not come with me. Safer for you to stay back here.'

I nodded and watched her as she went out, dragging the case behind her through the soggy mat of autumn leaves as she made her way back towards Sid's reception hut. *Best not hang around in here*, I reflected. I slipped out of the caravan and scrambled back through the surrounding hedge to a vantage point on the edge of the nearby woods from where I could observe Kate's departure from a distance.

The delivery van drove in. As Kate approached it with the suitcase, a convoy of police vehicle hurtled up the driveway. A couple of police officers quickly had her handcuffed. A posse of police officers spread around the caravan park, sealing off the perimeter. I could see both Detective Sergeant Travers and Robin Smith among them.

I would have liked to put some more distance between us, but with patrolling officers only a few feet away from my hiding place, I daren't make any move in case I was spotted. I observed the police squad taking apart the caravan park, searching every nook and cranny, including the caravan on plot 47 where we had both been only minutes before.

'What are you lot looking for?' Sid protested plaintively. 'You're wrecking the place.'

'You only need to tell us where Gordon Garage is hiding, and we can end the search,' said Robin Smith impassively.

When the police activity had died down somewhat, and I could risk moving away, I decided to walk home instead of returning to the university.

I arrived to find a grim-faced Detective Sergeant Travers waiting for me in the kitchen with a frightened-looking Amelia.

Amelia looked at me, her face showing a combination of confusion and alarm. I looked back, fighting my own shock at being faced with the long arm of the law, conveying what I hoped, probably in vain, would come across as cocky assurance and control.

'Ah, Professor, we've been waiting for you,' said Detective Sergeant Travers.

'Oh, I see. Why's that?'

'Could you tell me your movements today?'

'Right now, I've just walked over from the university.'

'What, on foot?'

'Yes. Autocabs aren't operating at the moment.'

'Some people absconded from the TICA near Dunwick. Would you know anything about that?'

'No.'

'One of them was Kate Stillworthy, who is still your wife, I believe.'

'Is that right? Is she still at large?'

'No, she was apprehended earlier this evening.'

'Right.'

‘You wouldn’t know anything about that, would you?’

‘No.’

‘Another person who is still at large is Gordon Garage. Can you tell me anything about his whereabouts?’

‘Sorry, I haven’t a clue.’

Chapter 20
Insurrection

Gordon Garage's whereabouts were revealed when he was reported as leading a march towards the Cenotaph in London to celebrate Remembrance Day.

"March of Hate" proclaimed the main news headline.

Gordon Garage, disgraced Toxic Influencer and leader of the outlawed Forward England party, is at the head of a mob of fascist thugs determined to turn the clock back to an era of British imperialism with a commemoration of militarism around the Cenotaph in central London.

In their rampage of hate and destruction, Forward England thugs have overrun the offices of Dolphins, an organisation devoted to the rights of gender-diverse young people. In this attack, a Dolphins employee identified as Fred Glibbins has been brutally mutilated and murdered.

Trans-exclusionist Kate Stillworthy is reported to be present on this march of hate.

The news about Kate took me by surprise, because the last I knew, she had been arrested and would presumably have been in police custody. Somehow, she must have been set free. I tried to go online to reach out for any more information about Kate, only to find that social media and email were blocked.

I resolved to join Gordon Garage's march to see whether I could track her down.

Having tried to book an Autocab and been informed that all public transport had been suspended due to security concerns, I set off towards Dunwick on foot.

Police roadblocks had been set up around the urban area of Dunwick, but as I knew the public footpaths in the area, I was able to avoid them.

Once I was in Dunwick, I followed along with some small groups of people making their way in the direction of the small park where I had seen Gordon Garage before addressing his supporters, within which were several coaches adorned with Union Jacks, "Lest We Forget" and "God Save the King" banners. A large hand-painted placard said, 'Transport to the Cenotaph.' I joined with the people stepping into one of the coaches, shuffling along to fill the available seats. A musty dampness hung in the air as the moisture from soggy clothes soaked into the dusty cloth of the seat upholstery. I exchanged nods with my neighbour as I took my place. Full to capacity, the coach moved off.

'Who are you here to remember?' my neighbour enquired.

Pursing my lips, I pondered this question. 'It's my wife, I suppose.'

'Your wife? She wasn't killed in a war, was she?'

'No. Actually she is still alive; at least, I hope so.'

'Why are you coming to the Cenotaph, then?'

'Because my wife might be there; I'm hoping so, anyway.'

'It's someone in her family you're commemorating, then?'

'Sort of. Who is it for you?'

'Me great-granddad. He was a fighter pilot. Battle of Britain.'

'Heroes, all of them, that generation.'

The coach came to a halt. We were in a congested outer London suburb in a line of vehicles, mostly coaches and minivans carrying folk like us, bound for the Cenotaph. Ahead in the distance, I could just make out flashing blue lights on some police vehicles blocking the road.

Hundreds of people were piling out of the vehicles and advancing on foot towards the police roadblock. For a couple of minutes, I could hear angry shouting and jeers, then a roar, tinkling of shattered glass, metallic thuds and scraping. A flashing blue light juddered from side to side and then flopped over as the vehicle it was mounted on was tipped over. The temporarily disembarked people walked back to their vehicles. Engines started up, and the convoy of coaches rolled forward.

As we passed through the dismantled roadblock, I could see at least three police officers on the wet ground with another half a dozen of their colleagues applying first aid. Several other officers stood aside, helpless and forlorn.

'Why are they so determined to stop us remembering our people?' exclaimed my neighbour.

'They say it's all militaristic, jingoistic, that sort of thing.'

'What do they mean by that?'

'Well, with bands and uniforms, making war seem like something good.'

'It's our heritage, our nation fighting back against tyranny. You can't just cast that aside.'

'What happened to your great-granddad?'

'Shot down over the Kent coast. They fished his body out of the sea.'

'You must be proud of him.'

'Very proud.'

'The government lot are saying being proud of those soldiers, sailors and airmen is glorifying war.'

'Fucking government. Bastards, the lot of them. We're behind Gordon to get rid of them. Clear them out. Them and all their 99 different genders and all that crap.'

'Do you think Gordon will be able to do that? They had him locked up until recently.'

'Yes. With us ordinary people behind him, they won't be able to stop him. We won't stand for it no more. We'll get them out.'

As we approached Hammersmith, the convoy of coaches again came to a halt. Ahead of us were blue flashing lights. There was a general groan of 'Not Again!' from my companions in the coach. Hundreds spilled out onto the street. This time, the police presence was more substantial, dressed in riot gear, shields and batons and numbering a couple of hundred officers. Even so, they were heavily outnumbered by the Forward England people who must have numbered well in excess of a thousand and were in no mood to be thwarted. Battle ensued. Many were felled by batons, but the crowd rushed forward with determination, pushing the police line back and then overrunning it. The police routed and the road cleared, and our column was free to move on.

We had sustained casualties. A couple of coaches were cleared to take the injured to hospital, while the remainder pressed on towards the Cenotaph.

'We've got them on the run now,' said my neighbour confidently. 'They can't stop us now. We'll be taking over, right on into Whitehall, you'll see.'

I shook my head. 'They won't give up easily. This could get very ugly.'

'What? You scared or something?'

I reflected for a moment. 'Not really. I'm not so bothered about me, but I've got my daughter to consider.'

'Couldn't your wife look after your daughter if anything happened to you?'

‘Probably not. They already had my wife locked up in one of those TICAs, you know the Toxic Influence places, and so I’m having to look after her on my own.’

‘What’s your wife done to be put in one of those places?’

‘She said that there were only two genders, and you get your biological gender when you’re born and can’t change it however much you may want to.’

‘What’s wrong with that? It’s just common sense.’

‘Those in authority find it objectionable, and she got locked up for it.’

‘If she’s locked up, how come you expect to find her here?’

‘I heard that she had got out. Don’t know how, or even if it’s true, but if she has, I want to find her.’

Nobody opposed us as the coaches pulled into Hyde Park to offload the many thousands who had come in from all points of the compass.

My neighbour and I remained together as we joined the immense multitude making its way slowly in the direction of the historic centre of the British imperial government in Whitehall.

‘How are you going to find your wife amongst this lot?’ he asked.

‘I don’t know. I’ve an idea she might be somewhere near Gordon Garage. They knew each other well in the TICA.’

‘I can’t see us getting very close to the action, the way things are.’

‘You’re probably right,’ I acknowledged.

The huge throng milled around for some time, vaguely aiming towards the central road junction of Knightsbridge and Piccadilly but failing to make any progress.

There was some vague shouting from that direction. At first, I thought nothing of, putting it down to some in the crowd venting their passions.

Then, far from advancing towards Wellington Arch and Green Park, the crowd was being thrown backwards, projected by an opposing force.

From the midst of the mass of people, I couldn’t make anything out, so I heaved myself up into a tree, clambering up into the branches, from where I could get a view.

There was a double line of hundreds of police officers standing in front of the crowd with batons drawn. Members of the crowd were shouting and throwing rocks at the police.

The police line began to advance, the officers banging their batons on their shields. A roar came from the crowd, who surged forward straight into the police line, which quickly gave way.

A voice came over a public address system. 'Get back or we will open fire!'

About thirty yards behind the broken police line was a line of soldiers armed with automatic rifles.

Most people in the crowd froze at the sight of the weapons, but some continued to harry the outnumbered police officers.

'Take aim,' said the voice over the public address system. The soldiers raised their rifles and pointed them in the direction of the crowd.

'Halt or we will open fire!' reiterated the voice.

There was a muttering from among the soldiers in the line. Some lowered their rifles.

'Fuck this. God save the King!' shouted one of the soldiers.

'God save the King!' shouted several other soldiers.

'Clear the path. Let them through,' ordered the original rebel soldier.

The soldiers swept over to the side of the walkway, pointing their rifles in the direction of the remaining police officers.

The crowd roared and surged on through, passing Wellington Arch and on into Green Park.

It took me a while, but somehow, I managed to squeeze through as far as Whitehall. The security guards were helpless to prevent mobs of people from breaking into and occupying the various government offices.

I had been aiming in the general direction of the Cenotaph, expecting to see some kind of formal ceremony of commemoration, but even had such a ceremony been originally planned, any sense of order and organisation had long since broken down.

I caught sight of Gordon Garage for a moment, proudly striding into Downing Street at the head of a mob of cheering supporters.

There was no sign of Kate, nor any likelihood of my being able to find her, even if she was there somewhere within this huge multitude, so I decided to make my back towards Slough by whatever means I could.

I set off on foot, covering a couple of miles as far as Cromwell Road in South Kensington before I was clear of the mobs that had descended upon central London. There were still no Autocabs so, hunched down under my coat against the drizzly rain, I put out my thumb in the vain hope that someone might give me a lift.

After about five minutes, I heard a horn. Turning to look, I saw a vintage van which looked somehow familiar, but I couldn't immediately remember why. The driver leaned over to talk to me. 'Where can I take you to, Professor?'

Of course, it was the black-market plumber who had fixed my shower promptly and for a fraction of the cost of a bona fide professional.

'Back to Slough, if you're going that way.'

'No problem; jump in.'

'That shower I fixed for you, is that still alright for you?' asked my chauffeur.

'Yes, perfect. Thanks.'

'What brings you to London today?'

'I came up with the Remembrance people.'

'That's causing quite a stir. I heard that they'd taken over most of the government buildings in Whitehall.'

'Yes, I was there.'

'But you're not staying for the fun.'

'No, I'm trying to track down my wife. I heard she would be there, but I didn't find her.'

'There's about a million people out there on the streets. Trying to find anyone amongst that lot would be like finding a needle in a haystack unless you knew where to look.'

'I know, that's why I'm on my way back.'

'I didn't have you down as a Forward England supporter. Thought, being a professor and that, you'd be a leftie.'

'I always thought I was a leftie, too, until recently.'

'What made you change your mind?'

'Not sure I have changed my mind, at least not entirely. I feel it's not me that's changed, it's what we seem to mean by social justice that's changed, and I haven't changed with it.'

'How do you mean?'

'We were supposed to be supporting the working class, whereas these days, the left seems to consist of the privileged middle class with strange ideas which, far from helping ordinary people, are oppressing them.'

'You're right there. It's people like Gordon Garage and Forward England who represent ordinary people.'

'What brought you into town?' I enquired.

'Job for Mr Sharmoni. Installing a public address system in Downing Street. Gordon Garage is going to use it later.'

Not sure exactly where to look first, I had my kind driver drop me off a discreet distance from the Lakeside Caravan Park. I approached carefully, fearful that the place might still be infested with police. All was quiet, but I remained cautious, slipping in through the hedge to avoid surveillance.

I found Sid, his face flushed and hands drained white from the cold, wearily fixing the smashed-up door of one of the caravans.

'Hello Sid, that looks a bit of a mess.'

'Too right it is. Bloody vandals, those rozzers.'

'They did that when they raided yesterday, I suppose.'

'Yes, that's right. Trashed the place. They got Kate. Surprised they didn't get you and all.'

'I got out just in time. Saw them come in, though.'

'You must be clairvoyant.'

'No, just lucky. But it's Kate I'm here about. Saw them arresting her, but then I heard later she was out somehow.'

'Yeah, they put her back in the TICA, but then the Forward England folk came along and broke in. Let everybody out.'

'Any idea how I might get in touch with Kate?'

'No, not a clue. The TICA's all empty now. Wouldn't know where to start finding any of them.'

'Thanks all the same, Sid. Hope it won't too much bother getting this place straightened out.'

Where now? I wondered. Perhaps Kate had managed to find her way home. I set off once more on foot.

There was no Kate there when I arrived, but there was Detective Sergeant Travers sitting up in a rigid posture and a stern expression, sitting in the kitchen with Amelia, who was now looking more bored and irritated than frightened.

'I am making enquiries concerning the whereabouts of Kate Stillworthy,' said DS Travers. 'You wouldn't be able to tell me anything, would you?'

'No, but I might be able to assist in connection with Gordon Garage.'

'What can you tell me?'

'The last I saw him, he was going into Downing Street.'

DS Travers frowned in annoyance. 'It is Ms Stillworthy I am mainly concerned about right now.'

'So am I. The last I heard about her, she was in your custody. What did you do to her?'

'Since then she has absconded. We need to get her back.'

'What for?'

'To protect public safety from her hateful activities.'

'Well, sorry, I can't help you.'

I was in a quandary. I didn't want to leave Amelia, but I wanted to find Kate, too. DS Travers showed no signs of leaving, I guess deciding to wait it out until Kate arrived.

I figured that, although it would be annoying and frightening for Amelia to be left alone with the horrible Travers woman, at least she would be safe, the police presence protecting her from the tender mercies of bands of outlaws. If I remained, Kate may turn up at any moment to be re-arrested. Best if I could reach Kate first and keep her away.

'I've got business to be getting on with elsewhere,' I announced.

'Must you go, Dad?' asked Amelia plaintively.

'Afraid so, love. Don't worry, I'll be back soon.'

'It's not nice, being here without you.'

I stood up and gave her a hug. 'I know. I would rather stay here with you. But there are things I have to do. DS Travers will look after you.'

Amelia wrinkled her face and peered at DS Travers with distaste.

'You'll be alright. Be brave for Daddy, okay?'

Kate may have tried to reach me at the university, I reflected. At the very least, going there might provide me with a better appreciation of the situation.

I arrived to find the Willow Brook entrance now wide open with people coming in and out as they pleased, unchallenged.

Evidently, there had been some kind of battle, with debris lying around, broken barriers and ambulance paramedics tending to injured people, shivering from shock and cold.

The chief security guard was in the security kiosk placidly, looking on as people came in and out.

'Hello,' I said as passed through the wide space where there had previously been a barrier.

‘Hello, Professor,’ said the security guard, as unruffled as a country yokel leaning on a gate observing a herd of cows chewing the cud in a field.

‘What happened?’ I enquired.

‘A mass of Forward England supporters forced their way through.’

‘Couldn’t you stop them?’

‘We tried to hold them at first, but there were too many of them.’

‘What’s with all this mess?’ I enquired, gesturing towards the carnage and casualties scattered around the place.

‘That was from a fight between a crowd of students and the Forward England folk. Made quite a mess, blood spilled, as you can see. Some died. They took the bodies away earlier.’

‘None of you security guards got hurt then?’

‘Nah. We kept out of it.’

‘You don’t seem overly bothered by it.’

‘Not our fight. If they want to kill themselves, good luck to them.’

Outside the Asima Shankar Laboratory Complex, there was an ongoing confrontation. A group of students led by Shamina Chakrabarti was outside, attempting to force their way in but prevented from doing so by an opposing group within the building led by Eddie Donagal.

Mz Chakrabarti was bloodstained and bandaged with heavy bruising on zir face, seemingly unaffected by zir injuries as ze urged her supporters on, screaming abuse about imperialist Fascist scum. Eddie’s mop of curly hair bobbed around wildly as he strenuously pushed back those shoving to get in.

I clearly wasn’t going to be able to get through, and I didn’t wish to get involved in the fracas, so I turned around towards the Oppressed Peoples Memorial Complex. There, I found the entrance guarded by Forward England supporters, middle-aged, bald-headed men with pot bellies wearing poppies and Union Jack armbands.

A little way behind, Jenny Colepepper was standing, vigilant and warily keeping an eye on things.

There was no sign of any opposition to the Forward England control of the building complex.

‘Hello, Ms Colepepper. There seem to have been some changes around here,’ I observed, casting my eyes over the Forward England goons.

‘Yes, Professor; it’s been an eventful few hours.’

‘These fellows seem to be in control, is that right?’

‘Yes, and not just here. From what I’ve been hearing, it’s all over the country.’

‘What’s to be done about it?’

‘Minimising bloodshed is what I’m focused on.’

‘How is that to be achieved?’

‘I’m working with the Forward England people to keep order as much as possible.’

‘I see. So, they’re pretty much in control, then?’

‘Yes.’

I made my way through to the history faculty, where I found Liz barricaded in her office. She threw her arms around me, holding onto to me tightly. Gone was her easy self-confidence. She was a frightened little girl holding on to her hero daddy.

‘Jim, it’s so good to see you. I’ve been so worried by what’s been happening.’

‘It’s alright, Liz. There’s been a lot happening, but it seems fairly quiet around here at the moment.’

‘It wasn’t earlier. It was horrible. Tremendous noise and shouting, mobs rampaging.’

‘Yes, I know. I’ve seen it.’

‘Jim, I need you. Look after me.’

‘Of course, as much as I can.’

‘It’s not safe here, in the university. Could I come over to your place, until things quieten down?’

‘Well, okay, but before that, I need to get back to check out the situation at the laboratory complex.’

‘May I come with you?’

‘Of course.’

Back at the Asima Shankar Laboratory Complex, the confrontation between the rival groups led by Shamina Chakrabarti and Eddie Donagal had settled down into a stand-off, with some desultory exchange of shouting, but without any active fisticuffs.

This changed as the imposing figure of Nelson appeared accompanied by three of Mr Sharmoni’s other mountainous minders. They pushed their way in between the warring parties.

'Come on, out of it,' said Nelson gruffly. 'Let's have some order. No fighting.'

'Fascist scum,' screamed Mz Chakrabarti, zir voice so loud and shrill I thought it might break glass.

'Enough of that,' said Nelson as he struck her with the back of his huge hairy hand, sending her sprawling backwards onto the ground. Mz Chakrabarti's followers backed away in fear.

'Mr Sharmoni wants some order round here,' said Nelson. There was a note of authority and certainty in his voice that left no doubt that there would be painful repercussions if Mr Sharmoni's wishes were not met. 'Now, clear off.'

Mz Chakrabarti stood up again, dazed, casting zir eyes around for support, but there was none. Zir followers had melted away. Helpless, ze stumbled away after them.

'Someone here to see you, Professor,' Nelson informed me.

I followed Nelson's gaze to see Kate coming up from where she had been waiting, while Nelson and his boys had cleared the way.

Liz grabbed hold of my arm tightly, digging her fingers into my flesh. 'What's she doing here?' she exclaimed.

'Oh, Kate, I've been so worried about you,' I said. I tried to walk towards her, but Liz clung onto me, holding me back.

I shook Liz off and ran towards Kate, taking her in my arms.

Kate hesitated, looking over my shoulder towards Liz, who was looking back, eyes blazing with fury.

'What's going on with her?' asked Kate.

'Nothing much really; it's you I care about.'

'I don't believe you,' said Kate. 'You've been carrying on with her, haven't you?'

'Well, okay, I had to, for appearance's sake.'

'You didn't have to do anything, least of all with her, that bloody Jezabel.'

Kate broke away from me and strode over in Liz's direction. 'What have you been doing with my husband?'

'You were split up. That's what he said, anyway,' protested Liz.

'You got me set up and out of the way so you could have him, you cow.'

Kate struck Liz hard across the face. Liz immediately struck back. Battle ensued within a windmill of flailing arms, but not for long. Nelson stepped in, taking each woman by the scruff of the neck. 'I said, no fighting. That means you too.'

Liz wriggled free from Nelson's grasp. She looked over at me enquiringly. I looked over towards Kate. Liz looked at me imploringly. I took Kate's hand in mine. Liz huffed a deep sigh of defeat, turned and stormed off fast back towards the Oppressed Peoples Memorial Complex.

Kate held onto my hand possessively, but not cordially. Her eyes drilled into me accusingly. 'How could you?' she said with seething anger.

'I'll explain later,' I said. 'First thing is to get you home.'

'You've got some explaining to do, that's for sure.'

Explaining from the doghouse, I reflected, but no time for that now. I turned to Nelson. 'Earlier on, I had a police presence at home, looking for Kate.'

'Leave it to me,' replied Nelson. 'We'll have it cleared before you get back there.' I had an image of Nelson and his boys wielding a huge can of anti-police spray to clear the infestation from the premises.

Autocabs were running again, so Kate and I took one home. I was hugely relieved to have her with me again, as I believe she was, yet the atmosphere between us was as frosty as a wintry day in Siberia.

'How could you?' said Kate again.

'I had to be seen with someone to allay suspicion.'

'How do you mean?'

'Suspicion that I was in league with you about the trans-exclusionary thing.'

Kate looked pensive. 'You do agree with me about that, don't you?'

'Yes, of course.'

'I know you always said that to my face, but is that really how you felt?'

'Yes, it is, but it wasn't something I dare say in public.'

'So, you just say what you think people want to hear. Where are your principles?'

'My principles are looking after Amelia and keeping her safe.'

Kate pouted her lips and considered. 'Alright. You couldn't risk anything for Amelia's sake.'

'No, I couldn't.'

'But getting together with that harlot. Did you really have to do that?'

'Being seen with her was a good cover, that's all. I just did what I had to do.'

Kate made a face. 'The thought of you with her. It's disgusting.'

I had the Autocab stop a little way from home.

‘Stay here,’ I said to Kate. ‘I’ll just go and check if it’s safe. If I’m not back in five minutes, take off.’

‘Where would I go?’

‘Good question. I suggest going back to the university, finding Bill Englebirt and telling him I asked him to look after you for a bit.’

I approached the house cautiously, finding a spot where I could peer in through the kitchen window hopefully without being seen. No sign of any police presence.

I let myself in.

‘Amelia?’ I called.

‘Here, Dad.’ She bounded out from the living room.

‘No police then?’

‘No, a couple of big men came. They said something to that DS Travers. She looked frightened. Then she left.’

‘I’ll be right back.’

There was an explosion of joy as Kate and Amelia were reunited, temporarily sweeping aside the jealousy arising from my having been with Liz.

‘When you were picked up by the police at the caravan park,’ I enquired once the passion of us being reunited as a family had settled down, ‘what did they do to you?’

‘Grilled me for hours about the whereabouts of Gordon Garage.’

‘Yes, he has been a real thorn in their side.’

‘They had this idea that he and I were somehow in league with one another. They referred to it as an axis of hate.’

‘Talking of which, I have a message here saying that Gordon Garage is about to address the nation.’

I switched on the television, and Gordon Garage’s face appeared and he began to speak with the commanding solemnity of an aspiring statesman.

‘I am speaking to you from the Cabinet Room of 10, Downing Street, having taken on the heavy responsibility of interim Prime Minister at the request of His Majesty the King.’

‘The royal standard is raised once again over Windsor Castle in place of the detested emblem of LGBTQ+ nonsense flown there by the now deposed treasonous regime, marking the return of His Majesty King William and the Queen into their rightful place of residence as our sovereign.’

‘England’s heritage has been restored, just as it was by King Charles the Second following the despicable treasonous rule of Oliver Cromwell.’

‘We’ll be seeing no more woke jobs, such as Learning Safety Officers in schools, no more thought police controlling what we can say.’

‘Our new watchword will be “Free Speech for All”.’

Chapter 21
The New Order

At home, I remained in the doghouse over my relationship with Liz, but Kate occasionally allowed me out on parole for good behaviour.

'How is school these days?' I asked Amelia while we were sitting down together for breakfast.

'Alright, I suppose.'

'Not been getting into trouble for saying the wrong things.'

'It's not a problem anymore.'

'Why's that?'

'Celia Englebury isn't there now.'

'What happened to her?'

'Don't know exactly. The school just said she had gone.'

'There must have been a reason for her to go.'

'They're saying that she was sent to a TICA.'

'I thought that they'd got rid of TICAs,' said Kate.

'They're still there; just had a change of name,' I explained. 'They're now Treasonous Indoctrination Containment Areas. The initials are the same, so they're still TICAs.'

'Oh, I see,' said Kate.

'Lesson for you there, Amelia,' I said. 'They still lock you up for saying the wrong thing, only the rules have changed.'

'But Gordon Garage said that we now have Free Speech for All,' said Amelia.

'Don't believe everything people say.'

'But what can we say?'

'You can say the things that the old government didn't like, about gender and all that, but if you say anything against the king, for example, or the armed services, watch out. You'll be in a TICA before you know what hit you.'

'You won't be going back into a TICA, Mum, will you?' said Amelia anxiously.

'Not if I can help it,' said Kate.

'In that case, you'll need to mind your Ps and Qs,' I observed.

'What do you mean?'

'It was shooting your mouth off that got you into trouble before, and Amelia has been taking after you.'

'What, standing up for my principles for what was right? Is that what you mean?'

'You didn't have to be quite so provocative.'

'At least, I have some principles,' said Kate coldly.

'What's that supposed to mean?'

'When did you stand up against the authorities?'

'I put my parental responsibilities first.'

'But you didn't prioritise your marital responsibilities, did you?' retorted Kate.

Kate and I glared at each other. I looked over at Amelia and shook my head. 'Let's not discuss that now.'

'Can we clear the air on the Liz thing?' I said once we had taken our places in the Autocab we were sharing to take us to the university.

'Alright.'

'We need to be careful what we say in front of Amelia.'

'Yes, you're right.'

'I know you don't like me being with Liz, but whatever I had going with Liz had nothing to do with my commitment to our marriage.'

'Oh, so it's okay now, to cheat and have affairs and expect it not to affect our marriage.'

'I did what I had to do.'

'You just had to go and shag that harlot, forced into it at gunpoint, I suppose.'

'I had to think of Amelia.'

'What has Amelia got to do with it?'

'You know perfectly well. With your highfaluting principles, you made yourself persona non grata. With all the mud flying around, it threatened to stick to me, if I hadn't distanced myself from you. I wouldn't have minded, but if I had been thrown into the TICA with you, Amelia would have been taken away into care.'

'Why did that mean you had to jump into bed with Liz?'

'I didn't divorce you because I love you, but not divorcing you meant that I would always be under suspicion of being in league with you. Liz provided cover.'

'So, you do still love me?'

'Yes, of course I do. More than anything. But I love Amelia, too. That means that I can't afford your ever-so-precious principles.'

'How can I be sure Liz is out of the picture?'

'Last I heard, since she lost her post when Harvey Bentling was reinstated as a history professor, she has moved on to a senior lecturer role at Royal Pentonville College, so our paths aren't likely to cross very often. Besides, we're back together now, and there is no need for us to pretend anymore.'

'Alright. But I'll need time to get used to it.'

'What have you got on today?'

'I've got a meeting with Harvey Bentling to discuss reinstatement of texts for the library.'

'How are you both finding it, picking up the reins again after being reinstated?'

'There is some sullen passive resistance from some who don't like it, but most are supportive.'

'For sure, not everyone is going to like it.'

'Both Harvey and I have a huge agenda to take care of. Both philosophy and history have huge political connotations and have been massively distorted to fit into the prevailing ethos.'

'I saw Jeremy Fitzregal has done alright for himself, appointed as head of research in the English Culture Agency.'

There were no demonstrators at the Willow Brook entrance of what the newly painted sign proclaimed as Eton University, where Kate and I parted, she taking the tram to the newly renamed Historic Eton Administrative Complex.

I lingered to chat with the friendly chief security guard.

'Quieter for you here than it has been,' I observed.

'Yes, the new police chief for the Slough area has things under control so we don't get any trouble.'

'Who is the new police chief?'

'You'd know him. It's Nelson, used to be Mr Sharmoni's minder.'

'It's Lord Sharmoni now, isn't it? With him being Home Secretary.'

'Yes, they're all lords now. Gordon Garage, too; he's a viscount. Don't know what this lord thing is all about.'

'It's Gordon Garage bringing back the House of Lords.'

'Oh, right. Like he brought the king back.'

'Yes, it's like a bygone age suddenly coming back, except it could never be quite the same as it used to be, just old names given to new things.'

'Better than all the strange stuff we've had recently.'

'Too early to say, I think.'

Weak sunshine shone onto the frosty ground as I wandered the short distance to the newly renamed Herbert Pethering Laboratory Complex.

It was good to see Herbert Pethering's reputation re-established. Fortunately, we had been able to put his statue back because, when it had been replaced by one of his administrative assistants, Enid Clompton, instead of having it destroyed, Eddie Donagal and I had hidden it away in a corner and wrapped it up in some old carpet. I didn't know what had happened to the replacement statue of Enid Clompton. As for Asima Shankar, I only vaguely remember her as being a trade union activist, campaigning for the employment rights of lab assistants as far as I recall.

Robin Smith from the Health Security Agency was there to see me, suave and impassive as always.

'Have you been affected much by recent changes?' I enquired as I walked up with him to my office.

'Our role remains to serve the government of the day, whoever that is.'

'Some changes in priorities, I imagine.'

'Priorities are always under review.'

We collected some coffee, which I supplemented with some chocolate biscuits when we adjourned to my office.

'What priority do you have for me this time?' I inquired as we took our seats.

'You would agree that a sense of unity and national allegiance across the population would make the nation stronger and more cohesive.'

'Personally, I'm not convinced that having everyone agree about everything is healthy.'

'You're not in favour of discord and disunity, are you?'

'I'm in favour of free discussion and debate so we can make rational decisions.'

'There is research showing that some psycho-active substances produce mystical and religious experiences in people.'

'Yes, that's true.'

'Perhaps they could also promote patriotism.'

'They might. There is some overlap between religion and patriotism.'

'We would like you to assist us with research in this area.'

I didn't feel comfortable, but it would not have been prudent to refuse point blank. 'Let me think about it.'

'Don't think too long.'

Jenny Colepepper had asked to see me, so I made my way over to her vantage point on the top floor of the central administration building.

Our conversation wasn't going to be about the laboratories, I reflected, because Kyle Fichner had been reinstated in his role as the facilities manager.

'The university needs to maximise our commercial opportunities,' Ms Colepepper informed me crisply.

'I see. How can I help?'

'Science departments, such as yours, will need to play a strong role.'

'What did you have in mind?'

'To begin with, are we protecting our intellectual property? When we make discoveries, we need to make sure that we have patent protection or commercial partnerships.'

'You're right. I'll make sure to pass that on to the research teams.'

'Protecting the IP isn't enough. We need to be exploiting its commercial potential, too. Making partnerships with pharmaceutical companies.'

'I'll reach out to my contacts in the industry.'

'Good. In our current situation, this will be important.'

'What's brought this about?' I enquired.

'We are projecting a big drop-off in student numbers from next year.'

'Why? Has something happened to damage our reputation?'

'It isn't just us. It is the higher education sector in general. The government is taking an axe to what it refers to as red tape. About half of what are currently graduate professions will no longer require degrees and will have on-the-job training instead. For a start, it will probably mean the closure of the Artisan Skills faculty. Also, the government is removing support for what they call Mickey Mouse degree subjects, which are almost half our arts degrees.'

'Oh dear. That sounds drastic.'

'It isn't only us. They're taking a chainsaw to just about everything. Risk assessments, equal opportunities, employment quotas, unfair dismissal, anything green.'

'Yes, I heard something on the news, someone complaining about absurd, supposedly green regulations, as they put it.'

'We're in for some hard times. It's going to be tough.'

My psychiatric clinic at Dunwick Park General Hospital continued as usual.

Carl, or was it Carla, Gellsten was back to see me, dressed in jeans and a tee shirt that could have passed for either sex or none.

'Good to see you again, Carl…or should I say…Carla.'

'Good of you to see me, after the bother I caused you. I'm very sorry about that.'

'That's alright. It's all over now. With the new government coming in, the whole thing's been dropped.'

'Truth is, I don't think I want to live anymore. But I couldn't go until I'd said sorry for making all that bother for you.'

'Oh, dear. Well, please don't do anything drastic until we've had a chance to talk through the situation. Things can always be straightened out. You'll see. And you're forgiven, okay.' I offered him/her my hand and we shook.

'Now,' I continued. 'What's happening about your transition? Are you going to be Carl or Carla, going forward?'

'I don't care. I don't want to go on, so it doesn't matter.'

'What makes you feel that way?'

'After what I saw at the Tavidown place, life is just too awful. I can't stand it anymore.'

I wondered what terrible thing the Tavidown Clinic might have done. 'What was it that you saw which shocked you?'

'It was that day when Gordon Garage took over. I was at the Tavidown with that Dr Ezra Bengold, then a load of Forward England blokes pushed their way in.' Carl/Carla put his/her hands over his/her eyes. 'It was horrible.'

'What happened?'

'They got Dr Bengold down on the floor, punching and kicking him and stuff, then they got his trousers down and they chopped off his cock and balls. He was screaming something terrible. Blood everywhere. They said, 'Now you know what it's like, having some of your own medicine.' He was just screaming and screaming, so they kicked his head in 'til he stopped. Dead, I think, when they were done.'

'Did they do anything to you?'

'No, they just said, "Think yourself lucky. You had a narrow escape; just get out of here", so I did. I scarpered.'

'What happened after that?'

'They burned the place down. There was already smoke pouring out when I left.'

'That really was terrible. I can understand why you are in shock over it.'

'See, I'm just trouble. I dropped you in the shit and then that happened to Dr Bengold, and that was after what happened to Johnie Dorritt, all because of me.'

'You didn't do anything to Johnie Dorritt, so that's not your fault, and I'm in the clear now, and I've forgiven you. And Dr Bengold, well that was politics; nothing you could have done.'

'I'm just a waste of space, causing people problems.'

'No, you're not. You're on a home appliances installation course. You're going to do well at that, I'm sure. You'll be fine.'

'Nah. They're cutting the course short. At the end of the year, it finishes.'

'What you mean, just chucking you out?'

'No, they're transferring us to on-the-job apprenticeships.'

'Well, that's alright. You'll still have a job at the end of it.'

'I won't have anything. I won't be around no more.'

'Tell you what, let's pretend. Supposing you did decide to go on for a while, in that case, which would you prefer to be Carl or Carla?'

'I don't care. It doesn't matter.'

'Humour me. Which would you prefer?'

'Dunno really.' He/she stared into space while he/she tried to figure it out. 'Don't really want to be a bloke after seeing what blokes did to that woman in Dunwick, to Johnie Dorritt and Dr Bengold.'

'Not all blokes do things like that.'

'Suppose not. But then I don't want to be like some of those blokes dressing up pretending to be women. They look ridiculous. Wouldn't want to be like them.'

'If it feels right to them, that's what matters.'

'Still don't know, really.'

'Look Carl, Carla, I'm here for you, whichever way you want to go. What I want you to do is this. Have a good think about which you want to be, Carl or Carla, make up your mind and let me know when you next come in. Do that one thing for me before you do anything else. The least you can do for me after the bother you put me through. Is that a deal?'

'Alright, Professor, I'll do that. For you.'

In the evening, I popped in to see Bill Englebirt in his Godolphin House apartment. Stiff gin and tonics in hand, we settled down into the dust-laden sagging easy chairs with their collapsed springs.

'Saw Jenny Colepepper today,' I said.

'What, you as well?' said Bill.

'So, you saw her too?'

'When are you going then?'

'Going where?'

'Out of here.'

I was perplexed. 'I'm not going anywhere as far as I know.'

'What did she want to talk to you about?'

'The university is looking at some hard times, so we need to do more to exploit our commercial potential.'

'She said the same to me about the hard times,' said Bill, breathing out heavily, 'but for me, my time here is up. I have to retire.'

'That's not so terrible, is it? Nice to be able to put your feet up. It'll give you a chance to focus on some research of your own free of the administrative burdens.'

'I don't think I'll get the chance to do any research, unfortunately.'

'Why not? As emeritus professor, you'll still be here with the run of the place.'

'I won't be. I'll have to leave this flat, and I won't have an office here, either. They're going to be renting out any spare space, and Godolphin House is included in that. Spare space in the laboratory complex will be made available to commercial partners.'

'That's very unfair. We have always looked after our people, and our emeritus staff have always been an asset to us.'

'Times have changed,' sighed Bill.

'They certainly have. A throwback to an earlier age. Restoration of monarchy and all the rest. Who would have thought.'

'There was never a consensus for the breakup of the United Kingdom, abolition of the monarchy and all the rest in the first place. There were millions who hated what had happened and just waiting to reverse it.'

'In hindsight, that has been proved right, but at the time, those reforms seemed to be simply the tide of history, logical and irreversible.'

'I suggest it only seemed logical and irreversible to the metropolitan elite living in their bubble of the universities and other institutions remote from ordinary people.'

'By metropolitan elite, you mean people like us,' I observed.

'Yes, exactly. Rather like eighteenth-century French aristocrats living in their artificial palace world in Versailles, oblivious to the concerns of the struggling starving French peasantry.'

'So, you see a parallel between Gordon Garage's recent coup and the French revolution.'

'They have a lot in common.'

'Including some shocking atrocities.'

'What do you have in mind?'

'The mutilation and killing of someone in the Tavidown Clinic, for one.'

'I didn't hear about that.'

'Neither did I, until one of my patients told me what happened.'

'Gruesome, I suppose.'

'Yes, it was. I expect you can imagine what they did.' I spread my legs apart and looked down.

'Yes, I can imagine.'

'Your comparison of our universities with Versailles is apt, full of artificial glitter in contrast to the gritty grime of the world outside, populated by effete dandies imagining themselves to be oh-so-superior to the ignorant hoi polloi outside.'

'Very true.'

'Unfortunately for them, come the revolution the university dandies are like livestock waiting helplessly to be slaughtered by predatory wolves.'

'Perhaps it's just as well I'm going to be leaving, in the circumstances,' mused Bill.

'A lot of colleagues have left us recently.'

'Your Liz being one of them.'

'Yes, but at least she has found a decent position elsewhere, unlike some.'

'How are things between you and Liz?'

'She and I are history. I'm back with Kate now.'

'How does Kate see things?'

'I'm still in the doghouse about Liz, but we'll get over it, I think.'

'I heard some folks have ended up in TICAs. I'm thinking of Shamina Chakrabarti and Cheryl Biggetty, for example.'

'They were never going to be tolerated by Forward England.'

'What happened to Gordon Garage's promise of "Free Speech for All", I wonder?'

'Nothing really changes. TICAs are still there. Just different people in charge and different people put away.'

'Reinforces my instinct to keep well out of politics,' mused Bill. 'It's a dangerous business.'

'What I find most depressing is that all we have been offered is an uncomfortable choice between hideous extremes. The insane quasi-religious puritan dogma on the liberal left versus xenophobia and tribalism on the right, leaving no space for rationality, pluralism, genuine diversity and freedom of expression.'

www.ingramcontent.com/pod-product-compliance
Lightning Source LLC
LaVergne TN
LVHW011207250125
802092LV00007B/160
9781035877645